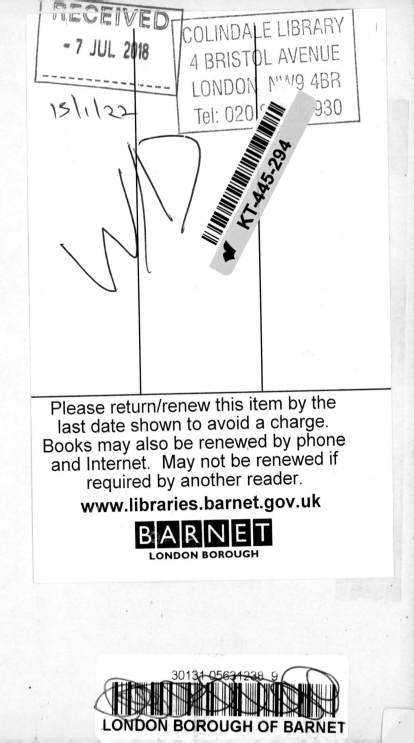

ABOUT THE AUTHOR

The Extinction Trials is S. M. Wilson's first teen series.
She lives with her family on the west coast of Scotland.

susan-wilson.com
@susanwilsonbook
#ExtinctionTrials

Books by S. M. Wilson:
The Extinction Trials
The Extinction Trials: Exile

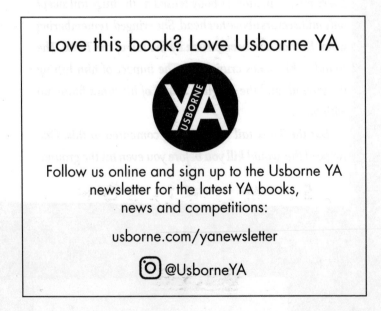

THE

EXTINCTION

TRIALS

EXILE

S. M. WILSON

<u>**USBORNE**</u>

UNCHARTED
TERRITORY

JUNGLE

MARSH

FOREST

MOUNTAINS

DESERT

PILORIA

This book is dedicated to my mum and dad,
Ian and Joanne Wilson, who have continued to support
my writing, are my biggest fans and champion my stories
everywhere. God blessed me with wonderful parents.

This book is also dedicated to my own three personal heroes,
Kevin, Elliott and Rhys Bain xxx

First published in the UK in 2018 by Usborne Publishing Ltd., Usborne House,
83-85 Saffron Hill, London EC1N 8RT, England. www.usborne.com

Text © Susan Wilson, 2018

Cover images: eye © Waravut Wattanapanich / Shutterstock;
palm leaves © Malden / Shutterstock

A CIP catalogue record for this book is available from the British Library.

JFM MJJASOND/18   ISBN 9781474927352   04342/1

Printed in the UK.

PART ONE

EARTHASIA

ONE

LINCOLN

Everything was white. And he hated that more than anything.

Bright lights and whiteness seemed to make the sick look even sicker. It was certainly the case for his sister.

He was tempted to close his eyes as he hurried along the corridor of the medico care centre, just to stop the glare of the whiteness. Even the labs weren't this bright. Their walls were a drab grey. He was lucky to get away from his work there. They were so busy right now. His visit to the dinosaur continent, Piloria, a month ago had quickly been forgotten. Life was back to normal – if you could call it that.

But no wonder. Lincoln hadn't won anything. He hadn't aced the final test. He'd almost lost out on this chance of care for his sister. If Storm hadn't stepped in…

He shook off his thoughts as he hurried the last few steps towards the door to Arta's room. As if she'd heard his approach, it swung open and Storm stepped out into the corridor.

For the briefest of seconds, her violet eyes met his. In less than the blink of an eye, the smile fell from her face and her hand dropped from waving goodbye to Arta back to her side.

He could see something forming on her lips, but then she changed her mind, spun around, with her long brown hair fanning out, and stomped off down the corridor.

He could swear she left an icy blast in her wake.

One month on and she still hadn't forgiven him. Still hadn't forgiven him for trying to save his family.

Storm was now staying in a house. Hardly anyone had a proper house in Ambulus City. The trouble with Storm's was that it now sheltered all the brothers and sisters of Rune and Kronar – their two teammates who had died on Piloria. Lincoln's sister, Arta, should also have been there, but she'd been so sick she'd only made it to the care centre.

Sixteen people in one house. He almost shuddered to think of Storm moving from her own small room in the Shelters to her new crowded home. The noise levels, the chaos, the fights between siblings – Storm was used to none of this. She had switched from one extreme to the other.

She was lucky though. Space was at such a premium on Earthasia that the majority of families lived in the cramped tower blocks or caves. He and his mother were still in the caves. Another family had even moved in alongside them. They slept in shifts. It was claustrophobic.

But at least Arta had health care now. The whole week

he'd been on Piloria that was all he'd really cared about – winning the prize that could save her life and praying she'd survive until he came home.

He swallowed and pushed open the door. Arta was lying against the white sheets, her skin so pale she almost blended in with them. Her face broke into a smile as she saw him and she winced as she shifted against her pillows.

One month. That was how long she'd been here. And even though part of Storm's rewards had been health care for her and her "family", the Stipulators had already started to grumble about Arta being so unwell and taking up so many resources.

But although Storm seemed to hate Lincoln for his betrayal, she didn't carry that hatred over to his sister. In fact, she was a formidable advocate. She argued with the health staff at every opportunity. Any time she thought Arta's care fell short, she reminded them of her time on the dinosaur continent. She told them about the T-rex, the deinosuchus, the pterosaurs, the raptors. She told them about how many Finalists had been lost – sometimes in graphic detail. According to Arta, it always seemed to help the medico staff focus their efforts on trying to get her blistering skin disease under control.

"Lincoln." Arta's voice came out as little more than a gasp. Despite the health care, her disease was still progressing, although slower than before. She held out her fragile hand towards him.

Her arm was bound with bandages, cream smeared over

her hands. Cracks were visible in her paper-thin skin, and her fingers were red and swollen.

Lincoln took his sister's hand as gently as possible. "I'm sorry, I couldn't get away from the lab any sooner. It's so busy."

She nodded, then winced. Even tiny movements were becoming painful. "What's happening?"

He shook his head as he sat down in the chair next to her bed. "There's just so many more people working there now. Maybe a thousand. Some days I can barely move. Apparently it's the same in all the labs on the continent."

Arta wrinkled her brow. "Is everyone working on the same thing? Is it all the dinosaur DNA?"

Lincoln's stomach gave a little flip. The dinosaur DNA that Storm had been so against letting the Stipulators have. It still made him cringe that he'd tried to hand it over and steal the credit for himself.

"Do you really get to work on it yourself?" asked Arta.

He smiled and shook his head. "Not really. I get to do more minor things. Preparing slides. Pulling off reports. Checking rates. They are so desperate to find something. To find anything they think will kill the dinosaurs. It's round-the-clock work."

His sister gently brushed her fingers against his. "Are you getting any sleep?" Her voice lowered. "Are you getting any food?"

He gave her a weak smile. "Some. Regular rations are fine." He tried his best to appear brighter. "Your cheeks have

12

filled out a little. Did you manage to eat today?"

It was easier to turn the conversation back around. His body still hadn't adjusted. There had been unlimited food during the Trials and on the ship to and from Piloria. While on the dinosaur continent they'd existed on ration packs and whatever they could find, but the surprise was that a whole host of other foods seemed to grow there – some rich, some odd, and some that had strange effects on the body. It was so different from their own continent, Earthasia – here, the land had been overworked and food production was at a minimum.

Since that final Trial when they'd arrived home – the Trial to claim ownership of the dinosaur eggs, the Trial that he'd lost – Lincoln had been back on normal rations. The hunger pains he felt now almost made him wish he'd never been exposed to the unlimited food.

Arta gave a nod. "I had some soup. And something creamy. I'm not quite sure what they called it. But it was sweet. It was nice."

"Good." He glanced towards the door. "What did Storm want?"

Arta looked uncomfortable. It didn't matter how much Lincoln wanted to shield her, she'd seen his behaviour. She'd watched him try to claim the eggs as his own, then take part in the Trial to try to win them again. She knew exactly what Storm thought of her brother.

"She visits every other day. She checks my skin, my breathing." Arta gave a little smile. "She argues with the medico. She tells him he has to do better. She keeps asking him about a cure." Arta's voice got quieter. "But we both know there's no cure. Apparently one of Rune's brothers – Cornelius – is getting sick too."

Lincoln felt a prickle down his spine. What if the health care he'd risked everything for wasn't enough? Maybe it was time to try something else. *Anything* else. He pushed his hand into his pocket and kept his voice low. "I found something. I don't know, but maybe it's worth a try."

Arta pulled back as he held out a scrap of cloth to her and a pungent smell filled the room. "Eurgh. What is that?"

It didn't look – or smell – entirely pleasant. The contents, a coiled leaf, had decayed and practically turned to mush, melding with the ointment inside it. "This is what we used on Piloria for healing my dinosaur bites." He paused as he tried to find the words – neither he nor Storm had mentioned Blaine's existence to anyone since they'd come home. Lincoln didn't know how to start telling the story of the exiled Stipulator who survived alone on Piloria and had made this medicine.

She wrinkled her nose again as he pulled up his trouser leg. "Look, the wound on my leg healed really quickly. No infection." He shook his head, as he still couldn't really believe it himself. "I thought it was only for deep wounds. Mum tidied my bag away when I got back, and I just found it again last night. Maybe it could help your skin."

She shook her head. "You want me to smell like that?"

He held up his hands. "Well, are the other creams helping?

14

Do you feel any better?" It was hard to keep the frustration from his voice.

She paused for a second then licked her lips. "I don't know. I don't think so. They're trying five different ones. One for each limb and another on my back and chest." She sighed. "I'm not sure any of them make that much difference." She stared down at her bandaged arms and lifted one a little. "They take these off and everything just looks… the same."

He smiled as he held up the decomposing leaf again. "Then give mine a try. Just on a small patch of skin. Pick a spot and we'll see what it can do." He tried his best to sound convincing. "The smell isn't that bad."

He opened the leaf to expose the ointment and the waft almost overcame his senses. Piloria. He could practically hear the noise of the insects, feel the warmth in the air and sense the earth shake beneath him with the thundering footsteps of the dinosaurs. He almost gagged.

Arta wrinkled her nose for a few seconds then pointed at the crook of her arm. "Okay, you can put a tiny bit here. But that's all. And you better find somewhere to put that or it will stink out my room. They'll wonder what the smell is."

Lincoln walked around to the other side of the bed and smeared a little of the green ointment on the inside of Arta's arm. He opened the door of the storage box next to her and rummaged among the care-centre gowns, depositing the wrapped-up leaf near the back.

He hesitated. "I might not make it in tomorrow. So

remember where it is. And put a little more on. You never know. It might just help."

She shook her head. "I don't believe you – but I'll try." He bent to kiss her cheek and she whispered in his ear, "Tell Mum I'll try and hide some food for her tomorrow."

Lincoln shook his head. "Don't, it's too dangerous. They're already suspicious of this arrangement. We mustn't give them any reason to refuse you care." He gently squeezed her shoulder. "I'll try and get back tomorrow."

Arta sighed and sagged back against the pillows. Entertaining two guests in a row was clearly too much for her.

He closed the door quietly as her eyes flickered shut, and took a deep breath. Arta didn't look better. One month of health care and unlimited rations hadn't had the effect that he'd hoped for.

Had the journey to the dinosaur continent all been for nothing?

TWO

STORMCHASER

She couldn't go back to the house. The noise was overwhelming. Instead, she'd come to the only place that gave her a little solace, a familiarity that she craved – the loch.

She'd gone from living alone to living in a house with fifteen other people.

When the Stipulators had offered preferred housing for the winner of the eggs, they'd assumed it would be a person with one family. Not the equivalent of three. But when she'd stood on that stage being declared the winner, and looked at the large families of her dead comrades, she couldn't just do nothing. There had been no thought. No reasoning behind it. So now she had Rune's and Kronar's brothers and sisters filling the home that she'd been given. And they were loud. They fought all the time. Sometimes they cried. And they didn't all attend school the way they should, even though it was only one day a week.

One of Rune's sisters was sick with the blistering plague, and now one of his brothers was falling ill too. But they were nowhere near as bad as Arta. They only had to go to the care centre one day a week for some creams, so far. Storm was just hoping they wouldn't get any worse.

She hadn't thought any of this through. She hadn't thought at all. She'd just acted on instinct and let her heart rule her head. Now, she was paying the consequences.

Maybe, if their parents had been allowed to stay with them in the house, there would be some element of control. But that was impossible, it would expose her lies. After all, she'd claimed that she and all her supposed siblings were the product of the same absent father.

Only her father wasn't absent. Her father was the Chief Stipulator. The one who'd sent them all to Piloria on a virtual suicide mission, to collect dinosaur eggs for their DNA. The man who'd never admitted who he was. Who'd left her to fend for herself when her mother had died.

Storm settled down at the edge of the loch and took a few deep breaths. Her shoulders ached and her head thumped. Winning all the rewards hadn't changed the fact she still had a job to do. After an assessment at school, she'd been working the hay bales since she was twelve. The hard, physical work suited her. She'd deliberately performed badly on every subsequent assessment the school had given her. She didn't want to end up in the factory like Dell, or the lab like Lincoln, and performing badly meant she remained in her menial job. Which was exactly what she wanted.

Lugging hay bales had always seemed like solid work. She liked being outdoors. But even the hay bales were changing consistency. They were less densely packed. The land here was virtually barren. Overworked and overused, with no nutrients left, the crop fields in Earthasia were almost as grey as the buildings.

Coming from the green openness of Piloria back to the never-ending buildings of Ambulus City had affected her more than she'd realized.

If she closed her eyes for a few seconds she could remember it. The bright shades of green she'd never seen before. The splashes of colour – red and orange – in the middle of the jungle. Grass for as far as the eye could see. If she focused really hard, she could remember the rich smells, and the noise of the rustling leaves. Was it wrong to miss the landscape of Piloria?

Even now, at the edge of the loch, the backdrop of buildings against the purple sky seemed to be closing in on her.

"Hey." Dell thudded down beside her. "How did I know you would be here?"

She let out a deep breath and leaned her head on her knees. "Because I can't hear myself think at home?"

Dell shifted on the shingle. "Them's the breaks."

Storm swallowed. When she'd been standing on that stage after the Trial, with adrenaline surging through her system, she hadn't thought about Dell – the only person who'd felt like family in the last six years, since her mother

19

died. She hadn't thought about Leif – her fellow competitor – and his brothers and sisters. Rune and Kronar had been lost on Piloria. They'd lost their lives to try to provide for their families. It had seemed only fitting that she claimed all their brothers and sisters as family members, to share in her prize.

But the truth was, in the heat of the moment, she'd forgotten about those closest to her, about Dell and about Leif too – even though he'd been right next to her. She'd saved Lincoln's sister but not Leif's family, even though Lincoln had betrayed them. It was unthinkable. Even to her.

But it was too late now. The moment had passed. She couldn't take it back.

In quiet moments like this, she tried to rationalize things. She tried to tell herself it was impossible. How many brothers and sisters could she actually pretend to have?

"Sorry, Dell," she said quietly.

He didn't answer. He just stared out across the loch. They'd had this angry conversation on more than one occasion. It was old now.

She started to trace patterns in the shingle with her fingers.

"Has Milo come back?"

She shook her head. "I still haven't seen him," she murmured, her eyes scanning the surface of the rippling loch.

Everyone on Earthasia was terrified of dinosaurs in all their forms. Even the quiet plesiosaurs that lived in this loch. But Storm wasn't. She didn't believe the propaganda they were fed by the Stipulators. Not all of the creatures were mindless beasts. Milo wasn't. He'd saved her life when she'd nearly drowned in the loch a few years ago.

Dell shook his head. "I don't get it. How can a creature that's lived in this loch for as long as you can remember appear in the sea at your final Trial? It just doesn't make sense."

She licked her lips, winding her hair around the fingers of her other hand. "I have no idea. I always suspected there was a link from this loch to the sea. I know where the caves are that Milo nests in – maybe they connect to the ocean. But" – she picked up a piece of the shingle and tossed it into the loch – "I can't give you a reasonable explanation for any of it."

"You mean there's no reasonable explanation why one plesiosaur helped save your life, and another helped you win a contest?"

He couldn't keep the mocking tone from his voice and she tried not to cringe. They'd had this conversation too, at least a dozen times. There was no love lost with Dell. He hated all dinosaurs. Always had. Always would. He believed everything that the Stipulators had ever told them. Piloria was a continent of monsters, a continent that the humans needed in order to try and survive. The place she'd been sent with the other Finalists to try and steal dinosaur DNA from. It hadn't helped that she'd told him some of the stories from Piloria. She'd been so overwhelmed when she'd got back that she'd just offloaded, telling him about the raptors,

21

the terrifying T-rexes and the deinosuchus that had dispensed with Rune in one bite. The wonder of the land, the scents and the colours, and the gentler, quieter dinosaurs had still been in her head, but had kind of got lost among the more dramatic tales.

She held up her hands. "I never said it was the same plesiosaur in the sea—"

"But you think it was Milo," he cut in.

Storm shrugged. She was too tired for this. Too tired to go home to the house of a hundred children, who were so excited by not being hungry any more that food seemed to litter the house. The Stipulators had already visited on a few occasions. It was clear they didn't believe the family story in the first place, although luckily they were too focused on the dinosaur DNA to investigate any further yet. But several times the Stipulators had pushed their way inside and started making threats about being "wasteful".

Storm understood. Food wasn't in plentiful supply. Being wasteful was shameful and shocking. Old habits died hard – she couldn't leave her plate unfinished. She'd spoken to Rune's and Kronar's brothers and sisters about it almost every day since they'd arrived, but the leadership skills she'd shown on Piloria didn't seem to translate back to her new home.

She'd never had a brother or sister. She didn't feel designed to be part of a family.

Dell put his hand on her shoulder. "It's your last day tomorrow. You should be happy."

She looked up and tried to smile. Tomorrow was her sixteenth birthday. The last day she had to attend her one day a week of school. No more tedious classes where everyone was taught that the dinosaurs were a threat to human survival. No more whitewashing of the facts. No more propaganda that they should wipe out the dinosaurs and take Piloria for human occupation. She was tired of all that now. After tomorrow, she'd work full-time, like all other adults on Earthasia.

"I know. I should be. And you're only a few weeks behind me. We'll both be free."

Would full-time work really be more freeing than school? She wanted to think so. The idea should have made her feel more hopeful.

But it didn't.

Nothing felt the way it should right now.

She should be happier than most. She'd won food, housing, health care and more energy rations. Other people would be celebrating.

So why wasn't she?

THREE

STORMCHASER

The last trip to school felt monumental.

One form. That's all she needed signed to release her from school and throw her into constant work. The same job in the same city, day after day, for the rest of her life.

She filed into class with the other students. Dell was right next to her. But their eyes were fixed on one spot. Cala's desk. The young girl who'd been sick before Storm had gone to Piloria.

She'd still been here for a couple of weeks when Storm had come back, with the rattle in her chest becoming worse day by day. Then she'd vanished. Storm's stomach gave a flip as she saw that the seat remained empty. She knew that Cala wouldn't be taking her seat again. They'd seen it over and over.

The instructor glared at them all. "Sit down," he growled. He started issuing instructions, walking up and down the rows, but he slowed as he reached Storm's desk.

"Stormchaser Knux."

She smiled. She could smile in school today – she didn't need to come back. "Yes?"

He reached out for her form and gave her a smile of his own. It felt like a giant insect was creeping down her spine. "You finish today."

She wasn't quite sure if it was a question or a statement. "Yes?"

His smile spread across his face. "You've been reassigned."

Her heart dropped like a stone. "What?"

The instructor raised his eyebrows. "It appears that a test you did for the Trials showed there are a few skills you've been concealing in your school assessments."

Her breath caught in her throat. She'd forgotten about the written test. It hadn't even felt like a test. It had been a map, with routes to calculate to the dinosaur nests on Piloria. She'd found it easy, but a huge number of candidates had been sent home after it.

Storm felt sick. The instructor had always known she was deliberately underperforming. He just hadn't been able to prove it – until now.

He scribbled on a slip, scoring through her current work assignment and writing something else. "It seems the Stipulators have taken an interest in you. You're to report to the parliament building tomorrow."

Now she really couldn't breathe. "What?"

She stared at the form in front of her. The instructor

started to walk away, and she noticed all the wide-mouthed gapes from her classmates. Then he threw one last comment over his shoulder: "What they'll actually find for you to do there, who knows?"

He couldn't help with the disparaging words. He'd never liked Storm. Never encouraged her. Barely tolerated her. And she'd almost enjoyed duping him.

Now, it seemed he had the perfect revenge.

She'd been found out.

FOUR

LINCOLN

He'd never seen chaos like it. The temperature in the lab had reached an all-time high. He was too far down the pecking order to know what was really going on, but tempers seemed to be fraying at an alarming rate.

The DNA work to create a virus to kill the dinosaurs was being given top priority across the continent. The rumours were that samples from the velociraptor, T-rex and pterosaur eggs had been shared out between the main labs in each of the four hundred zones on Earthasia, to allow work to be completed more quickly. Plus there were extra bodies working in every lab, twenty-four hours a day.

And the commotion in Lincoln's lab was even worse.

His lab was part of T-rex central. It was all anyone talked about – the genetic make-up of the terrifying T-rex. But they talked about it as scientists. Not as people who'd actually seen the creature in the flesh. Not as someone who'd shared the same land and walked through the same grass as the predatory beast. Someone who'd got close enough to smell the stench of the rotting breath from its mouth, and seen the blood drip from its teeth.

The memories still woke Lincoln up in the middle of the night, drenched in sweat, his heart thudding against his chest.

No one actually knew what that was like. No one except Storm, Leif and the few other survivors. But Storm wouldn't look at him, Leif had disappeared back to Norden and he'd no idea what had happened to the others. There wasn't anyone to talk to about it. There wasn't anyone to understand what the T-rex egg had felt like when it was clutched to his chest, the shell rough under his fingertips – the ripples on its surface, the weight of the stolen treasure. The people in this lab had weird and fanciful ideas about what a T-rex really was. They spoke with excitement about the treacherous beasts. They knew they were dangerous and deadly. But they didn't truly understand the terror. Not the way he did.

Lincoln glanced around the noisy lab. He was surrounded by a sea of grey overalls – the standard laboratory uniform. It was scratchy and uncomfortable, and in this crowd, unbearably hot. The heat was beginning to remind him of the temperature on Piloria. He shrugged off the thought. It seemed that everything right now was reminding him of the other continent.

All these people...all these people were trying to unravel the mysteries of dinosaur DNA, when they could be searching for a cure to the plague – the disease that had crippled his sister and had already killed his father. The disease he desperately wanted to cure.

The trouble was, the Stipulators had no intention of curing the plague right now, because it was the one thing that helped keep the ever-increasing population under control. Arguing that they should be working to cure it would earn Lincoln a one-way ticket to the mines. How would that help Arta?

He pushed aside his frustration as he tried not to think about how useful the collective minds in this room could actually be in finding a cure. Then he elbowed his way through the crowds to a machine and typed in the figures he'd been given. His tasks were simple. Prepare a few slides. Put some data in a machine. Note the numbers that came out and take them to head scientist Lorcan Field's office.

A few minutes later the machine spat out a thin strip of paper that he ripped off. Lorcan's office was already littered with so many of these strips that it looked as if there had been a paper explosion. On a continent with virtually no space, and no trees, paper was something of value. The waste annoyed Lincoln more than he expected.

He juggled his way through the lab workers towards Lorcan's office. Boxes were piled everywhere in the room, some of them open, spilling their contents onto the floor. There was hardly any space. Lorcan had his back to him, his white coat and shoulder-length wild grey hair on display. One of his hands was frantically chalking figures on a board which was already covered in letters and numbers that Lincoln couldn't begin to connect together or understand. Lincoln lifted his hand, then hesitated. Lorcan Field always seemed a little crazy to him – always absorbed in a world of his own. Maybe science did that to people.

Lincoln finally knocked on the door. "Dr Field?"

Lorcan spun round, sending more papers flying across the floor.

He barely acknowledged Lincoln – just reached over and grabbed the strip from Lincoln's hand, as he continued to mutter.

Lincoln sighed and turned to leave. "Oof!" He'd walked straight into something.

The firm, broad chest and black cloak of a Stipulator.

He raised his head and stared into a pair of familiar violet eyes.

"What are you doing here?" sneered Reban Don, the Chief Stipulator for their zone.

The Stipulators were used to ruling by intimidation. They were almost revered. But Lincoln had seen a whole new side to things in the last month. He wasn't so afraid any more. He wasn't so intimidated. Last time he'd been nose to nose with Reban Don had been after the first set of Trials, when Reban had nearly "forgotten" to name him as a Finalist. Lincoln had challenged Reban that day. But then it had been out of frustration, and desperation to get to Piloria and win health care for his sister. Now, he was tired of it all.

He knew who Reban Don was: Storm's father. Even though,

as a Stipulator, he'd obviously never admitted it. It was the First Law – Stipulators weren't supposed to have families. They were supposed to focus solely on their role and devote all their time and energy to keeping order and governing the zones. There were stories. Of the families of Stipulators who broke the law disappearing, quickly followed by the Stipulators themselves. At first he'd thought it might all be rumours, but then Lincoln had met Blaine, a Stipulator who'd been abandoned on the dinosaur continent – his punishment for having a family. Left to die with the dinosaurs. It made a change from the usual fate for criminals – being sent to the mines.

But even though he now knew there was some truth in the rumours of punishments for Stipulators, when it came to Reban Don, Lincoln simply had no love for the man.

Lincoln met the steely violet gaze with a glare of his own. "I work here. Didn't you know?"

Reban's nostrils flared in anger at Lincoln's impertinence, then he pushed past him. "Lorcan, you're needed at the care centre."

Lorcan had gone back to the chalkboard but he turned quickly, this time with full focus. "What?"

Reban gave a brief nod of his head. "It's Tarin. She's been taken in."

Lincoln hadn't made his way completely out the door. He felt a sharp push as Lorcan Field rushed past him, his white coat flapping as he ran down the corridor.

Lincoln kept his head and his pace steady as he returned

to the main lab. Tarin? Wasn't that the name of Lorcan Field's daughter? Had she been struck down by the plague too? It seemed odd that the Chief Stipulator had chosen to come and deliver the news. Any of the Stipulators could have done that.

But it felt as if things were changing around here. The fields of power were shifting. Lorcan Field and the other head scientists were the people who could solve their problems now. They were the ones who could find the key to the dinosaur DNA, so the cramped and starving people of Earthasia could find a new home on Piloria. The Stipulators were no longer the ones with all the power.

Maybe Reban Don had a reason to try and keep Lorcan Field onside...

And more importantly, if Lorcan's daughter was ill, maybe Lincoln had finally found an ally in his fight for a cure.

FIVE

STORMCHASER

Arta smiled as Storm pushed the door open gently. "Hey, two days in a row. What's up?"

Storm tried to find a suitable excuse, but nothing sprang to mind, so she just smiled and sat down at the edge of the bed. She visited Arta regularly to keep up the pretence that they were sisters and stop the Stipulators getting any more suspicious. But that wasn't the only reason she came here. For some odd reason, she liked Arta Kreft. Lincoln's sister was kind and smart, with a wicked sense of humour. Storm had never really had a female friend before.

Sometimes Arta said or did things that reminded Storm so much of her brother Lincoln that it actually made her flinch. Now Arta's green eyes sparkled. They were just like her brother's too. "Are the Nordens driving you crazy again?"

Storm groaned and sagged her head down on Arta's bed. "You have no idea." She looked up again and put her hand on her chest. "*I* had no idea. I had no idea how much these kids really need a parent." Her voice changed as she finished the sentence, as the irony gripped her.

She'd found herself alone at a relatively young age. She'd had to learn to survive in the Shelter.

Arta patted Storm's hand gently. Her own fingers were still red and swollen. "They need rules. They need boundaries. They must have had them in Norden. Right now they just can't believe their luck!" She leaned forward a little. "Are you regretting your decision?"

The obvious answer was no. But it took Storm a moment to form the word.

Arta looked hurt. "Are you sorry that you said we were your family?"

If Storm could punch herself right now, she would. She shook her head fiercely. "No, of course not. But it's hard. I've been alone for so long that I guess I've forgotten what family means for some folks." Her voice grew quieter. "Or maybe I've never really known." She held up her hands. "Even here, in Ambulus City, there aren't that many big families. I guess in Norden it must be…different."

Arta gave her an understanding smile.

Storm ran her fingers through her tangled hair. "You're the one person I actually think I could share a house with without going crazy, and you're not there, you're…" She looked around at the bright white walls, then sighed. "You're here."

Arta nodded. "And you've no idea how much I wish I

34

wasn't." She winced in pain as she adjusted position on the bed.

Storm cringed. "I know. I'm sorry, I'm being selfish. I'm just tired and frustrated, I guess." She took a deep breath. "I got bad news at school today."

"What kind of news? I thought today was your last day?"

Storm licked her lips. She was still trying to get her head around it. "It was. It is. But I've been reassigned."

"From the hay bales? Isn't that good?" Arta's voice sounded bright.

Storm shifted in her chair. Arta didn't know that Storm had deliberately flunked her assessments so she'd be assigned such a lowly job. For most people it would be a nightmare.

"You don't know where they want me to go," she groaned.

Arta leaned forward and smiled. "It has to be the lab," she said confidently. "They're sending everyone to the lab right now. It's so busy there."

The irony almost killed Storm. Before winning her Trial she'd rebelled: tried to destroy the eggs, and told the Stipulators to leave Piloria alone. She was lucky the baying crowd hadn't been able to get to her – they would have killed Storm for her unpopular views. "There's no way they'd put me in the lab," she said. "I'm too big a risk." She raised her eyebrows. "Think of the harm I might do."

Arta frowned for a second. "So where are you going then?"

"Parliament."

"What?" Arta's eyes practically stuck out from her head.

She said the word again, as if she didn't quite believe it. "Parliament?"

Storm was still in shock too. She felt sick just thinking about it.

"What will you do there?" asked Arta.

"I have no idea. What am I qualified to do? Nothing really. Unless anyone wants to ask me questions about Piloria. But then, no one really wants to know about Piloria. All people want to know about is how to kill the dinosaurs."

Arta looked at Storm carefully. She tilted her head to one side and said, "Lincoln talks about Piloria."

Storm tried to hide the smile that threatened to appear on her lips. This was the second time Arta had mentioned Lincoln. She wasn't very subtle.

"Does he?"

Arta tilted her head further. "Yes, he does." She frowned again as if she was thinking hard. "Sometimes he tells me things about the land. The trees. The flowers. The colours." Arta squeezed her eyes closed for a second. "I wish I could have seen the colours."

Arta on Piloria? Her stomach clenched as a wave of protectiveness swept over her. Storm couldn't bear the thought of this pale girl being exposed to the creatures there. She had barely made it out alive; someone as fragile as Arta wouldn't last a day.

But she'd only just been dreaming about the colours on Piloria herself. It was odd. She'd been so relieved to finally leave the dinosaur continent, but now? Now, the shades of grey on Earthasia seemed even bleaker than before. She didn't doubt Arta would love the beauty of the place. But the colours and landscape couldn't mask the danger of the continent.

Arta hadn't picked up on Storm's reaction, however. Her expression changed and the tone of her voice softened. She looked at Storm with sadness. "Then he clams up. He won't talk about the dinosaurs. He won't talk about his scars. And he won't talk about the others."

The others.

Rune and Kronar.

Her teammates, maybe even her friends, who had died on Piloria. Died on a mission it turned out she didn't believe in.

Storm stared at the white wall. "Sometimes it's better not to talk about things. Sometimes it's better just to forget." She didn't want to talk about what had happened to Rune or Kronar either. Her mind spun in circles every night as sleep evaded her and a thousand different outcomes taunted her.

Them crossing the lake safely. Kronar not being sick and alerting the deinosuchus to their presence. The T-rex not appearing at the lake. Kronar standing in a different spot – one which meant the T-rex's powerful tail couldn't send him flying through the air.

Her nightmares were frequent, leaving her thrashing around her bed and waking up slick with sweat, her heart hammering in her chest. But in the little period of time just before she fell asleep, Storm's mind always drifted off to the vibrant colours, smells and happier memories of Piloria.

The shades of green she'd never seen before. The pops of orange or red in bushes around her. The diplodocuses drinking in one of the shallow pools of water, flicking water over their young with their tails.

Things that she might never see again. Things Arta would never see.

Arta gave her a pointed look. "But talk is all I can do."

The sentence was short but Storm felt the impact. Arta could barely move her arms or legs without pain. What must it be like to be stuck in here all day staring at white walls?

Storm glanced across the room. There was an older lady in the bed opposite who seemed to be permanently sleeping. She nodded towards her. "Does she ever wake up?"

Arta gave a shrug. "Rarely. And only to moan and ask for something for the pain."

"Do you know who she is yet?"

Arta frowned. "I think she's related to one of the Stipulators. He's come in a few times to visit." She shifted uncomfortably. "He always looks at me as though I shouldn't be here."

Storm straightened in her chair, her anger flaring. "Well, you should be. Has he faced a T-rex? Has he had to climb a tree to escape raptors? Who is he to look at you, anyway?"

Arta shifted uncomfortably again. Storm wasn't sure if it was because of what she'd said or because of the pain.

"Are you feeling any better?"

When Storm had seen the frail figure of Arta near the stage and claimed she was her sister, she'd imagined that a few weeks in the medico care centre would make her magically better. How foolish was that?

Everyone knew this was a progressive disease. She'd seen enough kids in school with it to know better. Kids whose skin peeled and blistered until it became bleeding and infected. Kids whose chests started to rattle and wheeze. Kids who started to cough up blood. Kids who eventually never came back.

Kids like Arta.

Arta gave a tight smile then her eyes brightened slightly. "Actually, I am. Or at least one part of me is."

Arta uncrooked one arm and rubbed at the thin patch of green slime covering her skin there. Storm frowned and stood up, leaning over the bed and putting her face closer. The smell was instantly recognizable.

"What?" Storm looked around, as if some creature from Piloria were about to jump out at her from the perfect white walls. It was a jolt. A vivid reminder of where they'd been and what they'd discovered.

She reached out to touch the green substance, as if to confirm it really was what she thought it was. "Where did you get this?"

"Lincoln," said Arta simply. "He found it in his backpack when he emptied it." She laughed. "One month, and he's only just emptied his backpack. Apparently it was once a proper leaf with the ointment inside, now it's just a pile of mush. Granted, it does smell rotten. I didn't want to try it, but he made me promise to put it on one tiny spot." She smiled as she admired that small patch of skin. "And I have. The skin isn't bleeding any more. For me, that's better."

"Can I?" Storm's finger was poised just above the patch. Arta nodded, and Storm gently rubbed a little of the green away. Sure enough, the skin wasn't at all perfect. But it wasn't cracked, blistered and bleeding in the angry way that the rest of Arta's skin seemed to be. Storm had walked in one day before when Arta's bandages were being reapplied. She'd seen what lay beneath the cream-coloured wraps. It wasn't pretty.

Storm shook her head and sat back down. "He used that stuff on the T-rex bite, didn't he?"

Arta nodded. "And the pterosaur-claw wound. He said it healed both."

Storm was stunned. But maybe she shouldn't have been. Maybe she just hadn't been paying attention. Blaine had given her that ointment for her bleeding feet. At the time he'd said something about hiding the smell of the blood, but her toes had healed within a few days.

Hadn't he also told them about using the same leaves on a wound of his own that should never have healed?

"How much do you have left?" she asked. She tried to remember how much they'd been given... Blaine had put some ointment into a large leaf and made a kind of pouch for Lincoln.

Arta's voice wavered. "Not too much. But I'm only using a tiny bit at a time. If I used any more I'm sure the staff would smell it. I'm not too sure that they want to find a cure for this disease. At least, not one they'd want the rest of Earthasia to know about. I've heard them having conversations about it. So I wipe this off when I know they are due to come and change my bandages."

Storm let out a breath. Arta was so much wiser than her years. "But they'll notice. They'll notice that one tiny patch of skin is healing better than any other."

"Then they'll think that one of the five other creams they're using on me is finally working." She glanced towards the door. "Anyway, they're far too busy right now to notice what's happening to me."

"What does that mean?"

"Someone else came in. A girl. She must be someone important, because all the staff went rushing to her room. She's across the corridor."

Now Storm was curious. "Who do you think it is?"

Arta sighed. "I have no idea. I heard a name – Tarin – but that's all. She looked about the same age as me as they wheeled her past."

"What's wrong with her?"

Arta lay back against her pillows. "What's wrong with anyone they bring in here?"

Storm looked over at Arta's closed door. Another person with the blistering plague. She opened her mouth to answer, just as a commotion started outside. She couldn't help herself. "What's going on?" she murmured as she walked over, cracked open the door and peered out.

The sight stopped her dead. Lorcan Field was in the room

41

across the corridor. He was ranting and shouting, pointing to a young woman in the bed. The room was full of people – several of whom were Stipulators.

Somehow, the care centre was the last place Storm had expected to see the head scientist. He barely ever left the lab. Word had it that he even slept there.

But if she was surprised to see Lorcan Field, it was nothing to her shock at seeing the man who glared at her as he slammed the door shut.

Someone she hadn't seen for the last month – not since the final Trial.

Her father.

SIX

LINCOLN

Something had changed.

The atmosphere in the crowded lab had been frenetic since the T-rex DNA had arrived. But this morning, it was like walking into a completely different place. Lincoln's footsteps faltered.

He'd never experienced silence in the lab before.

A number of the senior scientists were standing near the main doors. They waited for everyone to shuffle in, gesturing for the squashed lab workers to move over and create more space.

After a few seconds of everyone staring at each other in puzzled silence, Lorcan Field walked into the room.

Lincoln swallowed. He hadn't told anyone what he'd heard yesterday. It didn't seem wise to indulge in idle gossip about a sick child – he knew that better than anyone.

Lorcan addressed the room. "There's been a change of plan.

43

We've had some success with the dinosaur DNA. We understand enough about it to try to develop a virus that could be effective."

Lincoln shifted on his feet. This didn't sound like Lorcan. Normally he bubbled with enthusiasm. "*Could be* effective" didn't sound like a phrase he would normally use.

Lorcan continued, his voice picking up speed. "But that will be another laboratory's job from this point forward. We will be looking at something new."

He unrolled a large piece of paper. "We" – he gestured to the scientist next to him to hold the other side – "will be looking at human DNA. DNA, genomes and chromosomes. We already know the basics. This time we will be looking at the abnormalities in genes that cause the disease that is ravaging our population – the blistering plague."

He ignored the stunned faces. "More specifically, we'll be examining the genes that affect the skin. We need to discover if this disease is a discrete mutation in a single base in the DNA of a single gene, or a gross chromosome abnormality involving the addition or subtraction of an entire chromosome or set of chromosomes."

Lincoln had no idea what Lorcan had just said. But several of the senior scientists looked stunned.

Lorcan kept talking. "We need to find out if the condition is hereditary. If it's an immune disorder. We need to find out if it will always develop, or if it's triggered." He stopped talking and took a deep breath. "And then, we need to find out if we can cure it."

44

Lincoln could swear that if a grain of sand dropped on the floor in that moment he would have heard it.

No one had ever taken any interest in the blistering plague. No one had ever looked for any kind of cure. The health care that Arta was getting was reserved for very few people, and even then, it was just thought of as a treatment, not a cure.

There were murmurs among the stunned crowd. The guy next to Lincoln leaned across and whispered in his ear: "Has he lost his mind? The Stipulators will go nuts if we try and stop the plague. We don't have enough resources for everyone as it is."

Every hair on Lincoln's neck bristled. He knew why Lorcan was doing this. He understood.

Lorcan was doing this for selfish reasons. He only wanted to help one person. He only wanted to help his daughter, Tarin.

Just like Lincoln only wanted to help his sister, Arta.

He didn't understand the science of any of this. But he did understand the desperation.

And if there was any chance of Lorcan finding a cure, Lincoln was going to be right by his side.

SEVEN

STORMCHASER

As she walked up the platform towards the parliament building, her stomach rolled and she almost vomited the eggs she'd eaten for breakfast all over her smart new shoes.

When she'd got home from the care centre yesterday there had been a pile of pale-blue folded clothes waiting for her, along with the shoes. *Parliament uniform.* It had made her blood run cold.

Storm had seen people wearing these clothes. She'd recognized an intelligent guy who'd been a few years older than her at school when she'd visited the parliament building once before. But all he'd seemed to do was follow a Stipulator around and whisper in his ear. It didn't seem like much of a job.

She hadn't been quite sure what to do with her hair. When she'd flung hay bales, her hair had always been tied in a knot on the top of her head. It was probably expected that she'd look smart for whatever her new role was. But that tiny little edge of resistance was still present in her. So she'd washed her hair and left it down. She could feel it swinging from side to side as she walked. She gave a little smile and wondered how long it would take someone to tell her to tie it up.

As she walked up the steep slope towards the parliament building her stomach flip-flopped over and over. The building looked like it had actually grown from the trees. It was set high up in thousand-year-old branches. Somewhere, there was an ancient law that banned the destruction or removal of these trees. She had no idea why. With space at such a premium, every other tree had been removed for the creation of farmland or housing.

But these ones had been saved. The red-brown brick colour of the parliament building blended with the thick trunks, and over the years dark green vines had threaded their way around the structure, almost like a spider's web. The building had a haunted look, an imposing look, as if the only wild trees and plant life left on Earthasia were actually fighting back and trying to pull the building down into the ground. She only hoped she wouldn't be in there when it happened.

Like everyone entering the parliament building, Storm had to go through security checks. Then she presented herself at the main reception point.

A sharp-faced woman scowled at her. "Yes?"

"I've been assigned here."

"Name?"

"Stormchaser Knux."

Something flickered in the woman's eyes. Then her face curled into a smile, similar to the school instructor's. "Ah, yes, I remember who you are." She pointed to a door across the atrium. "You're to report to Octavius Arange."

Storm blinked and turned around. There were black cloaks everywhere. Parliament was where the Chief Stipulators for all four hundred zones met. Scattered among the black cloaks were people dressed in the same uniform as her. But no one looked like her. No one else looked as if they were about to jump out of their skin.

No, they were all calm. Most appeared ruthlessly efficient, talking into a Stipulator's ear, or giving instructions to one of the other staff. Who had honestly decided that this would be the best place for her?

Storm threaded her way through the crowded atrium, arriving at the door that the receptionist had indicated. There was no sign. No designation.

Everything about this seemed so odd. She'd been given a name she didn't recognize. *Octavius Arange?* She didn't exactly trust the woman at the reception point. Her father was the Chief Stipulator for this zone, and worked in this very building. Could he be behind this? *Please don't let this be Reban Don's room.*

Yesterday was the only time she'd seen him since she had completed the final Trial and been declared the winner. He hadn't spoken to her, contacted her or looked in her direction since they'd stood on the stage together. What kind of a person did that? Storm hadn't known whether to be relieved, disappointed, or both.

Her hand trembled as she raised it to knock on the door. She pulled it back, wiping her clammy palms on her trousers, straightening her shoulders and tilting her chin. She wouldn't let herself be intimidated. It didn't matter how daunting this place was. It didn't matter how many black cloaks there were around her. None of these people had been on Piloria. None of these people had survived what she had.

She lifted her hand again and knocked on the door sharply. There was a muffled reply.

She pushed open the door gingerly, wary of what would meet her inside.

"Hurry up!" This time the voice seemed to boom, filling the office space. "And close that door behind you. It's too noisy out there."

She tried not to let her jaw hit the floor. There, sitting on a strangely shaped chair and hunched over a high desk, was the oldest man she'd ever seen. Small and wizened, he had saggy and transparent skin. His hair was snow-white and pulled back from his face. She'd seen this man before, when she and Dell had delivered a parcel here from the lab, but she'd no idea what his role was.

"Well, are you coming in or aren't you?"

Storm closed the door behind her, then leaned against it.

"Come here." The old man beckoned her with a long,

gnarled finger. She couldn't take her eyes off it. How could a man so small have fingers so long?

She took a few tentative steps towards him.

He wrinkled his nose. There was a reading aid balanced across his face and hooked around his ears. "Maybe you're not what I thought."

Storm glanced over her shoulder to make sure he was speaking to her. But the room was empty. It was only her – and the oldest man on the planet. "Ex…cuse me?" she stuttered.

He gestured to a small square brick box to the right of his high desk. "Come closer." She took another few steps, then he pointed at the box. "Go on then. Get up."

Storm stepped tentatively up onto the box, wary of getting too close to the old man. She inhaled as she stepped up, breathing in the strangest aroma. He smelled of…something. Something she didn't recognize. Oldness. Mustiness.

The old man leaned towards her as he adjusted the aid on his face. Clearly the purpose of the box was to let him see people more closely. "Octavius Arange. Captain Regent for parliament." He gave her an approving nod. "I requested you."

"What?"

"You." He pointed at the pink sheet in front of him – the slip she'd had signed at school. "I requested you. I needed a replacement for the last aide. He was useless. It was like being handcuffed to an idiot." He raised his eyebrows. "I asked…for you."

Storm was stunned. "What? Why?" She glanced around the room and sucked in a breath. The wall opposite was lined with wood. Real-life wood. And the wood had been made into shelves. Shelves filled with books.

She didn't hesitate. Just jumped down from the box and walked over to the wall, her hand raised in front of her to touch one of the spines. "You have books? I've never seen so many! Where did they come from? What kind of books are they?"

She kept moving as she talked, turning her head sideways to try and read the titles. "We only had a few textbooks in school. But they were damaged. Falling apart. Not like these."

She'd hated the books in school. But these books were different. Pristine. Now, she understood what the smell was. Now, she understood that the old man, who spent his life steeped in this room of books, practically had the smell of them emanating from his pores.

She was truly and utterly jealous.

She'd never, ever coveted possessions. But these beautiful books were pulling her in, sparking her brain and her enthusiasm in a way she'd never felt before. What wonders did they hold in their pages?

She stroked the spine of one. It was dark blue with gold writing. *The Continent of Monsters by Chief Stipulator Magnus Don.*

Octavius surprised her by appearing at her side. Now she understood how short he really was. He barely reached her shoulder.

He was smiling. "Go on, take one down."

She couldn't contain her pleasure. "Really?" She didn't wait for him to reply before lifting out the blue book. It creaked as she opened the pages, and the aroma swept over her again. It was the strangest smell – grassiness, acidity and mustiness, with an almost sweet tang. The pages of the book were a dark cream. Immaculate. These were old books – ones that had been loved, cared for and held in safe regard.

She'd expected words, but instead this book was full of sketches. Page after page of dinosaurs. And while the illustrations were beautiful, as she flicked through the pages, it became clear that some of the detail was entirely wrong.

She frowned. "How on earth…?" She couldn't find the words she really wanted to say.

Octavius's gnarled hand covered hers. "You made an interesting choice. Almost instinctive." He gave a gentle laugh. "I think you'll find most of the details in that book are wrong. Some not even close to correct. If we still had books, we could create an updated edition. We know so much more about the dinosaurs now." He shuffled back across the room.

Storm followed him, the book still open in her hands. "How old is this? Where did it come from?" She'd always known that the old, tattered books in school weren't the only ones to exist – it made sense that some other books must have been preserved. But she'd never seen anything like this before.

Octavius stepped onto the box and tried to perch back up

on his chair. It wobbled precariously and she grabbed one chair leg, steadying it until he sank back into the seat. He shuffled some of the books on his desk. "That book is almost seventy years old." He waved one hand. "There are others, older. You're welcome to look at them sometime, when you've finished your work."

Storm stared at the books.

A world of ancient information. Things she'd never known and never had a chance to be told. There was no guarantee any of it would be accurate. But most people learned these sorts of things from their family. Something Storm was sadly lacking.

Storm ran her hand over the thick blue cover of the book. Maybe looking at these would help fill the part of her that felt as if it were missing.

"Whenever you're ready, Ms Knux."

Storm jerked to attention. Octavius had an amused tone to his voice. But she knew he could be fearsome. The one time she'd seen him before, she'd witnessed him roaring at the Chief Stipulators. What was even more interesting was – they'd paid attention.

What did it mean to be Captain Regent?

She gulped and walked over to the shelves and replaced the book with a hint of regret. Then she turned back to face him. "I'm ready, Captain Regent Arange." She glanced around again. "What exactly is it you want me to do?"

His smile disappeared. "You're my new aide. I want you to assist."

She blinked. "With what?"

He handed her a sheet of paper. "This is a list of your duties. It's not exhaustive. There will be other things I require from you."

She scanned the list. It was full of administrative tasks. Some routine, some even a little insulting. Collecting graphite for him. Making carmon or bartoz tea. She held up the list. "Why…why do you think this is something I'll be good at?"

She couldn't get her head around it. She could name a few people from her class at school who would excel at these kinds of things. But no one would ever have volunteered Storm's name for a job like this, a role where she would basically be required to serve someone.

This was about as far away from lugging hay bales as she could get. She wasn't normally intimidated, but this building with its winding vines, this room with its wood and books, all seemed like another world. She stammered out the question on her mind. "Maybe if you tell me what it is that you do…then I'll be able to understand what I should do?"

For a second something clouded his face. Was it anger? Then he waved his hand in a dismissive manner. "I forget where you come from. I'm the Captain Regent. It's my job to keep the Chief Stipulators in line. To stop them from spending all their time fighting. To" – he paused for a second as if he was thinking, then gave a nod of his head – "find a way to steer them in the direction we need to go."

Storm was amazed. Octavius made it sound like he ran

the parliament. How come she'd never heard of him?

He must have read her mind. His hand waved again. "You only ever hear what your Chief Stipulator tells you at the announcements. It can take days, weeks, sometimes years to come to those decisions." He held up both hands questioningly. "The people don't need to know that. They just need to know what happens next."

She wrinkled her brow. "H…how…how did you get that job?"

He laughed. "They voted for me. They have to vote for me every six months. For some reason they never vote for anyone else."

She was still confused. "What does that mean?" Her breath stilled in her chest. "Were you a Stipulator? *Are* you a Stipulator?"

He watched her carefully. "Don't I seem like a Stipulator?"

She blinked. How did she answer that question without being banished to the mines? He was tiny. He didn't have the imposing gait of all the other Stipulators. They were universally tall, wide and physically strong. Octavius?

He raised his eyebrows. "What?" His voice was louder than before. She'd made him angry.

She stared at his wrinkled trousers. "You…you don't wear a black cloak." It was the first thing she could think of. It didn't really matter how ridiculous it sounded. "You don't wear the uniform of a Stipulator."

He nodded to a drawer. "Open that."

Her palms were sweating again. She wiped them on her

trouser legs before pulling open the drawer. Inside was something dark green with gold edging.

"Take it out," Octavius said sharply.

She was nervous. She tried to stop her hand from shaking as she touched the lustrous dark-green fabric. It was thick, luxurious. As she lifted it out, the material fell open, revealing itself as a cloak. A cloak perfectly sized to fit Octavius's diminutive frame. The gold trim ran all the way around the edge. It was beautiful and surprisingly heavy. How must it feel to wear something like this?

"That's my uniform. The Captain Regent wears green to stand out from the crowd." He gave a crackly laugh. "Black was never my colour."

Storm didn't know quite what to say. She didn't really understand all this. The man she'd mistaken for some kind of messenger was actually the backbone of the parliament?

She started to carefully refold the cloak and put it back in its place. Something as beautiful as this should be kept safe. As she tucked it into the drawer she looked up, surprised to find that Octavius's eyes were still on her.

His head was tilted to the side, as if he were thinking about something else. "Your hair," he said. "I like it. It suits you. Don't tie it up." He stared off to the side for a moment. "Reminds me of someone."

She couldn't think of a suitable reply. And the look on his face was strange. As if he was remembering something from long ago.

Storm slid the drawer closed. Although there was an

56

occasional odd flash of something behind his eyes, Octavius seemed reasonable. Formidable, but not completely scary. She licked her lips. "You've got a very important job. You must have a lot of responsibility. Why…why on earth did you pick me?"

There was silence for a few seconds, then Octavius tapped the side of his nose. "Because, Stormchaser Knux – winner of the dinosaur eggs, conqueror of the Trials, daughter of Dalia Knux and one of only a few people to have survived Piloria – I thought you were" – he paused as he stopped for breath – "the owner of the most interesting eyes I've ever seen."

A chill slid down her spine as Octavius continued. "As for the list? That's what you'll be telling people are your duties." He raised his eyebrows again. "The reality? That will be a little different."

EIGHT

LINCOLN

"This is not the agreement. This is not what you're supposed to be working on." Reban Don's voice was distinctive.

"Our arrangement has changed. I have other priorities now." Lorcan sounded almost dismissive.

"We need all our resources focused on finding a way to kill the dinosaurs. We need the land." There was a huge thud. "We need to stay on task."

"Whose task? It's not mine. I have no interest in the dinosaurs any more." Lorcan was yelling now.

But Reban roared back. "It's your job to have an interest!"

Lincoln was working at a station near the office. The door to the office was wide open. He heard Lorcan's voice drop. There was something quite chilling in his tone.

"*I* decide what I do. Not you. Not any of the Chief Stipulators. I've done your work for years. Plant growth.

Food supplies. The virus work is almost completed anyhow. We won't be able to progress any further until we can test it. *Now* I have a new priority. *Now* I'm going to focus on human DNA. I'm going to focus on finding a cure for the plague."

"You can't do that," hissed Reban.

Lincoln jumped as Lorcan appeared at the door. He had the strangest expression on his face. In all the time that Lincoln had worked in the lab, Lorcan had always seemed entirely focused, often in a world of his own, frequently not noticing anyone or anything around him. Now the look on his face was defiant. As he walked out the door, he threw a parting shot over his shoulder at Reban: "Try and stop me."

Lincoln put his head down sharply. The last person's gaze he wanted to meet was an angry Reban Don's.

But this was everything he wanted to hear. Everything he was working towards. Yesterday he'd spent twenty hours in the lab, hoping his small part in the workload might make some kind of contribution towards the goal – the cure.

As Reban swept out of the office, his cloak billowed behind him. "This isn't over," he snarled at Lorcan's disappearing figure.

Lincoln froze, as if a cold breeze had just swept over his whole body.

Last time he'd heard Reban say those words it had been a threat to Storm after she'd claimed victory at the final Trial.

And it had seemed every bit as ominous then as it did now.

NINE

STORMCHASER

She'd been here for nearly a week now. One bizarre and puzzling week.

Her main role seemed to be that of a dogsbody. She brought Octavius Arange hot water with carmon leaves a dozen times in the morning, then by mid-afternoon he changed to peculiar-smelling bartoz leaves. She shuffled and reorganized papers, and ran errands.

Her blue uniform seemed to make her invisible – she'd already overheard three Stipulators plotting against the Chief from Norden. Ever since then, she'd been listening carefully, trying to find out anything she could about the Stipulators' plans for Piloria and infecting the dinosaurs. But it seemed that parliament was still waiting for news from the laboratories. Patience was not a virtue that Storm possessed. The waiting was driving her mad. And the craziness of parliament wasn't helping.

When they weren't plotting against each other, the Stipulators argued constantly. Sometimes Storm and the other aides would spend all day rushing between them, taking messages, before the Stipulators would finally appear themselves, with a sweep of their black cloaks, and their voices would fill the atrium. On occasion, Octavius would leap down from his perch and his tiny legs would cover ground rapidly. Storm had learned not to follow him. Seconds later Octavius's voice would boom above any others. Sometimes the exchanges would be finished in a few seconds, sometimes not. On one occasion there had even been a punch swung by one Stipulator at another.

Storm was astonished. In her mind, the Chief Stipulators were above fights, above arguments. When Reban Don came and made announcements to the people of Ambulus City he was terrifying. People obeyed without question.

She'd thought that all the Chief Stipulators agreed on everything. She'd thought they practically had one voice. But perhaps the ever-increasing pressure to find more land and more food was causing rifts. Maybe an explosion was coming.

"Stormchaser?"

Octavius's voice broke her from her thoughts. She'd just made more of the carmon drink for him. The smell was beginning to permeate her clothes.

"Storm," she replied firmly.

He shook his head. "I don't know why you insist on trying to shorten your beautiful name." He waved his hand at her.

"Stormchaser is the name that your mother chose for you."
He gave a knowing smile. "Sounds like you came out angry.
So we will respect your mother's wishes and use your given
name."

Something about the way he said the words made her
catch her breath. Had he known her mother? She still
couldn't quite put her finger on things with Octavius. He
was strict, he worked hard, and she suspected he never slept.
He was always here before her in the morning and was still
here when she left at night. He could snap at times. She'd
learned quickly not to question him too much – he had yet
to reveal what her true task would be, even though she'd
asked many times. But what was most interesting about
Octavius was the way he played people. He had their respect.
He watched. And he listened.

Like now.

"Stormchaser, I want you to deliver a message for me."

She nodded and walked over to his high desk, ready to
receive whatever he had ready. But he shook his head.
"Nothing written. I just want you to *give* the message." He
emphasized the word *give* with a nod of his head.

"Who is it for?"

"Reban Don."

She flinched, conscious that he was watching her
carefully.

"I…I'm not quite sure where his office is," she stuttered,
frantically trying to search for another excuse. The last thing
she wanted was to be face-to-face with the man who wouldn't

admit he was her father. She'd managed to avoid him so far.

His gaze stayed steady. "I'm sure you will find it." He raised his eyebrows. "If you can make your way around Piloria, then a room in this building won't take too much energy to find."

Was he being sarcastic? Baiting her? She straightened her back and tried to look confident. "W…what's the message?"

She could swear he almost smiled. "I want you to let Reban Don know that he has to deal with Lorcan Field. He needs to get him under control. And soon. Other Stipulators are complaining. They're saying Reban's losing control."

The effect was instant. It was like a million little bugs crawling over her skin. "What?"

Reban Don was more than a little bad-tempered. She could only imagine how he'd react to a message like that.

Octavius's face was completely sincere. He looked back down to the rest of his work. "Just deliver the message."

Storm's feet were rooted to the floor. She couldn't move. She couldn't speak. Her mouth just wouldn't form words.

After a few seconds, Octavius looked up again with his pale eyes. "Is there a problem?"

Her tongue was stuck to the top of her mouth. *Of course there's a problem!* she wanted to yell. Reban Don would likely destroy anyone who took him a message like that.

She hadn't seen him since she started here. People mentioned him all the time. She knew he was around. But she hadn't actually *seen* him yet. Did he even know she was working here? The prickly feeling on her skin grew worse. Surely there was no way he had anything to do with her being here?

She'd blackmailed him. She'd stood on that stage in the auditorium and spat her mother's name at him when she'd thought she was about to be sent to the mines. It had been risky. She'd only suspected she was his daughter – she hadn't known for sure. But his reaction had told her everything she needed to know.

He'd helped her. He'd told her to challenge Lincoln. To argue that the eggs he claimed were his actually belonged to her. She hadn't even known the option to challenge existed. But even though he'd helped her, the look on Reban's face had been anything but friendly. She'd managed to stay out of his way ever since winning the final Trial. She wasn't too sure what a Chief Stipulator would do to someone who had information that could threaten their position.

But he hadn't looked for her either. He hadn't come to find her. He hadn't asked about her mother. He hadn't asked where she'd stayed, or what had happened.

When Storm had looked into those violet eyes of his, they had been a clear mirror image of her own. And all that had done was intensify her hatred for him.

"Stormchaser?"

She folded her arms across her chest. "I don't think Reban Don will take a message like that well."

Octavius didn't even raise his head from his papers. "Neither do I," he replied.

There was nothing else to say. Her feet took her to the door. She stepped outside into the bustling atrium. She made her way over to one of the collection points, checking for any messages for Octavius and pouring some water for herself. She was stalling, trying to keep her temper in check.

There were a few other aides chatting at the collection point. They nudged each other when they saw her. She'd noticed them whispering about her before. At first, she thought it was because she was new. Then she thought it was because they recognized her from the Trials. Now, one dark-haired guy who looked a few years older than her finally stepped forward.

"Where did you come from?" he asked.

"I'm from here," she answered. "Ambulus City. I've lived here all my life."

"Are you related to Octavius?" asked another.

"No."

"Then how did you get the job? No one just walks into a job like that."

The statement made her uncomfortable. "Apparently I scored well in some test," she answered blandly.

There was only one aide she vaguely recognized, the guy who'd been a few years above her at school – she thought his name was Corin. It was obvious from his stare that he found her familiar, but couldn't place her. "What did you do before?" he asked easily.

She smiled widely. "I lugged hay bales."

She watched as their jaws collectively hit the floor. Then,

apart from Corin, they turned back towards each other and started whispering again.

"How do you go from hay bales to being the aide to the most important man in here?" she overheard.

"She's far too young."

"Forven was nearly forty. If he hadn't been so useless, she would never have got this job."

"It should have been mine," hissed another voice. "I was next in line for that position."

Corin took her elbow.

"Ignore them. You might have noticed that everyone's pretty stressed out here. Things are getting really bad, you know."

She gulped. "What do you mean?"

"The parliament chamber." His brow furrowed. "Haven't you heard the Chief Stipulators?"

She narrowed her gaze and turned to face him. She'd never been inside the actual parliament chamber. Who needed to, when everything seemed to happen in the atrium anyway? But she'd watched with a tiny bit of wonder as all the Chief Stipulators in their black cloaks filed into the grand hall once a week. She'd made a point of counting them. Three hundred and seventy-six men, and twenty-four women. This place sucked. She shook her head and focused her attention back on Corin. "Why? What's being said?"

He shrugged. "I just think there might be some changes in the future. People are getting tired. They're getting tired of waiting, tired of living on top of one another, tired of constant rations." Right on cue, his stomach gave a loud growl. "Aren't we all?"

She felt a flicker of guilt – after all, she wasn't stuck with normal rations. But then, she had earned her rewards. She sighed and looked at the corridor of blank doors. "Which one is Reban Don's office?"

He laughed. "You're going there? I wouldn't advise it."

"Why?"

"Parliament just finished. They spent most of the time shouting at each other. I don't think he'll be in the best of moods."

She shrugged. "Well, I don't imagine his mood will improve any when I give him this message."

Corin shook his head. "Good luck then." He pointed down the corridor. "Down there, first door as you turn the corner."

She finished her water and headed down the corridor. The lights were dimmer here, casting shadows.

Why was everyone so unhappy with Reban Don? What was it that Lorcan Field was doing? Her heart gave a little lurch. Maybe Lorcan had said that the dinosaur DNA was useless – that the plans for a virus wouldn't work. Maybe this could actually be good news instead of bad…

Storm turned the corner and steeled herself as she walked towards the door, lifting her hand and knocking before she had a chance to change her mind.

"What is it?" came the shout.

Storm shook her head. This had *disaster* stamped all over it.

She felt a surge of adrenaline. She'd survived for seven days on Piloria. She'd faced raptors and a T-rex. She'd seen a megalodon. She'd had the heart-wrenching experience of seeing her friend killed by a deinosuchus.

Reban Don was only a man. And not a very honourable man at that. Against the scale of a continent filled with dinosaurs, he was nothing.

And with that thought, she pushed open the door.

His room was eerily empty. It was almost as if he didn't want to leave anything around for people to see. He didn't have shelves full of books like Octavius. His desk was on a raised platform but the smaller desk where she guessed an aide would normally sit was empty. Didn't he have one?

Not that she cared.

He started, obviously surprised to see her standing there. He was leaning across a pile of paper, a piece of graphite in his hand.

"What are you doing here?"

She stifled her smile. "Octavius Arange sent me with a message."

He stiffened in his chair. "Why on earth would Octavius Arange send *you* with a message?" His eyes narrowed as he recognized her blue uniform.

"I'm his aide."

"Since when?"

"A week ago."

He didn't say anything. Just held her gaze. She could almost see the cogs in his brain whirring. Any thought she'd had about Reban Don being the person to bring her here vanished. It was clear he knew nothing about it. He muttered under his breath: "What a surprise. Octavius wants Ms Piloria all to himself."

"What?" She couldn't help it. What kind of comment was that?

He ignored her question. "What's the message?" he snapped.

She took a deep breath. "Octavius wanted me to tell you to get Lorcan Field under control. He said the other Chief Stipulators are complaining."

Reban's nostrils flared. "That's it?"

She'd expected more. She'd expected him to shout and scream. He was obviously angry, but he had an unexpected air of calm around him. She was almost a little disappointed.

"Yes, that's it," she replied.

"You can go." He waved his hand. An act of dismissal. Another one. She tilted her chin and put her hands on her hips.

"That's all? That's all you're going to say to me?"

He put down his graphite and raised one eyebrow. "What exactly would you like me to say to you?"

The rage that she'd tempered for so long bubbled to the surface. "Maybe some kind of an explanation? Maybe some acknowledgement of who you actually are? Or is that too much to ask of Chief Stipulator Reban Don?" She couldn't help the mocking tone in her voice.

He stood up, thudding his hands on the desk. "You should

watch what you say out loud, Stormchaser Knux," he hissed. "You have no idea how much danger you could be in."

"From who? And is it me or you that you're worried about?"

She could see the veins bulging on his forehead as his face grew redder and redder. "Be careful who you trust. People aren't quite what they seem."

She walked over to the desk. Even though he towered above her, she wasn't intimidated. "Don't worry, I learned that a long time ago."

She turned on her heels and walked towards the door.

"Storm," came the voice behind her. "Be careful."

Her footsteps faltered but she was determined not to stop, determined not to give him any further acknowledgement. She'd delivered Octavius's message.

The sooner she got away from this man the better.

TEN

LINCOLN

It was unusually cold as Lincoln made his way home towards the caves. He was worried about his mother – she'd been looking exhausted and strained, working extra hours while worrying all the time about Arta. The other family that had moved in with them were difficult and untidy. Tunics lay unwashed on the floor, dirty bowls were scattered across the eating area and the cave had a strange odour now. It had always smelled damp. But now it almost smelled mouldy.

Without Arta there the cave felt strange. When Storm had declared Arta her half-sister he'd been so relieved he hadn't considered anything else. But now he realized that to keep up their current charade, Arta would never be able to come and live with them again.

Home just didn't feel like a home any more.

And from what Arta told him about Storm, she was struggling with the changes since their return from Piloria too.

But something was giving him just the tiniest bit of hope. Today, when he'd looked at Arta's arm, it had seemed a little bit better. Maybe he was imagining it? Maybe he was just seeing what he wanted to see. But he was almost sure there had been an improvement. The skin wasn't quite so red in the crook of her arm, and the cracked skin there actually looked as if it might seal and mend.

He hadn't said anything out loud – because he didn't want to draw any attention to the ointment or to create false hope – but his mind was currently on overdrive. Could an ointment from Piloria actually help the blistering plague?

He jostled his way through the thronging bodies in Ambulus City. For most of the workplaces, shifts had just changed.

The crowd was claustrophobic. Some people just walked blindly forward, exhausted from the long hours, banging blank-faced into other people and shouldering them out of the way. Thankfully, due to the starvation rations, most of these people had no weight behind them.

A woman appeared directly in front of Lincoln. He tried to sidestep her, but she moved back into his path. He tried again, and she moved again. "Sorry," he muttered.

But she reached out and grabbed his arm. "It's you," she said, her face tense.

"What?"

"It's you, isn't it? You're Lincoln Kreft." He instantly felt uncomfortable and glanced from side to side to see if anyone had overheard. Nobody in the crowd made eye contact, except one. A boy who looked the same age as him, with brown shaggy hair. Lincoln blinked. Although he was certain he didn't know this boy, there was something achingly familiar about him. He wasn't quite sure what it was. The almond-shaped brown eyes?

Lincoln shook his head. "Do I know you?"

It was clear the woman and boy were together. The woman took his hand and squeezed it. "You were there. You were there on Piloria. I need to know. I need to know what it's like."

Lincoln tried to pull his hand away. He had no idea who this woman was. Was she some kind of weird fan of the Trials? Or the Finalists? Lots of people had asked him questions about Piloria. About the dinosaurs. But no one had approached him quite like this.

He pulled his hand away sharply and held it against his chest. "It's a continent," he said abruptly, "and it's got dinosaurs."

The boy leaned forward and gripped Lincoln's shoulder tightly. "Could someone survive there?"

"What do you mean?" Lincoln instantly felt more on edge.

The woman and boy glanced at each other. "We…might know someone who was sent there."

Sent there. A strange thing to say. Finalists won their places. They weren't *sent* to Piloria. Lincoln only knew one person who'd been sent there…

His eyes widened as realization struck. He stared at the

woman again. She was older than the picture he remembered…
and the boy? He'd only been a child in the sketch stuck to the
wall in Blaine Thredell's makeshift hut. The sketch had been
of the woman and her two young children. A boy and a girl.

He'd known Blaine had a family in Ambulus City. But in a
city of a million people he'd never expected to see them – to
meet them. The surprise was like being plunged into the cold
sea at the bottom of the pterosaur cliffs. He couldn't speak.

The boy shook him. "Well?"

Tears glistened in the woman's eyes. She glanced around
to see if anyone else was listening. "My partner. He was sent
there nine years ago."

Lincoln was numb. The one thing that Blaine had revealed
he longed for, but had never been granted, was news of his
family. And this boy had to be his – with his brown shaggy
hair and brown eyes, he was almost a living image of his
father. It was just like looking at a younger version of the
slightly mad man who'd been abandoned with the dinosaurs.

"I've been watching you – following you," the woman
muttered, averting her eyes from his. "I needed to ask. I
needed to speak to you."

"Wh…who…was your partner?" he managed to say. He
needed confirmation. He needed to know that this wasn't
just some random mistake.

"Blaine, Blaine Thredell." Both voices spoke in perfect
unison.

It was like being in a bubble. The mass of people around
him, the chattering noise and echo of machinery seemed to

vanish into the background. All he could see right now was the woman and boy in front of him.

Lincoln's father had died only a few years before – another victim of the blistering plague. Lincoln had a number of special memories of him. But this boy in front of him hadn't seen his father since he'd been around five. He must have spent the last nine years wondering about him. Wondering if his father was dead or alive.

The thought of it was like a fist punching into Lincoln's heart. Blaine's manner had worried him. His behaviour had been erratic. But one thing had been crystal clear: Blaine loved this woman and their children. He'd lost his position and his life on Earthasia because of them.

The Stipulators already knew Blaine had survived on the continent. But they were determined to keep that fact a secret – Blaine had told them that much. Which meant that telling people about meeting Blaine was the easiest way to make an enemy of parliament. So Lincoln, Leif and Storm had agreed not to mention him to anyone. Lincoln hadn't told his mother, or his sister, or any of the Stipulators who'd interrogated him about his time on Piloria. He hadn't mentioned Blaine at all. But could he really deny the man's existence to his partner and his child?

Lincoln squeezed the woman's hand back and pulled her towards one of the Blocks. There were cameras in the streets. People were watched. He didn't want to draw attention to himself, or them. The boy looked furtively around, then dodged between the crowds and followed.

The Blocks were so close together that only a little sun filtered down between them. Lincoln pulled the woman against the side of one of the buildings. In the shade it was less likely they would be spotted. Her lips were trembling.

"What? What is it?"

The boy appeared by his mother, his face pale, his fists clenched at his sides.

He looked at the anxiety in their eyes. He could lie. He could make up some kind of story. But wasn't the truth always best? He'd learned what lies and deceit could do. It had cost him the two people he'd come to think of as friends on Piloria.

The woman placed her hand on his chest. "You have to tell us," she pleaded.

He nodded slowly. "Blaine…he's still there. He's alive."

"He's alive?" the woman shouted. Several heads turned in their direction.

"Sshhhh," Lincoln urged.

"He's managed to stay alive on the dinosaur continent?" Her eyes were wide as the thoughts clearly kept tumbling around in her mind. "Do the Stipulators know?"

Lincoln nodded.

The boy spoke up. "They won't bring him back? Surely if he's managed to stay alive all this time then he's earned the right to come home?"

Lincoln sighed, trying to decide how much to share. "What are your names?"

"He didn't tell you?" The woman's voice wobbled.

Lincoln chose his words carefully. "He had a hand-drawn picture of the three of you. I saw it, but I didn't ask your names."

The hand against his chest was trembling. The woman spoke. "This is our son Caleb, our daughter is Jesa and I'm Kayna."

Caleb narrowed his eyes. "He's really survived on Piloria all this time?"

Lincoln nodded again. "He has. He was injured to begin with. But he managed to find food and water and survive until the ship returned a year later." He left out the extent of Blaine's injuries from the T-rex. The fact he'd originally been unable to walk and it had taken a whole year for his gaping wound to finally heal.

"So why didn't they let him come home then? Surely he'd suffered enough punishment?"

Lincoln ran his fingers through his hair. "The Stipulators don't want it to be known that anyone can actually survive that length of time on the dinosaur continent. They're so fixed on killing the dinosaurs and wiping the place clean for themselves. If Blaine comes home and the news spreads, people might start asking questions about the virus plan."

"And so they should. So they leave him there? On his own?" Kayna was angry.

Lincoln held up both hands. "Hey, it wasn't up to me. But Blaine has made some sort of arrangement with them."

Caleb looked suspicious. "What kind of arrangement?"

Lincoln shrugged. "Blaine was vague. He just said that he gave them information. He had lots of detailed drawings of

77

the dinosaurs and notes on them. Maps with their nests, their habits."

"And what do the Stipulators give him in return?"

"They take him supplies every year. When we landed, they left a crate on the beach for him. But that's not what he really wants. He wants to see you all again. I think he's accepted they won't let him come home, but he still wants to know about his family."

Lincoln could see how upset they were. He was beginning to regret his decision to tell them. The truth was he could never really give them the answers they wanted.

"How can they do this to him?" Kayna burst out. "They sent him there and they won't even let him contact us?"

Lincoln could hear pure anguish and frustration in her voice. He tried to speak carefully. "He's a Stipulator. Or he was." He left the rest hanging in the air.

But Kayna knew exactly what he meant. "So this is my fault? My fault because we had a family." Her face was getting redder by the second.

Lincoln stepped back. "I don't make the rules. I don't make the punishments."

Caleb still looked angry. "So for years Finalists have gone to Piloria, seen my father and never mentioned him?"

Lincoln shook his head. "No. Not at all. He hides."

"He what?" Kayna and Caleb looked at each other in confusion.

Lincoln tried to find a more tactful way of putting it. "We met Blaine by accident. We'd been chased by a T-rex and we scrambled into a cave to hide. That's where we met Blaine."

"He lives in a cave?" Kayna's face filled with horror and Lincoln almost laughed out loud. *He* lived in a cave, with his mother and now another family. Kayna had obviously forgotten that people on Earthasia lived in caves too.

He shook his head. "No. But he's survived on Piloria for nine years. He's built a kind of home in the jungle. He knows what to do, he knows where to hide."

Kayna shook her head and wiped tears from her eyes. The information seemed to overwhelm her.

"I'm sorry," Lincoln whispered. "I'm sorry. I just thought I should be truthful with you. He still loves you all. He just can't tell you that." Lincoln paused. "I think if he'd known I would meet you, he would have given me a million messages for you." He closed his eyes for a second. "I wish I'd asked him. I wish I'd thought to ask him what to tell you."

Kayna's hands clasped one of Lincoln's and he opened his eyes. "But now I know. I've spent the last nine years imagining terrible things. Not knowing what to tell my children." She squeezed his hand so hard he almost winced, but then she released it and placed one hand on her heart. She nodded her head. "Now, I know. I know the person I love is still alive." Tears dripped down her face. "Now, I can go home and tell my daughter about her father. About the survivor on Piloria. About the only human who has survived on the dinosaur continent." She wrapped her arm around Caleb. "Now, I can tell my children to be proud of their father.

To be proud that he's survived." She gritted her teeth. "Even if he's been abandoned by the people he used to consider family."

She tugged at Caleb's sleeve, they exchanged a glance, then, in the blink of an eye, they disappeared into the crowd.

Lincoln was stunned. His heart was pounding against his chest. He stood for a few moments collecting his thoughts. Had that really just happened? He slid his hands through his hair as his stomach churned over and over.

He couldn't shake the feeling that he'd just done something wrong.

But it was too late now.

ELEVEN

LINCOLN

He didn't mean to be there. He was in the wrong place at the wrong time. Lorcan Field had finally decided to bring some order to his office and Lincoln had been assigned the prestigious task of picking up the mountains of paper strips from the floor. So when Reban Don stormed into the office he didn't notice Lincoln under the desk.

"Enough," growled Reban Don. "The other zones are becoming impatient. They aren't interested in the human DNA studies. They want to know if we can kill the T-rexes. They want to know when we can inhabit Piloria."

Lorcan's lab coat was dirty and smudged, his grey hair practically standing on end. Lincoln had no idea when the last time Lorcan had actually gone home and slept was. His every breath was being spent on trying to find a cure for the blistering plague. The lab workers had also been encouraged to work even longer hours. Mapping genomes wasn't for the faint-hearted. Lincoln had dropped a clay pot one day and instead of shattering into large pieces, it had virtually disintegrated into dust. From the little he understood about DNA, they were practically trying to map that dust, joining all the pieces together to make a complete pot again.

The initial excitement that Lincoln had felt was slowly fading. The work was tedious and even though the staff were putting in long hours, there didn't seem to be any results yet. His gut clenched. What if the cure came too late for Arta? If it came at all.

Lorcan had barely even acknowledged Reban's entrance.

But Reban wasn't so easily ignored.

He grabbed hold of Lorcan's lab coat. "I said, enough. It's time to stop this work. We need you to work on the dinosaurs. We need you to find a way to kill them! We need the land."

"I don't need the land. I don't care about the dinosaurs. Go away. I have far too much to do. There is so much to learn about human DNA. Do you know that yesterday we discovered which genes affect eye colour? There's more than one. We've only scratched the surface."

Reban shook Lorcan with every word he said. "It's time to stop. It's time to focus."

But instead of being intimidated, Lorcan sneered. "What are you afraid of, Reban Don? I know what DNA can show. I already know how to connect families. Are you worried I'll tell the world you have a daughter?"

Lincoln winced as Reban slammed Lorcan against the wall. "You have no idea what you're talking about."

Lorcan didn't seem to care. "Be careful, Reban. Don't push me. It isn't wise. I can reveal your dirty little secret to the world. What will happen to you then?"

Reban's teeth were gritted together. "I've told you. The Chief Stipulators will shut this lab down if you don't complete your assignment. The other labs are ahead of this one. If you can't perform, you're no use to us."

Lorcan shook his head and pushed hard at Reban's chest. "Then persuade them that I am completing the work. Or else I'll tell the world what you don't want them to know."

Lincoln could see the fury on Reban's face. He hated the fact he was cowering under the desk right now. But revealing himself could be dangerous. Revealing himself now would likely get him sent him straight to the mines. A certain death sentence.

Reban released his grip on Lorcan's lab coat, shoving him halfway across the room. "Don't threaten me, Lorcan. Not now, not ever." He turned with a sweep of his cloak and kicked the door open with his foot so hard that part of it shattered against the wall.

Lincoln shook his head. Thank goodness Reban hadn't seen him. Maybe he should try and warn Storm that she could be in danger? That someone else knew who her father was.

But how could he warn someone who wouldn't even look at him, let alone speak to him?

TWELVE

STORMCHASER

The corridor in the care centre was quiet, but as Storm pushed open the door to Arta's room she could hear laughter.

Arta's roommate had changed. The older woman was gone and in her place was a girl of around Arta's age.

Storm gave a hesitant smile as she walked into the room, clutching an orange fruit. "Hi, just thought I'd check on you."

Arta gave a bright smile. "I'm good." She lifted her hand. "This is Tarin. She got moved in here last night."

Storm gave Tarin a nod. Like Arta she was covered in bandages, except Tarin's wound all the way up her neck. Her blonde hair stuck out around her head and even with the bandages bulking up her body she still seemed thin.

"Nice to meet you, Tarin. I'm Storm. I'm..." For a second she was lost for words as her head sorted out the correct answer. "I'm Arta's half-sister."

Tarin frowned, as if the name was familiar and she was trying to place it. "Storm?" A few seconds later, realization hit. "You're Stormchaser Knux. You fought the dinosaurs!" Tarin clapped her hands together then winced.

Something must have clicked in her brain. She glanced over at Arta. "But Arta's only got a brother."

Storm's skin prickled instantly. The staff gave Arta medication for her condition. Sometimes it made her woozy. What had she said?

Storm spoke quickly. "Yes, I fought the dinosaurs – though actually sometimes I just hid. Arta and Lincoln have the same mum, but different dads. My father" – she almost cringed saying the word out loud – "is the same as Arta's. In fact I have quite a few half-brothers and half-sisters."

She was trying to keep things smooth. She had no idea who could be listening around here. She'd have to try and warn Arta later to be careful what she said.

Lincoln visiting too could complicate things. They hadn't spoken since the final Trial. She didn't *want* to speak to him. Not when he'd betrayed her. Then again, there was always a chance he could unwittingly tell a different story of how Arta was related to Storm. Did she really want their fight to impact on Arta's care?

But Tarin seemed to accept the explanation. She lay back against her pillows with a sigh. "Lucky you. There's only me. I think it must be fun to have brothers and sisters." Her voice had a wistful tone.

Storm resisted the temptation to answer honestly. She'd

dreamed, years ago, of having brothers and sisters. But dreams and reality were two different things.

She gave a smile and walked over to Arta, handing her the orange. "Here. Look, this came in the ration box today. I wanted you to try it. I think it's the same as a fruit we found on Piloria. It's lovely. But a bit messy. See what you think."

Arta held out her hand for the fruit and wrinkled her nose as she studied it. She banged it against her leg under the bedclothes. "But it feels so hard. How can you eat it?"

Storm shook her head. "You don't eat the skin. That peels off. The soft flesh is underneath. It breaks into pieces when you open it and there's lots of juice."

She was just showing Arta how to peel the orange when the door banged behind her. She turned around just in time to see Lincoln walk into the room.

The last person she wanted to see.

THIRTEEN

LINCOLN

Lincoln stopped mid-step. He hadn't managed to visit for a few days and had only planned to drop in for a short spell after another long session at the lab. He knew Storm visited Arta, but he hadn't expected her to be here.

Awkward.

Arta's lips turned upwards as she glanced between the two of them. He tried to act normally, even though he felt distinctly uncomfortable.

Arta patted the side of her bed. She had a bright orange fruit in her lap. He recognized it instantly. He wrinkled his brow. "Where did you get that?"

Arta grinned. "Apparently I've just got a little piece of Piloria. It came in Storm's ration box."

Lincoln stared at Storm, his mind racing. "That was in your box?"

If the fruit from Piloria could grow here, maybe other

plants could too. He glanced at Arta's arm. It was still covered. But a little spark of something flickered inside him. Was it working? Was the ointment doing anything at all to help?

Storm turned and headed to the door. "I need to go. See you later, Arta."

He couldn't help it, he reached out and brushed Storm's hand. "We should talk." He needed to tell her. He needed to tell her about Blaine's family.

She pulled her hand back sharply and gave him an angry stare. "We were done talking a long time ago."

Storm spun around and stalked out of the door, and his heart twisted in his chest. She still hated him.

Arta gave a sympathetic smile and held up the half-peeled fruit. "Want to help me with this?"

He sighed and settled himself at Arta's bedside – but the next minute all hell was breaking loose.

The girl opposite Arta started coughing. It sounded like a tickly cough, but became hoarser and hoarser, with her colour changing from white to red and then verging on blue.

Finally she gave an enormous cough, spluttering blood all over her bedclothes. Lincoln jumped to his feet just as a female care worker appeared at the door, who shouted for assistance.

Lincoln could hardly believe it when Lorcan Field burst through the doors, his eyes wide at the sight of the sick girl in the bed.

Lincoln stepped back. He'd known Lorcan's daughter was

in the care centre. He just hadn't realized that *she* was Arta's new roommate.

Within a few moments, there was a crowd around the young girl's bed. Lincoln crouched down next to Arta. He didn't really think he should be in here right now, but he didn't want to leave his sister alone with all this.

Lorcan was gripped by panic. He shouted at one care worker after another. The medico ran in, heading to the top of the bed.

Because of the mass of people, Lincoln couldn't really see what was going on. He slid his arm around Arta's shoulder. Her eyes were wide, her fingers at her mouth.

Words were flying.

"What are you doing to help her?"

"We're doing our best. You know there's no cure. This is a progressive disease. We don't know how to stop the damage to the lungs."

There was a little yelp from the bed opposite and both Lincoln and Arta jumped. Lincoln hated the sound of the other girl in pain. He could hear her ragged breaths, the way she was struggling to breathe. It could so easily be Arta.

"Why can't you help my daughter? This isn't good enough. You have to keep her stable. I can find a cure for this. I can. But I need time."

One of the other care workers mumbled under her voice, "But they don't all have time."

Lincoln stiffened, conscious that Arta could hear just as clearly as he could.

As Lorcan shouted louder, the staff seemed to get more nervous. More edgy.

"There must be something that can halt this!" He threw his hands in the air. "Anything!"

One of the care workers looked over at Arta, her gaze narrowing. Every hair on Lincoln's arms bristled.

The woman bent forward and spoke quietly to the other people around the bed. There was some more coughing. A shifting of positions. After a few minutes one of the care workers swept away the bloodied sheet and replaced it with another. The voices were low. Lorcan seemed to be holding his breath.

A couple of the care workers disappeared out of the room, muttering to each other. The medico stayed a bit longer. He looked as if he were giving Tarin some medicine – some kind of injection. As the crowd around the bed dispersed, Tarin became visible, lying back against the pillows, her face even paler than usual and streaked with tears.

Arta breathed an audible sigh of relief.

The woman who'd stared at Arta was still there, still shooting glances in their direction.

She moved next to Lorcan and tugged at his sleeve.

"Look at her hands," she said.

Lorcan looked confused. "What?"

The woman pointed at Tarin's hands. "Look, they're the only part of her that's healed."

Lorcan furrowed his brow and gently picked up Tarin's hands. After a few seconds examining them he started to nod.

"You're right. They do look better. They're not bleeding. The cracks are starting to heal. The skin around them has stopped peeling. There are no blisters." His voice started to sound hopeful. "What is this? Have you been using something different on her hands?"

Tarin blinked her dark eyes. She gave a tired smile, pulling her hands back from her father's in a dazed kind of way. She let out a little laugh. "It's magic. But it's not from them. It's from my friend." She looked over towards Arta.

Lorcan shook his head. "Who?"

Lincoln felt frozen. The ointment. It could only be the ointment. Arta must have shared it.

And it had worked. It had *actually* worked.

He couldn't help it. He held Arta's arm, straightened it and peeled back the covering, focusing on the crook of her elbow. The crook of her elbow that now looked entirely normal, with pink skin.

His brain crowded with a million thoughts. He should have visited sooner. He should have monitored exactly how the ointment was doing.

He closed his eyes for a second and could picture the inside of Blaine's makeshift hut. He could see the hotch-potch of things stuck to the wall. He could see all the hours of work, the individual sense of order with the pots of ointment and glue.

The ointment. The actual *ointment* that was helping Arta's skin. He should have asked Blaine so much more than he actually had. He should have watched more carefully as Blaine made it. He should have taken samples of the plants and leaves. He should have done anything that would mean he could get his hands on some more of the precious substance.

He was stupid. He was so, so stupid. He hadn't even asked Blaine how he'd made it. He didn't even know the name of the plant that had been used.

The whole time he'd been on Piloria he'd thought about helping his sister. That had been his sole motivation. His only goal. And now it seemed he'd let the one opportunity that actually *could* make a difference slip through his fingers.

He'd missed it. It had been right in front of him and he'd missed it.

The care worker looked pointedly in their direction. She gestured with her head. "It's them. They had the ointment. Arta started using it on her inside arm without telling us. I've no idea what it is, but her skin there has practically healed."

Lorcan crossed the room in three long strides. He grabbed Arta's arm himself – a little too roughly for Lincoln's liking – and his finger reached down and stroked the inside of her elbow. The skin was pale, but healthy. No breaks. No peeling. No bleeding. No blisters.

His voice had a tone of wonder. "What is this? What is it?" He tugged at the edge of one of Arta's bandages further up her arm, trying to see the skin hidden underneath.

Lincoln elbowed him out of the way. "Stop it," he said sharply.

Arta's gaze flicked from one to the other. She peeled back the rest of the bandages on her own.

She gave a hopeful, tentative smile. "It's the ointment. The one Lincoln gave me." She nodded at her brother. "The one you brought back from Piloria. I've only been putting on a tiny smear each day, but my arm feels so much better. I can bend it now without it hurting." She bent her elbow up and down. "I gave Tarin some to try on her sore hands. But there isn't much left."

But Lorcan was too excited to stop. "But this – it's working. What is it? From Piloria? We need some more. You only gave Tarin enough for her fingers. What kind of a person does that? She needs more. Have you seen how sick she is? You need to give me more. You need to share what you have."

He was babbling, carried away by the idea of a cure. His eyes were bright.

But the smile had dropped from Arta's face.

"I can't," Lincoln said bluntly.

He was still trying to work out how he could have been so stupid. How he could have missed the most important thing in the world. He'd been worried about dinosaurs, eggs and staying alive the whole time he'd been in Piloria. But the thing he'd wanted most had been right there the whole time.

The air rushed out of his lungs as Lorcan slammed him against the wall. Instinctively Lincoln raised his fists. He was strong. He was more than able to protect himself, but did he really want to do this? Particularly in front of his sister?

"What do you mean, you can't?" roared Lorcan.

Tarin let out a whimper. But Lorcan didn't seem to hear. He was busy directing his anger and frustration at Lincoln.

"Did you see? Did you see what just happened to my daughter? Wait a minute." Something seemed to register in his brain as he glanced up and down at the guy clutched in his fists. "I know you. I *know* you. You work in my lab. You're one of mine. You work in my lab and you won't give it to me?" He sounded incredulous.

Lincoln felt the rage burn inside him. He spoke through gritted teeth. "Don't you think if I had any more I would have given it to my sister? Why do you think it's just one tiny part of her that's healed? Don't you think if I'd realized it could really help I would have given it to her sooner? Brought it to you, to see if you could actually replicate it?" He pushed Lorcan back. Thoughts were rushing through his head. He felt like a failure. He'd left that ointment lying forgotten at the bottom of a bag for a few weeks after his return. When time was something Arta couldn't afford.

And now Arta had given away something that could potentially save her.

More than anything, Lincoln hated the way that made him feel.

But Lorcan didn't retaliate. No, he seemed to have only one thing on his mind. He scrambled over to Arta's storage box and started yanking all her things out, scattering them across the floor. Care centre gowns, tunics and undergarments spilled across the floor, followed by bandages that bounced in every direction.

"Stop it," Arta whimpered. "Stop it."

Lincoln stood rooted to the spot. He knew exactly what

Lorcan was looking for. He just didn't know if there was anything left to find.

As one of the gowns floated across the floor, a scrap of material landed on the ground. The tiny remnants of the leaf and ointment were mushed against the cloth. Within a few seconds the smell was unmistakeable.

Lorcan pounced. "Is this it?" His nose wrinkled at the smell, then his face started to fall as he realized how little ointment there actually was.

"There must be more," he said frantically, searching among the rest of Arta's things. A tiny clotted bit of ointment broke away and landed on the floor. Lorcan muttered as he stared at the fallen fragments. He dropped to his knees and tried to scoop them up. But the smear on the fabric was the only real part of the ointment that was left. Lincoln could hardly breathe.

What happened now? What about Arta? Without the ointment would even her small healed patch of skin just deteriorate again, and the disease progress?

Lorcan held up the tiny hard remnants in the palm of his hand. He turned to Lincoln. "This...this is it? This is all there is?"

Lincoln nodded.

Lorcan was shaking. Lincoln could practically hear his brain whizzing around, processing all his thoughts and deciding what to do next. After a few seconds Lorcan took a deep breath and blew it out slowly, then he stepped forward, lowering his voice so only Lincoln could hear. "Finally.

Something that might actually work. But let's keep this between us. If the Stipulators know you might have a possible cure for the blistering plague they'll do anything to keep you quiet. Me? I've already annoyed them, but they still need me to kill the dinosaurs. They can't do that alone."

Lincoln's heart was still thudding in his chest. What was in Lorcan's hand was all that was left of the miracle ointment. The tiniest remnant of something that might actually help. "We don't have any of the right plants. And I've never seen them growing on Earthasia. They were dark green – with a really distinctive smell." Lincoln let out a painful sigh and shook his head. "If only I'd known. If only I'd thought, I could have tried to bring some back from Piloria." The orange fruit sparked in his brain again. "Maybe we could grow them here?"

But Lorcan was studying the sample in his hand. "Let's see. I need to look at this in the lab. We might not need to grow the plants. I might be able to replicate this artificially."

For the first time since he'd come home, Lincoln's heart gave a leap. Finally, a chance to do something that might help his sister.

He hoped that Lorcan was right about making the ointment without the evergreen plants. Because unless some secret garden had a stock of them, there was only one place to get them. Only one place that could hold a potential cure for the blistering plague.

Piloria.

FOURTEEN

STORMCHASER

She was trying not to show any excitement. But every time Octavius left the room she was left surrounded by the old books. Right now she'd do anything for a bit of distraction. Anything to stop herself thinking about Reban Don, or Lincoln Kreft. The anger she felt for both of them continued to simmer just beneath the surface. Even Octavius was starting to frustrate her now. He still hadn't even told why she was really there.

Focusing on the books gave her something else to think about. It was like a whole new world. School had never interested Storm. Never engaged her mind. But all these books?

Since she'd got back to Earthasia things had seemed even blander than before. The whole place felt grey. Nothing like the bright lushness of Piloria.

She ran her hand over the cover of a thick book, wishing for just a second that it could transport her back there.

Maybe these books would tell her more about Piloria than she'd discovered in her time there. Okay, the dinosaur one wasn't entirely accurate, but at least it would feed her need for more knowledge about the dinosaur continent – and that in turn, would feed her soul.

She'd spent the last few nights at the side of the loch watching for Milo. But he was nowhere to be seen. She'd never gone this long without seeing the plesiosaur, not since he'd saved her life. Maybe it was because she wasn't swimming in the loch so much. Before, she'd never worried about the deep expanse of water. The loch was relatively clear – one of the Trials had even been in the loch.

For a second, the lake on Piloria flashed in front of her eyes, along with the vision of the deinosuchus with its wide jaws and endless teeth.

The downside of Piloria. In amongst the wonder of the landscape, there were still the terrifying dinosaurs. Her stomach gave a flip.

If only she could experience the beauty of Piloria without the near-constant fear of dying. If only she could think about the place without remembering the deaths of her friends.

A horrible prickle went down her spine. Was she actually wishing the dangerous dinosaurs dead? Was her mind adjusting to the way that the Stipulators thought?

This time the shudder didn't just go down her spine, it vibrated through her whole body. Was working in parliament somehow affecting how she thought?

She couldn't even bear to imagine that. Right now, these

books were the best distraction she could have. There was a whole world of information here which she had never been exposed to before. Maybe, if she looked hard enough, she would find something that could help her. Maybe even information that could help her to stop the viruses the scientists were creating to destroy the dinosaurs.

She rested her hand against the shelf. Wood. Even the feel of it was special. It had a smell. Even though the wood had been worked to be straight and flat she could still feel the grain and tiny notches under the palm of her hand. The boat on Piloria had been much rougher, with splinters everywhere to catch her skin. But the smell was the same. She closed her eyes for a second.

Octavius's voice sounded in a curious tone behind her. "What do we have here?"

She jumped and pulled her hand back. "Oh, sorry. I didn't see you there."

"Obviously," he said, nodding. Then he waited. He had a pile of papers under his arm and she held out her hands to take them but he shook his head and nodded back to the shelves. "What were you doing?"

She hesitated, trying to think of a suitable lie. But it was hard to formulate one in her head while Octavius was staring at her with those all-knowing eyes of his.

She sighed. "The wood. I like it. I like the feel of it. The smell of it. I can't believe we used to have trees everywhere and now we have virtually none. It just seems such…such a shame." She held up her hands.

Octavius nodded. "You must have seen trees as a child."

"Trees, yes. I just didn't realize you could actually make things from wood."

"Like shelves?"

"And boats." The word came out before she realized.

Octavius's gaze narrowed. "Now where would someone like you see a boat made of wood, I wonder?"

She gulped. Back on Piloria, Blaine had crafted a boat out of a tree trunk that they'd used to cross the loch. She hadn't told anyone they'd met Blaine. They'd all agreed it was safest not to. "Maybe someone told me about it once."

He gave a perfunctory nod. She had the oddest sensation that he knew so much more than he was admitting to.

Octavius thrust the pile of papers towards her. "Put these somewhere." He walked away with a wave of his hand. "Anywhere will do."

He climbed back up to his desk. "We have other work to do." He raised his eyebrows. "Now I know you a little better…" His lips curved into a smile. "Now I've seen your curiosity and your tenacity, it's time you found out what you're really here for."

FIFTEEN

LINCOLN

Lorcan was a man with a mission.

Once again he had gathered the lab staff together and instructed them that there had been a change of plan. Now, they were to spend their time analysing the sample for medicinal purposes. Lorcan wanted to know if they could replicate what was in the leaf – but hadn't given the lab staff any indication of what the sample actually was.

It sounded like a reasonable plan. Except, this wasn't a lab-made substance. This was a plant. Something that could be grown.

The guy working next to Lincoln looked up and murmured, "What happens next week? First it was dinosaur DNA, then it was human DNA and the search for the blistering plague, now it's try to replicate some green smush. Can't the guy make up his mind?"

Lincoln kept his mouth shut. He had a mountain of tasks

to do. Lorcan had questioned him to death about the ointment. What was the name of the plant? What did the leaves look like? How was it made? How quickly did it work? Trouble was – he couldn't remember that much about it. The only question he could answer truthfully was how quickly the ointment worked, and that only seemed to build on Lorcan's frustration.

Eventually he'd been dismissed, with the instruction to stay close and keep his mouth shut if anyone asked any questions.

A flicker of a black cloak caught his eye. He immediately turned away, not wanting to have to deal with Reban Don again. But this time it wasn't Reban Don. It was another Stipulator. One he'd never seen before. He had white-blond hair – a bit like the Nordens' – and pale blue eyes.

Lincoln frowned. Why would another Stipulator be here? It was easy to become invisible in a lab as busy as this one, with everyone dressed the same. He found a tiny space at the bench nearest where the Stipulator had stopped.

The Stipulator was talking in a low voice to a lab worker. "So this is it? This is what you wanted me to see?" The older man nodded. The Stipulator frowned. "Okay, explain again. What is it *exactly*?"

The lab worker pointed to the sequences and charts. "This is what we've discovered about human DNA. We can see which conditions are inherited from parents. We can map which traits – eye colour, hand use, heart problems, for example – come from which side of the family."

A strange look passed across the Stipulator's face. "But how do you know the DNA is correct?"

"What do you mean?"

"How do you know you have the right samples? How do you know these people are actually the parents of that child?"

The lab worker waved his hand. "Oh, that's the easy part. We can show how the strands match. It's the first step. We always check in case there's been a mix-up with the samples."

The Stipulator's gaze narrowed. "So if I gave you a sample of DNA from a child, you would be able to match it to the DNA of a parent?"

"Of course!" The lab worker started to babble, going into a huge amount of detail about the technicalities of DNA. Lincoln could see the Stipulator's eyes glaze over. The truth was he'd been lost himself after the second sentence.

The Stipulator tried to keep his frustration in check. "And human DNA, how do you get a sample? Where does the DNA come from?"

The lab worker blinked. "Body fluids. Blood, saliva. And other places, hair, flakes of skin, nails. We've been using flakes of skin to get the DNA for the people with the blistering plague."

The Stipulator was completely focused now. "So if I brought you some samples from two people and you analysed them, you could give me absolute, definite proof that one person was the parent of the other?" He seemed to be getting more animated by the second.

The lab worker started to look a little wary. "Well, yes. Of course. But why on earth would we want to do that? We're not working on the blistering plague any more. We've been told to focus on the new samples, that strange substance."

Lincoln cringed at the lab worker's words, hoping the Stipulator wouldn't question what "strange substance" they were working on.

But the Stipulator seemed not to hear him. He bent forward and kept his voice low. "You'll do exactly what I want you to do." He glanced around the room. "How long have you worked in this lab?"

The man looked worried now. "About fifteen years."

The Stipulator nodded. "Then maybe it's time for a promotion. Somewhere better to stay. Some more rations. You give me what I want and I can make life *very* comfortable for you."

It was a threat and a promise all in one.

Lincoln saw the lab worker gulp and struggle to find words. Of course he would want extra food. Everyone did.

But in the end he didn't even get a chance to say yes or no. The Stipulator just gave a brief nod of his head as he closed his hand around the man's trembling fist on the bench and tightened his grip. Lincoln winced. He was sure he heard a crack.

"I'll be back in a few days with the samples. How long will it take for you to give me the proof?"

The man could hardly speak. He was obviously in pain from the Stipulator's grip on his hand. "About five…days."

A broad smile stretched across the Stipulator's face. "Perfect."

SIXTEEN

STORMCHASER

She'd spent three days drawing maps. Detailed maps. Wracking every single part of her brain to try to remember things she hadn't consciously paid attention to. Her hand ached from constantly holding the graphite.

It appeared she had her purpose. The books she'd admired? Octavius wanted information from Piloria to update them all. He wanted to know about foods. Dinosaurs. He wanted to know if the creatures had revealed any vulnerabilities. He asked unending questions about how much she'd watched them. How they fed, what they ate, their nesting sites.

It seemed that Octavius had spent the first week getting to know her – before deciding if he could trust her and the information she could provide for his precious books.

"Tell me about the deinosuchus again."

Storm closed her eyes for a few seconds. Thinking about

the deinosuchus meant thinking about Rune and Kronar. Two friends gone.

Some parts of Piloria were best forgotten.

She sighed. "What do you want to know?"

Octavius pointed to the map, gesturing towards the lake. "So it lives here, you say?"

She nodded. "Apparently, yes."

"Colour?"

She wrinkled her nose. "Green, grey, sludgy. The colour is hard to describe, it was only out of the water for a second and I was mainly running in the other direction." She took a deep breath. "It had lumpy skin. Like scales. I remember that. And its mouth…" She shuddered. "It had a long jaw, with rows and rows of teeth. It was so powerful."

Octavius nodded as he scribbled some notes. "Why were you on the lake?"

She started. "I didn't say I was…on the lake. I was beside the lake."

"Do you always tell lies?"

She blinked. It came totally out of the blue. Just like that.

The door to the room swung open and one of the Chief Stipulators walked in. She vaguely recognized him. He'd been in the atrium a few times when she'd been there. She couldn't quite remember his name but he was the Chief Stipulator of Norden and he had the distinctive white-blond hair of the area.

"Don't you know how to knock, Silas?" snapped Octavius.

Silas ignored the question. He walked straight across the

room and looked directly over Storm's shoulder. She shifted in her seat. She hated someone trying to intimidate her and his large frame cast shadows over her work.

He scowled, his finger pointing square in the middle of the map. "Why are you wasting time with this?"

Octavius gave him a pointed stare. "I'm picking the best spot for you to stay when we have Piloria to ourselves." He gave Storm's shoulder a nudge. "Storm suggested the velociraptor nest site." He let out a little laugh. "You'd feel right at home, Silas, you have similar characteristics."

Storm was amazed. Octavius was around a third of the size of the Norden Chief Stipulator – in height and weight. But it seemed he was immune to the intimidation that Storm was currently feeling.

Silas leaned closer to Storm, his body weight pressing against her back. She cringed. He pointed to the upper corner of the map. She hadn't charted that area because she'd no idea what was there. They hadn't reached that far around the coastline.

"What's up there? Why haven't you mapped that area?"

She opened her mouth to speak but Octavius got in first. "What do you want, Silas?" He asked the question as if he were dealing with a troublesome two year old.

Silas threw Storm a disparaging look, but as he pulled back, his hand caught in her long hair.

"Ow!" Storm's hands flew to her head.

Silas gave her an almost-smile. "Sorry." He turned back to Octavius. "We need to talk. In private."

Storm was still rubbing her smarting scalp. She didn't like this guy at all.

Octavius was brisk. "If you have something to say, Silas, then just say it."

Silas gave a calculating smile as he looked between Storm and Octavius. "No, it might be more interesting if we wait a few days. Let's not rush into anything."

He strode out of the room without a backward glance.

Storm pulled her hands away from her head. "What was that all about?"

Octavius tapped his graphite on the desk. "I'm not sure," he said in a puzzled tone, "but Silas is someone to watch."

"What does that mean?"

Octavius shook his head. "I think he has designs on being Chief Stipulator for more than one zone. He's calculating. Has been for a long time." Octavius's eyes were still fixed on the door. "Sometimes nothing is quite what it seems." His eyes flickered back to Storm and she shifted uncomfortably in her chair.

This place got stranger every day.

SEVENTEEN

LINCOLN

The sky was bathed in shades of purple and violet as he made his way down to the loch. His heart gave a little lurch as he saw the outline of someone sitting on the shore.

There was no sneaking up on Storm. His feet crunched loudly on the shingle as he walked up and sat beside her. "I've been down here the last three nights. Where have you been?"

She didn't even deign to turn her head towards his voice, just shot him a steely sideways glance. "I've been busy. Some of us have jobs to do. Go away, Lincoln. This is my space, not yours."

"I have a job too. One that seems to change on a daily basis." He shifted to face her better. "Arta told me you were moved to the parliament. That seems a bit of a drastic change. What happened to the hay bales?"

"Are you going to go away?" she snapped in response.

"No. I'm not." Now he'd finally got her on her own he wasn't going to let this chance disappear. "So, if you want to go for a swim in the loch, I'll just swim alongside you." The words sounded braver than he actually felt. Storm had always sworn that this loch was harmless – and there had never been reports of anything untoward. But he still didn't relish the thought of swimming in the loch at night with unknown marine creatures. "You're not getting rid of me. So, tell me about parliament."

She let out an exasperated sigh. And it was music to his ears. Because it meant that she might actually talk to him again.

He didn't speak. He just gave her a little space. He knew Storm. He knew she'd need to fill the silence.

Their time on Piloria had built a friendship he couldn't forget. He'd seen her at her most vulnerable, her most open. She'd shared with him just how alone she was in this world.

Her fingers were tracing circles in the small stones. "Funnily enough, I didn't really get much of a reason for the change." She lifted her fingers in the air. "*Apparently*, I scored well in the written test for the Trials. So they moved me to a job they think is more suitable. Octavius said that he asked for me specially."

"Who is Octavius?"

"He's the Captain Regent for parliament."

Lincoln wrinkled his nose. "The what?"

She sighed. "You obviously paid as much attention as

I did at school. Apparently he keeps the Chief Stipulators under control. I didn't even know he existed."

Lincoln gave a half laugh. "Well, it's not like we hang out in parliament all the time. But this guy. You work for him?" Lincoln couldn't keep the incredulous tone from his voice.

"Yep." She tossed a few stones into the loch, sending little ripples out across the still water.

"Why did he ask for you?"

She thudded her hands down on the shingle and turned to face him. "Who knows?" She was frustrated by him. "What do you want, Lincoln? Why are you here? We have nothing to talk about."

He pressed his lips together. "Well, actually we do."

She turned away again and fixed her gaze on the water.

At least he'd made some progress. For the last few weeks, on the rare occasions they'd crossed paths, she'd refused to meet his eye, let alone talk to him. He'd been so worried about Arta, and felt so guilty about betraying his friends, that he'd accepted the silence. Arta's health had been his ultimate goal. But things weren't working out quite as planned.

"Like what?"

Her voice cut through his thoughts.

He shifted on the shingle so that he was facing her. She might not want to look at him, but he was going to look at her. "There's been a complication."

Furrows appeared in her brow. "What?"

He took a deep breath. "Blaine's family. They approached me in the street."

"What?" Now he had her full attention. She spun around to face him. "What on earth do you mean?"

He met her violet gaze. She had her hair down tonight. It hung in straight glossy sheets. It made her look different. More like a girl. Most of the time they'd been in Piloria her hair had been tied in a knot on top of her head.

He licked his lips. "I mean, they approached me in the street. I didn't know who they were at first. The woman – her name is Kayna. She had the boy with her – Caleb. He looks around the same age as us. It took me a few moments to recognize her from the sketch in Blaine's hut. They were desperate, Storm. I didn't know what to do." He chose his next words carefully. "Have you told anyone about Blaine?"

"No!" The words came out of her mouth just a little too quickly. Then she started to hesitate. "Well…not really. Not intentionally. But the Stipulators already know about him anyway. What difference does it make?"

Lincoln nodded. "They know he exists. They know he's alive. But they don't know *we* met him. They don't know we spoke to him."

"What did you tell his family?" Her voice sounded sad.

Lincoln sighed. "I told them part of the truth. I told them that he mentioned them – that he loved them. How he'd asked about them, and wanted to come home and the Stipulators had refused."

"How did that go down?"

"About as well as you can expect." He picked up some of the shingle and let it run through his fingers. "When they

112

asked me if anyone could survive on Piloria, I just couldn't lie to them. I couldn't pretend we hadn't met. But I wonder if telling them did more harm than good."

Storm pushed herself to her feet and folded her arms. He'd forgotten what being in her company was like. He'd blocked from his mind how connected they'd felt. How she'd seemed to sense when he was struggling with things, and how he'd been the same with her. He glanced towards her folded arms and had a flashback to the ship. The two of them, sitting in the dark near the engine room. She'd just told him about the scars on her back. How she'd fallen out of the boat on the loch with no one apparently noticing, been knocked unconscious and dragged under. How she'd woken with Milo, the plesiosaur, resting his head next to hers at the side of the lake and realized that he must have rescued her. How alone she was. And they'd sat for the longest time, leaning against each other with their hands intertwined. This was harder than he'd thought.

"So you couldn't lie to them – strangers. But you could lie to me and Leif. The people whose lives all depended on each other?"

He sagged his head forward into his hands. "Don't do this. Don't do this again. How much longer can we fight about this? You know I feel like crap about it all." He pushed himself up onto his feet too, stepping forward until they were only an arm's length apart.

She was still angry. He could practically see the flash in her eyes, even in this dim light.

"You've seen Arta. You know exactly how sick she was, how sick she *is*. Tell me, if she was your sister, that you would have done anything different. Tell me."

She stared at him. Almost willing him to look away. But Lincoln was steady. He put his hands on his hips and stepped even closer.

"You can't, can you? I think you've connected with my sister more than you meant to. She talks about you all the time." He let out the biggest sigh and ran his fingers through his hair. "But we've let her down." He shook his head. "All that way. Megalodons. Raptors. T-rexes. Pterosaurs. All that way to Piloria and we completely ignored the one thing that looks as if it might actually help. Maybe if we hadn't concentrated on the dinosaurs... Maybe if we'd spent more time exploring our surroundings, we would have found out the things that are most important."

The tension in his muscles released. He hadn't told his mother any of this.

"What do you mean?"

He held up his hands. "The ointment. The sludgy ointment that Blaine gave me for my wounds and your feet. I found it again and gave some to Arta. Her skin – it healed it. But by the time I realized how important it was, there was barely any left."

Her eyes widened. "You mean it really could be a cure for the plague?" She stared at him for a moment, then she let out a long slow breath as her shoulders slumped. "Oh no."

He hadn't spoken to anyone about this huge cloud of guilt

114

that was currently hanging over his head. Only someone who'd actually been to Piloria could understand how overwhelming it had all been.

"We missed it." She sagged back down onto the shingles.

"We missed it," he said too as he sat down beside her.

For a few moments no one spoke. They just both stared out across the rippling loch.

"I miss it."

"What?" His head shot up.

She licked her lips. Her voice was a little shaky. "I miss it. I miss the green. I miss the smells. I miss seeing the mountains in the distance with not a single building anywhere. I miss the colour. I miss finding different things to eat." She looked out over the loch. "But most of all, I just miss the place." A tear trickled down her cheek. "And I don't understand why I feel this way. I spent half my time there plain terrified."

Lincoln didn't quite know how to react. He reached out with his finger and brushed away her tear. "Don't." He couldn't bear to see her cry. He kept his voice quiet. "How can you miss the terror? How can you miss the fear? How can you miss going to sleep every night and not knowing if you'll see the morning?"

He was trying to understand – he really was. He'd been so focused on his family, his one priority, that he hadn't considered any of this.

She shook her head and gave a half smile. "Don't you get it? That's just it. I don't miss the T-rex, or the raptors. But I miss the place. The way it made me feel in here." She pressed her hand against her chest. "The wonder of it. The feeling of space. The feeling of possibilities. And I hate how that makes me think."

Something clicked in his brain. Storm had always said she didn't believe in what the Stipulators wanted to do. She'd questioned it all along. She'd been convinced they wouldn't be happy to just kill the dangerous dinosaurs, and were more likely to try and kill them all.

"You'd like to go back to Piloria," he breathed. "But you don't want them there. The T-rexes, the raptors or the pterosaurs."

She winced as if he'd slapped her. But he was just saying out loud what had obviously been playing on her mind.

He shook his head. "Come here," he said as he slung his arm around her shoulder and he felt her relax a little. "It's the nightmares I find worst. Piloria. It plays on your mind even when you don't think about it. I've had a nightmare every night since we got back." He sighed. "I have no idea what's going on right now. Arta, the ointment. We messed up big time. We should have brought more. We should have taken some of the plants. We had the potential cure for the blistering plague right in our hands and just didn't notice."

Lincoln watched the quiet surface of the loch as the sun dipped lower in the sky. "Things at the lab have been crazy." He licked his lips. "Lorcan's daughter is sick. She has the blistering plague too. He found out about the ointment. He wants to try and replicate it in the lab."

Storm's eyes widened. "Did you tell him Blaine made it?"

Lorcan shook his head. "I lied. Trouble is, the lie isn't too good. I told him we made it from some leaves we found on Piloria." He lifted his hand. "But I couldn't give him enough details – because I didn't know them. I didn't pay attention to what Blaine was doing, did you?"

He couldn't help the hopeful urge in his voice. But Storm shook her head. She grabbed some stones in frustration, squeezing them in her fist. "He was right next to me. Right next to me, making things in that darn clay pot and I didn't pay attention." She met his gaze. Her voice quietened. "I wish I had."

He nodded. "So do I."

"Do you think the lab stuff might work?"

Lincoln sagged a little. "Probably not. The ointment didn't come from a lab. It's a plant. A living thing. Even if we'd brought it here it probably wouldn't grow. Piloria is so much warmer, so much more humid."

"Maybe the next people who go could bring some back…"

"But that's nearly a whole year away! It's too long." He paused for a second. "You've forgotten, I've already lost someone to the plague. Once the signs started, my dad didn't even get a year."

She edged a little closer, letting her head rest against his shoulder and reaching her hand across to connect with his.

Something occurred to him then. He had to ask. "What about your father? Your job at parliament. Do you think Reban Don had anything to do with it?"

She let out a kind of exasperated snort. "I hope not. I've only seen him once, when I had to deliver a message. He couldn't wait for me to leave again."

"He's been in the lab – fighting with Lorcan."

"He's what?" She lifted her head from his shoulder and pulled a face. "What did he say? I heard he's been told to keep Lorcan in line."

Lincoln shook his head again. "I think there's trouble. Between the Stipulators, I mean. Reban said our lab was falling behind. And we are. One minute we're looking at human DNA samples – they're using hair, saliva and skin cells. The next minute we're trying to replicate the ointment. But I don't know how much Lorcan really tells Reban. Last I heard, they had the basis for some kind of dinosaur virus. They just needed to test it."

Storm sat bolt upright. "A virus for the T-rex – or a virus for all the dinosaurs?"

Lincoln pulled his arm from her shoulder and turned to face her. She still had her other hand in his. It almost felt like it had back on Piloria. When they were connected. When she trusted him. "I have no idea. I put numbers into a machine and prepare slides. I'm far too low down the pecking order to find out any more."

Storm looked thoughtful. "The Chief Stipulators have been fighting. Octavius says that one of them is ambitious. He wants to rule more than one zone. I haven't been there long enough to find out more. But the Stipulators seem to fight all the time. It's not like what I imagined."

"Nothing is what we imagined, Storm." He was staring across the loch again.

She finally pulled her hand away from his. He wasn't sure he'd wanted her to.

He rested his elbows on his knees. "I somehow thought if we got to Piloria, stole the eggs and got home, everything would be okay. Sometimes I think I'm reasonably clever. Then I realize I'm as dumb as the next guy. I've watched people die from the plague. I watched my dad die from the plague." His voice shook a little as he struggled to keep it steady. "I just never thought I'd have to watch my sister die. I'd do anything to stop that happening. Anything at all."

Storm didn't speak at first. She just followed his gaze, as he looked out over the loch bathed in purple.

She reached back and gave his hand a squeeze. "I know," she said simply as they sat together in the dimming light.

EIGHTEEN

STORMCHASER

Storm had never seen parliament so busy. The security lines snaked away from the entrance. She was used to the atrium being filled with black cloaks or pale-blue uniformed colleagues, but today it was bursting at the seams.

She pushed her way through to Octavius's office, finally catching her breath as she burst through the tightly packed crowd.

"There you are!" exclaimed Octavius. For the first time since she'd worked for him he was wearing his dark-green cloak. "Hurry!" He pushed a pile of papers into her arms. "Follow me."

"What's happened?" she asked, as they shoved their way back out of his office. Octavius walked quickly, his small stature seemingly an advantage as he darted among the jostling bodies. She struggled to keep up, struggling even more to keep him in her eye line. After a few minutes she realized where he was going.

The crowd was biggest around the entrance to the main parliament debating chamber. She'd never actually been inside it before. The heavy double doors were intricately carved and today they were wide open. The inside of the chamber was white. White walls and white seats. All except one. One grander seat at the end of the chamber was red. Some of the Stipulators were already in place, seated according to their zone. Their black cloaks were striking against the white backdrop. Octavius pushed his way past the numerous black cloaks around the door. It seemed many of the Chief Stipulators were either consulting with their aides, or with other Stipulators from their area.

She'd never seen parliament in session before. Was this what it was always like?

Octavius mumbled to himself the whole way across the chamber. Storm couldn't keep up with his short legs. When he reached the red chair he pulled out a little box on the side to help him up into it, then held his hands out for his papers again.

"What's going on, Octavius?" she whispered.

He looked her straight in the eye. "An unscheduled session was called. All the Chief Stipulators have to attend. There will likely be a vote."

Storm shook her head as she glanced around the rapidly filling chamber. "A vote about what?" Being in the chamber was intimidating. The space was bigger than she expected, amplified by the fact it was completely white. A few eyes settled on her, scowling. She realized she was now the only aide inside the chamber.

As she turned to ask Octavius the obvious question, it seemed he was expecting it. "You have to leave. Session starts in a few minutes. It could go on for hours. Wait in the office."

"Do you need anything else?"

He shook his head. She gave a nod and turned to go. Reban Don was near the entrance – he caught her eye as he strode angrily into the chamber. Her skin prickled. But not from Reban's gaze. No. It was Silas. He was watching Reban from the other side of the chamber, his arms folded across his chest, and murmuring to the Stipulators on either side of him. He was almost smirking.

The last few black-cloaked figures swept through the entrance as Storm left, and seconds later the doors boomed shut. For a few seconds the atrium was silent. Everyone stared at the closed doors.

After a few moments she heard murmurs from aides gathered near one of the collection points. She walked in that direction but just as she reached them they all headed another way. Corin was with them. He looked over his shoulder and slowed his step, grabbing her sleeve. "Hurry up, we only have a few moments."

She quickened her pace. "Where are we going?"

Corin shook his head as they turned the corner. "And don't speak from this second onwards. Only whisper." She wrinkled her brow as they filed down an older-looking set of stairs. The light disappeared behind her. The corridor seemed a little cramped and musty. The bodies jammed closer together as the corridor got more winding and the aides in front of her slowed down.

Storm tried to see around Corin's body to figure out what was going on. The others had stopped walking and turned to face the wall. Just as she was about to ask why, one of the aides reached up and slid open a little grate in front of her. The shock of white made her gasp out loud.

"Shhh," hissed Corin angrily. He put his finger to his lips and mouthed, "Not a word."

She blinked as her eyes tried to focus. Although the whiteness was startling, her view was a little more unusual. Mainly black-clad feet.

She lifted her hands up in question to Corin.

He leaned over and whispered in her ear. "This is how we find out what actually happens in parliament."

She shook her head in wonder as Octavius's voice boomed around them.

"Order! Chief Stipulators to order, now!"

The voices in the debating chamber fell quiet. Storm stood on her tiptoes. She only had a little gap to peer through – she tried to squint first one way, then the other. When she looked really hard to her left she could see a tiny flash of green. Octavius.

"Silas Jung. You called this session. What is your displeasure?"

There were footsteps. Silas was obviously moving to

another position. After a few minutes she heard his familiar voice. "We were promised Piloria. We were promised a virus that would rid of us the most dangerous dinosaurs – or all dinosaurs – and yet it seems that some of our laboratories have been using their facilities for other priorities. Some zones are not delivering what is required. I think it's time to look at the leadership in those areas."

Octavius's voice cut through. "That's not your decision to make. That's for parliament. Let's start with reports from each of the zones on their labs."

One of the assistants next to Corin groaned. "Four hundred reports?" He pressed his head against the wall.

But the reports went quickly. And they varied. Some zones reported being ready to test a virus. Some weren't at that stage yet. A few reported problems. The lab at Tarribeth City was ready to test the pterosaur virus. The lab at Corbeth City was ready to test the velociraptor virus. Octavius asked a few questions along the way and Storm could tell he was taking notes.

It finally reached Reban Don's turn. His voice was icy cold. "Ambulus City. The T-rex virus is ready for testing."

"What about your other issues?"

It was a question from Octavius. Storm held her breath. He'd asked other Chief Stipulators questions when they'd said there had been problems in their labs. But he'd never queried anyone who'd given a positive report.

Reban didn't seem fazed by the question. "Everything's under control. As I reported, the T-rex virus is ready for trial."

Silas Jung's voice broke through. "I've heard that the lab in Ambulus City has been spending its time working on human DNA instead of T-rex DN—"

"The work on dinosaur DNA is completed," Reban broke in angrily.

Octavius's voice was heard again. "Let us focus on the priority here. We have viruses ready to use on the dinosaurs, and sooner than we expected. I suggest we don't delay. Our initial plan had been to send them with the next set of Finalists to visit Piloria, next year. But there is no reason to wait. We can send another voyage to Piloria now. Let's see if the viruses work. Let's see if Piloria can actually be habitable for humans. Let us vote."

His voice boomed.

Storm shifted. She hadn't realized Octavius actually told the Stipulators what to do. He'd skipped around that part of his role.

The murmuring eventually halted. Silas was close enough that she could hear him muttering. He sounded irritated.

"All the ayes?"

She couldn't see what anyone was doing. But she heard the collective voices: "Aye."

"All the nays?"

Silence. Complete and utter silence.

"The motion is carried. Chief Stipulators, normally you would inform your subjects of government decisions. On this occasion, I suggest we wait until we know the results of the virus study. It would be better to tell our subjects good news."

No one spoke. No one argued. But this didn't seem to go to a vote. Octavius's suggestion just seemed to be agreed.

"Who will we send?" Storm didn't know where the question came from, but it seemed to spur renewed conversation around the chamber.

Octavius spoke over the voices. "It's an important question. We need to try and spread the virus. Who do we have to send?"

A voice cut through. "We can do Trials again. We can send new Finalists."

"Takes too long," called another. "We should use the people we already have."

"What people?" Octavius's question was louder than the others.

"The winners," replied the voice. Storm couldn't work out who the other speaker was. "The three who completed the final Trial. And the other survivors. They know Piloria. They know the terrain. The head scientists can give them instructions on how to distribute the virus. They can be on and off the continent in just a few days. It shouldn't be dangerous for them."

Says a man who has obviously never set foot on the continent. Storm's legs were beginning to shake beneath her. Back to Piloria? Back across the ocean at the mercy of the megalodon? The thought was terrifying.

She pressed her hands against the wall to steady herself.

But once she'd crossed the ocean? Then she'd be back – back on Piloria. Back on the land that stretched as far as the eye could see with no buildings, no structures. Green everywhere, trees, bushes and mountains. Colours and smells most people couldn't even imagine.

A cold hand rested on her shoulder. "Storm, are you okay?" Corin's forehead was creased with deep lines.

She couldn't reply, she was still listening to the chamber.

Octavius's voice was steady. "How can we send them back? Haven't they earned their right to peace? They've already visited the continent. They brought us the eggs."

"And now they can finish the job. They can release the viruses. It shouldn't require much effort. They know the land, they know how to stay safe. And, if the viruses work, there should be less danger than there was before. Fewer dinosaurs to eat them." This time the speaker was Silas. She could hear the smirk in his voice.

"And their reward?" She hated the fact she couldn't see who was asking the questions.

Silence in the chamber. It seemed that none of the Stipulators thought Storm and her friends should be rewarded for risking their lives again.

Silas's voice cut across the murmuring voices. "Wait. Before we agree who to send I have another matter for parliament to consider. Apparently the human DNA work has led to other discoveries." He paused for effect. "It seems that one of my colleagues has broken the First Law of the Stipulators."

The First Law – the one that said Stipulators weren't

allowed families, so that they would devote all their attention and energy to the preservation of their zone.

There was a collective gasp around the parliament chamber. But Octavius's response was calm. "Silas Jung, who do you accuse of breaking the First Law?"

There was an interminable silence. Storm was practically bouncing on her toes. Her occluded vision was beyond frustrating. She imagined all the Chief Stipulators were staring at each other suspiciously right now.

"I accuse Reban Don."

Storm could almost hear the smile in his words. The bottom fell out of her stomach. It was like a million little flies crawling across her skin. She swayed, then leaned forward, closed her eyes and pressed her head against the grate in front of her. This had to be about her.

There were murmurs around the chamber. Reban Don's voice was unmistakeable. "Your proof?"

Silas continued to sound smug. "The proof I have is new. It's based on the human DNA studies conducted" – he gave a short laugh – "by your own lab in Ambulus City."

Storm looked up.

Octavius's voice was grave. "What are these new studies? What do they show?"

There was a crumple of paper. Silas moved. He was now in Storm's line of sight. Triumphant. That's the word she'd use to describe Silas right now.

He was holding aloft a piece of paper. She was too far away to see what was on it.

"This. Conclusive proof. A match between a father and a daughter. One that cannot be denied. A DNA match. Reban Don and his daughter. The one he has hidden away for years."

The gasps beside her seemed magnified in the cramped corridor. "What?" said Corin.

Storm couldn't speak. This was all like a bad dream. How could there be a DNA match between her and Reban Don? Didn't that mean she'd have to have given a sample?

Silas.

Of course. Sickness welled at the back of her throat. Things that Lincoln had told her at the loch side all slotted into place. That's what Silas had been doing in Octavius's office. Her hair. He'd pulled her hair to steal a DNA sample.

Silas brandished the paper high in the air. "Proof. Isn't it time to invite his daughter here?" He turned to face Octavius. "After all, she does work in parliament."

A horrible, icy feeling tingled down her spine. She couldn't see Octavius right now, but she'd become familiar with his tendencies. He didn't like people trying to outsmart him – trying to make a fool of him.

She had a bad feeling about this.

After the longest pause, Octavius spoke. "The head scientists. They will confirm this data? This human DNA?"

Silas nodded. "Of course. Call your head scientist in. He will confirm what Reban has never acknowledged. Stormchaser Knux is the child of Dalia Knux and Reban Don."

There was an audible gasp around the chamber.

"The girl who won the Final?" exclaimed a voice.

129

"Send her to the mines!" said a second.

"Send them both to the mines!" came the next.

Storm's breathing faltered. Her lungs wouldn't let air in, and definitely wouldn't let it out.

Silas cut across the voices. "We must vote on Reban Don's guilt in breaking the First Law."

Octavius's voice was unerringly steady. "Agreed. Reban Don, face your accusers."

Reban's footsteps echoed across the parliament floor. Storm saw his black boots walk past the grate. Her stomach rolled. What did this mean for her?

When the noise came to a halt, Octavius spoke again. "On the accusation of breaking the First Law we now vote. Do you find Reban Don guilty? All the ayes?"

"Aye." It sounded almost unanimous.

She heard Octavius clear his throat. "All the nays?"

This time it wasn't silent. This time there were a handful of replies: "Nay."

Octavius paused for a second, then finally said, "The ayes have it."

The shouts started up again immediately. "Send him to the mines!"

"Him and his daughter!"

Something banged sharply on the floor. "Order, order!"

Silas let out a snort. "Let's face it. Reban's daughter can choose between Piloria or the mines."

There was a yell from inside the chamber. An explosion of rage. "SILAS!"

There was a blur of black. A scuffle, rolling bodies on the ground. She saw a flash of white-blond hair, big boots. Small flashes of skin. A thud. The distinctive sound of a punch.

"Enough!" roared Octavius.

Several more of the Stipulators rushed forward, trying to pull them apart. Reban's head was close to the floor. She could see him now as he was pulled away. His hands were around Silas's neck, grasping with all his might. Even though it was only a few seconds, Silas's face was already coloured, his eyes bulging with the sudden pressure. Reban's face was pure fury.

Suddenly he blinked, as if he had noticed her face at the grate. She gasped and stepped back against the wall behind her.

Reban started shouting at the top of his voice. "You're taking his word – his word about this science when you all know nothing about it. Silas is only interested in taking over Ambulus zone."

Reban was pulled to his feet by a Stipulator on either side of him.

Silas shouted in return, "You broke the First Law. You no longer have a say. You no longer have any rights. You'll be banished, you and your…daughter." He waved his hands. "Off to the mines." He added the last part with relish.

"Silence!" Octavius's voice dripped with rage. "The vote has been taken. Reban Don has been found guilty of breaking the First Law. The usual punishment for Stipulators…and their families…is the mines."

There were a few cheers around the chamber.

She'd heard of Stipulators being sent to the mines. Blaine was the only person she'd heard of who had been served a different punishment. She'd never heard of the *families* being sent to the mines, though. That part had been kept quiet. What had Lincoln said about Blaine's family? Was that why they'd disappeared and stayed hidden for years?

But Octavius wasn't finished. "But on this occasion I have another suggestion. We have a more pressing matter. Piloria. The dinosaurs. The viruses. We've already discussed sending the Finalists back. Stormchaser Knux is one of those Finalists. It is my suggestion that Reban Don be part of that journey too – be part of the team that goes to Piloria. The law says only that he must be punished. It's up to us to decide how. On Piloria he can oversee the planting of the viruses – after all, it will be in his best interests to ensure the team stays on task, seeing as he will be staying there for ever. If he survives, he can report back on the effects of the viruses." Octavius cleared his throat. "As for Stormchaser? She's already paid a great service to Earthasia by bringing us the eggs. If…" He paused for the briefest instant. "If she plants the viruses then I suggest she is allowed some leniency and can return." He waited a few seconds then continued. "Any objections? No. Good. It is decided."

A few of the Stipulators started to mumble again.

There was a noise. The pull of a box, then a light thump. A few moments later Storm glimpsed the edge of the heavy green cloak trimmed with gold.

"Make the arrangements," Octavius said as he started to walk away.

Silas growled, "How are we supposed to find the other Finalists?"

Octavius turned again. "Well, I have one, another is in the lab close by. It will be the responsibility of the individual Chief Stipulators to locate their own survivors from the previous expedition." Octavius gave Silas a little smile. "I believe the third Finalist is a Norden. I guess that's your problem, Silas, as the Chief Stipulator for that area. But don't worry, if you fail to produce your Finalist, you can always take his place."

The jolliness in Octavius's voice was fake. His words were a threat.

Within an instant, several of the Chief Stipulators in the chamber were on their feet and rushing to the door.

The aides crowded around Storm. All of a sudden she had their full attention. "You're going back to Piloria?"

"Did you know?"

"Reban Don is your father?"

"Did you plan this with Octavius?"

Storm was stunned. Her legs were shaking. She pushed down, willing her muscles to tense and steady her. "No… no," she answered, stepping forward and pushing them away.

She had to see Octavius. Had this always been his intention? Had he always intended to send her back?

Was this why he'd been getting her to compile information on Piloria – had he been preparing her?

As she paced back down the dark corridor, each step became more confident, more angry. Every muscle in her body was currently on fire.

If she was going back to Piloria, she was going back on her terms.

NINETEEN

LINCOLN

Everything happened so quickly. One minute he was minding his own business in the lab, the next minute there was a Stipulator on either side of him.

"What?" he asked, as they grabbed his arms.

Lorcan Field must have been alerted to their presence. He appeared behind Lincoln. "What are you doing in my lab?"

"We're taking Lincoln Kreft. It's an order from the Chief Stipulators. They need him to go back to Piloria. They need the Finalists to release the viruses."

"What?" Lorcan looked stunned.

But not as stunned as Lincoln was. His head started to swim. Piloria, the last place on earth he should want to go... but the place that seemed to hold the best – maybe only – chance of a cure for Arta.

Dinosaurs. Dinosaurs again. In the blink of an eye he

could see Kronar's crushed body on the ground, Rune trapped between the jaws of the deinosuchus. He could feel the thud of his heart, reminding him that every second spent there was a second at risk.

"Wait!" Lorcan said quickly. "Lincoln is a member of my staff. I need information from him before you take him. Leave him with me for a minute."

He grabbed hold of Lincoln's arm, pulling him towards his office and kicking the door closed behind them.

"Right," he said quickly. "As soon as you get to Piloria, I need you to collect samples." He started pulling collection pots from a box in the corner of the room.

"Get me leaves. Thousands of leaves. As many as will fit in the sample case. Get me a whole plant if you can. With roots! I need roots. In fact, get more than one sample with roots – and bring some soil too so I can see what nutrients are in the soil on Piloria. It's likely the soil is different from ours." Now Lorcan had started talking he couldn't seem to stop. "If you can, get Blaine to show you how to make the ointment."

Lincoln flinched. He'd only told Lorcan the truth about the ointment when they'd been alone. After days of questioning, his story had finally been unpicked, and he'd admitted the truth. Up until that point Lorcan hadn't known that an exiled Stipulator had discovered the healing properties of the leaf. But he didn't seem to have any concern that Blaine had been left abandoned on the continent – or that Lincoln was about to be sent back there without any consultation.

"Find out if there are any other ingredients." Lorcan was still talking; he looked up as he pulled out some smaller sample cases. "Get specimens of those too. I need everything. I need everything to recreate the ointment and produce more."

"You really think you can do that?" Every hair on Lincoln's arms stood on end. The lab looked at cells. They'd just created a virus – apparently. But could they actually look at the cellular make-up of an ointment and reproduce it?

Lincoln felt sick. He was reeling. Reeling from the prospect of having to go back to Piloria. Terrified even. But if it meant he had a second chance of getting more ointment to help Arta? Then it would be worth it. Because that's how his brain worked. He could only think about Arta. He couldn't think wider. He couldn't afford to.

The T-rex. The deinosuchus. His mouth was dry. For a few seconds, the horrors of Piloria flashed through his brain again. But he knew them now. He knew they were there. He could plan ahead. He could do this.

"You think you can cure the plague?"

Lorcan looked up sharply. He stopped stuffing things into a bag for Lincoln and gave him a pitying glance. He stepped over and touched Lincoln's shoulder. "I can't cure it."

"You can't?" Something icy gripped his heart.

Lorcan shook his head. "It is part of us – or part of most of us. That's what I've discovered. At least seventy per cent of our population has it in their DNA. What triggers it? I don't know." He shook his head and looked a bit glazed. "I just can't figure it out."

"So…nothing can help?" Lincoln couldn't help the tremor in his voice.

Lorcan met his gaze and smiled. "Of course something can help. The ointment. We can't cure this, but we can treat it. We can manage it. People who die from the blistering plague die from infection or blood poisoning when the skin is broken. The ointment? It's like a miracle. It heals the skin. It stops it blistering and breaking down. No open wounds – no infection or blood poisoning. The ointment is the closest thing to a cure we can get."

Lincoln's breath came out in a gush. He hadn't realized he'd been holding it. His mind was churning with information. There was so much resting on the steps he was about to take.

Lorcan squeezed his shoulder. "Get me fresh samples. I *need* fresh samples. The fragments we have…they've deteriorated too much. They aren't giving me the information I require. I can examine fresh samples in the lab and maybe find a way to grow some of the plants here. Get me as much as you can." Lorcan's eyes were gleaming.

There was so much at stake here. So much for Lorcan, and for Lincoln.

Lincoln stood steady. "On one condition."

"What?" Lorcan seemed surprised. He wasn't used to junior members of staff questioning him.

"I'm being sent back to release a virus for the dinosaurs. I'm not being sent back for samples." He chose his words carefully. "I will bring you samples, as long as I have a guarantee that you won't just treat Tarin, you'll treat my sister Arta too."

He let the words hang in the air.

Lorcan stepped closer. He was only a little taller than Lincoln, so they were virtually eye to eye. One side of his lip quirked upwards. He gave a little nod – almost in approval.

It seemed like he was seeing his lab assistant in a new light. He held out his hand towards Lincoln. "Get me the leaves and I'll make our girls a treatment as good as a cure."

For the first time in a long while, Lincoln felt a wave of hope. He reached out and clasped Lorcan's warm hand, shaking it. He glanced towards the door where the Stipulators were waiting for him.

"There's something else I need to do before I go."

Lorcan followed his gaze. "It seems unlikely they'll let you go anywhere. You're their prize right now." He tilted his head in question. "Family?"

Lincoln's heart clenched. Of course he wanted to see his mother and his sister right now. But every cell in his body told him he had a responsibility elsewhere.

His voice was tight. "Yes…but not mine."

Lorcan arched one eyebrow. He gave a nod of his head. "I may have another way out of here."

"That's just what I needed to hear."

TWENTY

STORMCHASER

The Stipulators spilled across the atrium in groups. It seemed that once they'd exited the chamber, no one was in a hurry to leave. After collecting her thoughts, Storm was ready.

She strode across the atrium, noticing the drop in voices with each stride. All eyes were on her, but she didn't care. When she reached Octavius's room she didn't knock before she entered, she just pushed the door so hard it banged off the adjacent wall.

Octavius blinked and looked up from his desk. It was almost as if the previous events hadn't just occurred. He waited as the door slammed shut behind her.

"You threw me to them. You practically volunteered me. You didn't even ask me. Was this your plan all along?"

Octavius stood up behind his desk. "I did not throw you to them, Storm. Your choice was the mines or Piloria –

and that's still your choice. Which would you prefer?"

His voice was steady but she noticed something odd. He was gripping the edge of the desk. As if he was trying to stop his hands shaking.

She couldn't stop the anger surging through her veins. "And Reban? That test shows he's my father – proves it conclusively? And his punishment is Piloria? Isn't it enough that I'm being sent back, why would you suggest sending him too? The last place I want to be is anywhere with that… man." She practically spat out the last word.

Octavius jumped down from his desk. Sometimes he could be more agile than she anticipated. He marched over to her. "Do you know the average life expectancy at the mines, Stormchaser?"

She shook her head.

"Two weeks. Two weeks! That's it. If Reban went to the mines he'd be lucky to last two weeks." Octavius was angry. She'd never seen him quite so enraged.

She straightened her spine. She was still trying to get her head around all this.

Octavius looked her in the eye. "I can't speak for Reban. I wouldn't want to. But I have reasons. Reasons for wanting to keep you both alive. You might hate him, Stormchaser, but you've told me about Piloria. You've told me, in all its glory, how dangerous it can be. Don't underestimate Reban Don. Don't underestimate what you can learn about each other. And remember, you get the option to come home. He doesn't."

The words she wanted to say choked in her throat. The last thing she wanted to do was learn anything about Reban Don.

And he was about to become another Blaine.

She could imagine how Blaine would feel about company.

There was a knock at the door. "Enter," shouted Octavius.

Two Stipulators were waiting. "We've come for the girl," one said.

Octavius waved his hand. "Wait outside, you'll get her when I've finished."

Storm felt her heart flip-flop in her chest. Already? They'd come for her already.

Octavius marched over to the desk where Storm usually sat. He pulled over the map that she'd been working on. Then he walked over to the library and ran his fingers along the spines of the books, finally selecting one and pulling it from the shelf. He opened the book and took out a carefully folded piece of paper.

Storm's eyes widened as he unfolded the paper and laid it down next to her own map. It took a few seconds for her to realize what it was. The lines were carefully drawn, mapped in detail. But the coastline was unfamiliar.

She leaned forward to get a better look. It was like part of a missing puzzle. She shook her head. "Where…where did you get this?"

Octavius gave a conciliatory nod. "I have means. I suspect the ship won't land at the same spot this time. They'll want you to reach the nests as quickly as possible."

She frowned. "But who mapped this part of the coastline?" Could it have been Blaine?

Octavius gave a shrug. "It takes seven days to reach Piloria. The Finalists only ever stay on land for seven days. The ship has to wait somewhere."

He pointed to a bay, a clear inlet along the coastline. "This area has always proved safe. The ship usually stays there while the Finalists search for food."

She was still confused. "But if this is closer to the nests, and safer, why didn't they drop us here instead?"

Octavius closed his eyes for a second and pressed his lips together. "It was the ultimate test, Storm. Only the worthy survive."

Her mouth fell open. "So they want people to die? It's deliberate?"

Octavius waved his hand a little. "Not entirely deliberate. But if fewer people return, then there are fewer people to reward." He gave a huge sigh. "I don't think you know just how bad things are. The extra rations for the families staying with you – that can't last for ever. Ultimately, they'll just stop."

"And the health care?" Arta was the first person that came to her mind.

Octavius gave her a sorry look. "I'm afraid I just don't know."

She sucked in a deep breath. Her mind was spinning. The events of today felt overwhelming. She tried to get things straight in her head.

"What if…what if I went to Piloria and brought back something else? Something to help the blistering plague?"

Octavius's face paled. "What do you mean?"

"Ointment – or leaves. Something to help Linc…I mean, *my* sister. For her skin."

Octavius's brow creased. "But you're going to Piloria to release the virus. To get us space. We *need* that space, Stormchaser. Now, more than ever."

"But no one could stop me, could they? I mean, if I go on that journey again, and release the virus, I can bring back whatever else I like?"

The frown deepened. "I would be careful. I would be careful who you tell of your plans. The blistering plague is the current reason that the whole population can still be fed – albeit with rations. You cure that…" He held up his hands and shook his head.

Storm tilted her chin. "So if I tell no one, I can still do what I want?"

Octavius walked slowly over to the maps. He used glue to delicately join them, blowing on it for a few seconds before refolding the map and giving it to her. He gave her a sideways glance and a little smile. "Too much of your mother in you," he mumbled.

But Storm's brain was already somewhere else. Octavius opened the door for the Stipulators. "Best not to keep them waiting." He gave Storm's arm a brief squeeze. "Good luck."

A Stipulator stood on either side of her, taking each arm and practically sweeping her along.

It took her a few seconds to realize what Octavius had just said.

It was like a cool breeze across her skin. *Too much of her mother in her?*

A memory pinged into her brain and her feet stopped moving as she recalled Octavius's words from the first time they'd met.

"Because, Stormchaser Knux – winner of the dinosaur eggs, conqueror of the Trials, daughter of Dalia Knux and one of only a few people to have survived Piloria – I thought you were the owner of the most interesting eyes I've ever seen."

This was before the announcement in chambers. Before the newfangled DNA test.

Dalia Knux.

She'd never told Octavius who her mother was.

How on earth did he know?

PART TWO

THE OCEAN

TWENTY-ONE

LINCOLN

The ship was docked ominously in the port. The first time he'd seen the *Invincible* he'd been impressed. Now, it just conjured up bad memories.

Lincoln stood for a second, staring out at the vast ocean. Seven days. Seven days on an ocean filled with creatures that could kill him in one bite.

He glanced at the rippling waves and tried not to shudder as his mind crowded with memories, including one of the megalodon that had attacked them in the middle of the ocean and eaten some of the Finalists and crew.

There was a noise beside him as a transporter pulled up. The grey door slid open and Leif tumbled out onto the dockside. His face was angry and bruised, his lip split and swollen. As he thudded onto the ground he let out a list of expletives, rolling and landing at Lincoln's feet.

Lincoln hesitated for a second, then held out his hand

to help him up. "Leif," he said simply.

Leif stared up from the ground, shielding his eyes from the sun. He scowled, ignored Lincoln's hand and pushed himself up.

"Is this your fault? Is it your fault I'm here again?" Leif spat the words out.

Lincoln shook his head. "Blame the Chief Stipulators. Piloria isn't on my wish list. Well, not really."

"What's that supposed to mean?"

There was a rumble next to them and another compartment on the transporter opened. Storm stepped out. She was dressed completely in dark green, with a black backpack on her shoulder. Her face lit up when she saw Leif.

She ran over and gave him a hug. "I'm so happy to see you." As soon as she said them, she obviously realized the error of her words. "Not like this, of course. I just mean in general. How are you? What about your brothers and sisters? How are they?"

Leif stepped backwards out of her embrace. "Hungry," he answered bluntly.

Lincoln cringed. Although Leif's face showed signs of being swollen, the rest of his body told a different story. He was more angular. His arms thinner. He almost looked... gaunt.

It seemed that the rations in Norden were even less than the rations in Ambulus City.

"Hey, hey, you!"

The voice came from behind them. They all spun around

towards it. A girl was running towards them. She had tangled, tight brown curls in a mass around her face. She was lean, dressed in brown three-quarter-length trousers, thick boots and a green shirt tied at her waist. A bag was slung across her body.

Lincoln looked at the other two in confusion, but they seemed just as bewildered as he was.

She thudded up to them, stopping and leaning right over, hands on her knees, to catch her breath. After a second she straightened up, tossing her mass of curls back. "Talk about giving someone no notice," she muttered sarcastically.

"No notice for what?" Leif held up his hands and looked at her in confusion.

She raised her eyebrows and gestured towards the ship. "Taking a journey."

Storm stepped forward. "I'm sorry, who are you?"

The girl tilted her chin and looked Storm up and down. "You're Stormchaser." She wrinkled her nose. "Weird kind of name." She turned around and looked at Leif with his shock of bright, blond hair. She smiled. "Well obviously you have to be the Norden. You're Leif." Then she turned back and looked at Lincoln. "So, that makes you Lincoln." She put her hands on her hips. "What's the point of sending a message? What's the point of trying to write down what you can say in person?"

Something clicked in his brain.

That place he'd had to go yesterday. That message he'd had to ensure was given. He'd darted through the streets and banged on doors in the area until he'd finally been pointed in the right direction. But the family hadn't been home. He couldn't wait. The Stipulators would already be searching for him. So he'd pushed something through the door in frustration.

He still couldn't believe she was standing in front of him. "You're Jesa."

She nodded. "Of course I am."

Leif threw up his hands. "Well, I'm lost. What on earth is going on?"

Lincoln was still a little stunned. But he couldn't help a smile. "This is Jesa. Blaine's daughter."

"What?" Leif's voice echoed around them.

Storm shook her head. "But…what on earth is she doing here?"

"*She?*" Antagonism dripped from Jesa's voice. "What is *she* doing here?"

Storm tried to find some other words but it was too late. Jesa moved a few paces to stand directly in front of her. "*She* is here to come to Piloria. After nine years, *she* is going to see her father again." She prodded Storm square in the chest. "And *you* won't stop me."

Leif shook his head. "You're Blaine's daughter, really?" He still looked completely confused. "But how did you know? Who told you?"

Leif gave Storm and Lincoln a suspicious glance. They'd all agreed not to talk about Blaine. Lincoln stepped forward. "I met Jesa's mother," he said to Leif. "Her mother and

152

brother approached me in the street. They asked me if anyone could survive there. They were desperate to know – I couldn't lie to them."

Jesa turned to face Leif. "We thought he was dead. We thought he'd died on the dinosaur continent. I stopped drawing pictures of him five years ago. I'll never forgive myself for that." Her voice had changed, the antagonistic tone was gone.

Storm reached over and hesitantly touched Jesa's arm. "How did you know to come here?"

Jesa blinked, as if coming out of her thoughts. "Lincoln. He left a message. He told us he was going back to Piloria and asked if there was anything we wanted to tell my father."

Storm gave Lincoln a half-frown. "But what now? She can't come, can she? The Stipulators won't let her."

Leif shook his head. "How do we know that? They might. I was grabbed from my house in the middle of the night. How do you think I ended up looking like this? I'm still not even sure why I'm here. No one could answer my questions. The Stipulators don't seem so organized right now." He held up his hands. "Look around you. Last time we were here this place was full of them. Apart from the ones on the transporter, I don't see any more."

Lincoln nodded. "You're right. Everything about this is odd." He glanced back over to the ship. "It looks almost deserted. And we know that can't be true."

Jesa put her hands on her hips. "Deserted is good. If they

153

say I can't get on board, I can stow away. I'm sure I can find a way onto a ship as big as this."

Lincoln glanced at her. Determined. Feisty. A lot like someone else he knew. He met Storm's gaze. He could tell she was trying to stop a smile appearing.

"Someone want to tell me why we're being forced to go back to the continent of death?"

Storm jerked at Leif's words.

Lincoln sighed. How could he summarize the last two months? "It worked. They've made a virus. Or three viruses. I don't really know. They need someone to trial them on Piloria to see if they actually work."

Leif pulled back. "They've made a virus already? I thought that would take years." He ran his fingers through his short hair. "And why us? We've already done our bit. It's someone else's turn. Who decided we should go anyway?"

"I did." All four jumped at the unexpected voice. Silas Jung strolled out from the other side of the transporter, his shock of white-blond hair against his black Stipulator garb even more startling in the bright light of day. He looked like the kind of guy kids would run and hide from.

Leif seemed to catch his breath. Of course. Silas was the Chief Stipulator from Norden. Leif would have seen him on many occasions before. But he wouldn't have expected to see him here. A wave of confusion swept his face.

Silas had a smug look. Conceit was particularly ugly on him. He looked down his nose at Leif. "The Chief Stipulators voted. We need the viruses trialled. Waiting until next year will take too long. It made sense to send people who already know the territory. We need results."

"And I need to stay alive." Leif finally spoke up. "My two friends already died on Piloria. I have no wish to set foot on the place again." He shook his head as he glanced at both Lincoln and Storm. "Piloria's the kind of place where you need to be with people you trust. People who have your back. People who can work together as a team." He shot them both a look of disgust. "Now the hellos are over, I can say that you don't have that here. We're not a team. We're not family."

Silas snorted. "Do I care? And yes" – he gave a laugh, glancing at Storm – "some of you apparently *are* family. I don't care if you decide to work separately and deliver one virus each. I just want to know it's done. I want to know the results."

Storm shook her head. "How do you know we can even do it? How do you give a virus to a dinosaur?"

Silas waved his hand. "The head scientists will fill you in. Just make sure you pay attention. There are to be no mistakes." He started to walk away then gave another laugh. "And don't worry about adding people to your merry little band. I'll give you a few more. Dinosaur fodder. I won't be doing a headcount. Except, of course, for one."

He gave a signal and the door at the very back of the transporter slid open. Seven Stipulators were inside. They bent down and dragged out a body. A very angry body.

Reban Don's ankles, wrists and mouth were bound.

His face and body were just as bruised as Leif's and he was wearing an odd set of scruffy blue and green clothes. His shouts could be heard beneath the gag. "You'd better watch your back, Silas Jung, I'll get you—"

He was silenced by a swift kick from Silas's boot. "That will be a bit hard – from Piloria. But I'll be coming along – to make sure you get off at the other side." Silas laughed and walked towards the other Stipulators, who fanned around him like some kind of guard as they strode off towards the ship.

Lincoln looked at the squirming body on the ground. Storm's face was tight – she could barely even look at Reban. He gave a sigh. "Jesa and Leif, meet Reban Don – Storm's father."

TWENTY-TWO

STORMCHASER

The ship left without any fanfare, as the sun was beginning to set in the sky. The atmosphere was odd. This time there weren't a hundred Finalists on board. This time there were only a few.

Storm could only hope that the other bunch of ragtag recruits who'd boarded the ship hadn't heard that Silas had labelled them dinosaur fodder.

They were a mixed age range dressed in an assortment of greys and browns, all with a bewildered look on their faces. A few muttered about being saved from the mines. Another few seemed to be opportunistic adventure seekers. Two were definitely previous Finalists – Froan Jung and Tena Koll. They looked just as happy to be here as Leif. "There were seven other Finalists," Storm hissed at Leif. "Where are the rest of them?"

Leif popped a piece of fruit into his mouth. "Maybe they

got lucky. Maybe they're dead already."

Storm shifted uneasily. The woman wasn't here. The one who'd been scarred by the raptors. Last time Storm had seen any of them had been during the final Trial, when they'd all been on top of the cliff. The Stipulators had decided visiting Piloria wasn't dangerous enough. They'd made the other Finalists stand with items on their head while she, Lincoln and Leif had thrown knives at them in the hope of winning the final Trial. And now, two of them were here again.

Lincoln had mentioned he'd recognized the uniform of some people from the labs. It seemed – although the voyage was supposed to be kept quiet – that a few of them had decided they didn't just want to help develop the virus, they also wanted to see it in action.

Whatever their reason for being there, Storm didn't care. She was more concerned with trying to quell the feeling in her stomach. The feeling of excitement.

Yes, she should be scared. Of course, she should be part terrified. She was also determined she would help find the plant leaves to assist Arta, and for Rune's brother and sister, Cornelius and Livia, and anyone else they could help. She was almost sure she'd be able to find that part of the forest again.

But just the thought of breathing in deeply and smelling that rich air, seeing the expanse of land before her eyes, the wonder of the landscape and the aroma of life on the continent made her skin tingle.

Storm took herself off to a bunk room. Jesa followed her. Inside the room were several backpacks.

She grabbed one and emptied its contents over the bunk. Jesa thudded down onto one of the other bunks. She stared defiantly at Storm. "Are you planning on mentioning my father at all?"

Storm hesitated. "I don't have much to tell. He helped us on Piloria. He's managed to survive there for the last nine years. He seemed...comfortable."

Exactly the opposite of how Storm was feeling right now. Blaine's behaviour had been erratic. After nine years virtually alone he'd made it very clear that he struggled to be in the company of other people. He'd even made a veiled threat that they shouldn't leave anyone behind.

"Comfortable? How can anyone be comfortable on the dinosaur continent?" Jesa asked angrily.

Storm started to repack the contents of the backpack. It was the same as last time. Several tunics, underwear and socks. A torch. Kindling. Rope and a harness, along with metal clips for climbing. Balm. A kit with some kind of chemicals. A mat and bedroll. A water canteen.

"He's made his own shelter. He's found a way to get clean water. He's made ointments. He's even made a boat from a tree. As for the things he can't make..."

Her voice trailed off. Maybe this wasn't the best conversation to have with Jesa.

But Jesa stood up and stepped right over to Storm. "How does he get the things he doesn't make?"

Storm licked her dry lips. "He trades."

"Who with?"

She should never have started this conversation. It wasn't going to end well. But there was no point in trying to avoid it now. "With the Stipulators."

"What?" Jesa's voice rose in shock. No one trusted the Stipulators.

Storm tried to make it sound a little better. "I thought Lincoln filled you in on all this?"

Jesa shook her head. "I wasn't with my mother and brother when they met Lincoln. Today was the first time I'd seen him."

Storm nodded and sat back down. "Piloria isn't like anything you've ever seen before. I could try and explain it to you, but it's best that you just see it for yourself. There might be dangerous dinosaurs. But it's much more beautiful than you could ever imagine."

"Are you crazy?"

Storm held up her hands. "Maybe? I don't know. Your father doesn't want to be there. He wants to be at home. With you. With your mother and with your brother. But he doesn't have any other option. There's no way off Piloria for him. He's had to learn to live there. The things that he can't make for himself, like sneakers or paper? The Stipulators leave him a supply every time they visit."

Jesa's eyes narrowed. "And what does he do to earn them?"

Storm shrugged. "Gives them information about the dinosaurs. I'm sure it was him who pointed out where the nesting sites were for the raptors, T-rexes and pterosaurs."

Jesa frowned. "So why aren't they just asking him to plant

the viruses? He knows the place better than anyone."

How did she answer a question like that? Blaine's behaviour was so erratic that there was no way the Stipulators would trust him to do something so vital.

Storm tried not to let herself smile. "I'm not sure that Blaine would do what the Stipulators want. He likes to make up his own mind about things."

Jesa nodded, as her stomach growled loudly. "Are you going to tell me what the deal is with you and Reban Don?"

Storm felt the hairs stand up at the back of her neck – instantly defensive. "There is no deal. He's never acknowledged that he is my father, and I'll never acknowledge that I'm his daughter. I don't want anything to do with him. You had your mother. You had your brother. My mother died when I was twelve and I was left in a Shelter. I had no one. What kind of a father lets that happen?"

Jesa stared at her for the longest time. It was almost as if she were trying to decide what to say. She pressed her lips together for a few seconds. It was the first time since they'd met that Jesa hadn't seemed confrontational. "They couldn't find us, you know. When my father was sent away, my mother took us somewhere else. We hid in another city for a few years." Jesa broke her gaze from Storm's and stared down at her hands for a moment. "Even if my father had sent a message home, it wouldn't have reached us. We weren't there. I'm not sure my father realized the risk of being found out. Oh, he knew the risk for himself. But for us, not so much. It would have been a death sentence."

Storm swallowed and sat down on the bed next to Jesa. This was the second time she'd heard something like this. "Are you really sure about that?"

Jesa nodded. "Oh, I'm sure. My father had a friend. Another Stipulator. Neither of them were Chiefs like Reban Don." Jesa looked off at the far wall. "His name was Kaden. He had bright red hair – as did his children. They stayed right next to us. I think Kaden and my father had some kind of arrangement. I think they covered for each other." She took a deep breath. "Anyway, as soon as my father was seized, we left. My mum said when we came back a few years later one of the neighbours told her that the Stipulators broke down the door of the other house. Kaden, his partner and their children were dragged out onto the street and never seen again."

Storm shook her head as an icy chill swept over her body. "I've never heard any of this. I mean, I've heard about the Stipulators being banished. But until yesterday, I'd never heard a single thing about their families being punished too."

Jesa looked at her curiously. "I thought you were smarter than this. Haven't you learned that you only hear what they want you to hear?"

Of course. Storm cringed. She didn't like the other girl in the team thinking she wasn't smart.

Jesa's stomach growled loudly again. Storm stood up. "Come on, I'll show you where we eat. There's no rationing here – at least, there wasn't last time." She stared across at the other empty bunks and gave a sad smile. "Last time I was on this boat heading to Piloria these bunks were filled. The noise annoyed me." She let her head hang a little as she tried not to let the wave of shame take over her. "And then on the way back? I hated the silence. It seemed to echo all around me. I moved in with Lincoln and Leif."

Jesa looked curiously at her. "And now?"

Storm shook her head. "Everything has changed. We felt like family before. We don't now."

Jesa stood up. "Well, you have me this time. And we have more in common than the boys ever will – Stipulators for fathers." She rolled her eyes then headed towards the door. "Probably a bigger virus than we could ever give the dinosaurs."

TWENTY-THREE

LINCOLN

It felt like a stand-off. Lincoln had selected one bunk, next to a wall, and Leif had chosen another as far away as possible. After a perfunctory glance into the backpacks that lay next to the bunks, there wasn't much more to do.

Leif had left the dorm room almost as soon as he arrived and Lincoln decided to do the same.

He walked outside onto the deck. There hadn't been a chance to see his mother or Arta before he got on the ship. He'd left messages with Lorcan Field and, surprisingly, he trusted him to deliver them. Now he watched as Ambulus City faded in the distance, its few lights glowing like stars in the dark sky.

It seemed they'd all had similar thoughts. Storm, Jesa and Leif were all leaning on the rail. Storm sighed as she glanced back at Ambulus City. "Imagine what it would look like if the whole place was lit up."

Jesa leaned back. "Imagine if we could actually produce enough energy to do that."

Leif turned to her. "What did your mother and brother say about you coming?"

For the first time since Lincoln had met her, Jesa didn't seem quite so confident. She didn't meet Leif's gaze. "I didn't exactly tell them."

"What?" Lincoln couldn't help himself.

Storm spun around. "You left without saying goodbye?"

Lincoln winced at her words. "So did I," he said quietly.

Jesa's eyes widened while Storm's flashed as she turned on them both. "You both have family who love you, and you didn't say goodbye?" It was more accusation than question.

Lincoln looked out across the ocean. His heart was twisting in his chest. "I had to make a choice. The Stipulators came to the lab for me. Lorcan let me sneak out another door. I had to choose between saying goodbye to my family or leaving a message for Blaine's."

For a few seconds he couldn't breathe. He'd hated having to make that choice. His mother would be devastated when he didn't return home. But he knew Lorcan would fill her in. And the important thing was that Arta was still safe, still being treated, while he found the medicine that could make her properly healthy again.

Jesa's eyes glistened. "I didn't know you had to do that," she said quietly. Her hand brushed his arm. "Thank you." He shook his head. He couldn't speak right now. "We'd already discussed the messages we wanted to send to Dad. I was supposed to just bring them to Lincoln – to find a way to slip them to him. But the more I thought about it, the more I realized it wasn't enough. What if this is the last time anyone gets to see him? Why should you get to see my father and I can't?" Her hands gripped the rail of the ship and she looked back at the fading sight of Ambulus City. "Caleb will be furious with me. He'll be mad he didn't think of it first. But I couldn't have told him. If he'd known, he would have come too. I couldn't leave Mum alone. At least if something happens to me, she'll still have him."

Jesa's stomach grumbled loudly again. "Come on," said Storm. She had a strange look on her face. Lincoln guessed she was thinking about families and he sympathized. Because Storm always thought she had no family. But now things had changed. Now, the closest thing she had to family was sitting, under guard, in another room on this ship. But would she even talk to him?

Lincoln didn't think so. And he could hardly blame her.

As Storm passed, Lincoln grabbed her arm. "We need to talk."

She frowned as she watched Leif lead Jesa inside. "What about?"

Lincoln waited a few seconds until the others had vanished. "Piloria."

She shook her head. "Have we spoken about anything else since we got on board?"

He took a deep breath and leaned on the ship's rail, looking across the dark ocean. "I need to do something

166

different when I get to Piloria, something that's not the task we're being sent for, and…I'm hoping that you'll help me."

There was a silence. And then she said the thing he fully expected her to say. "After the last time?"

He nodded. "I know. I know I kept secrets from you. I know I lied…by omission. You have no reason to trust me at all."

She was still frowning but the corners of her lips turned upwards. She stepped closer. "But you're asking anyway?"

He smiled as he nodded. "I'm asking because this is about Arta."

The smile fell from her face but she nodded straight away. Storm was one of the brightest people he'd ever met. He could see her slotting pieces of the puzzle together in her mind. "The ointment." She leaned on the rail alongside him.

"The ointment."

"What do we need to do?"

His insides squeezed. No hesitation. *We.*

"Lorcan asked me to get as many samples as I could. Ointment too, if Blaine has any, and specific instructions on how he makes it."

Storm nodded again in the darkness. "That sounds simple enough. We get to the shack. We load up on leaves. And we ask Blaine for more." She nudged him with her elbow. "Let's just hope he's in a good mood when he finds out we're back."

Lincoln looked out into the darkness. "There is that."

They stood for a while staring out at the unending ocean.

167

"I'm not sure about the viruses," she said quietly. "I know that's why we're here, but I'm still not convinced. I still don't think we should be trying to kill the dinosaurs."

Lincoln held on to the rail and shook his head. The last thing he needed to do was get into a debate with Storm. "I don't care about the dinosaurs. I only care about my sister." He took a deep breath of the salty air. "I do remember. I remember Rune. I remember Kronar."

"So do I." Her words were practically a whisper.

"I don't want to end up like that." It was the most honest he could be. "And I don't want anyone in our group to end up like that."

Her voice broke a little. "Neither do I."

Lincoln nodded. "Then how about you don't plant any of the viruses. You let the others take the lead."

She leaned back, her hands still holding the rail, her hair fluttering in the wind. "I don't know if I can do that, Linc."

He smiled. It was the first time she'd called him that since their last trip to Piloria. "Then we take things as they come."

He looked at her and her violet gaze locked with his.

This time, they wouldn't get in each other's way. This time, they both had at least one common goal.

She blinked and licked her lips, then repeated, "We take things as they come."

Lincoln was relieved. So far only Lorcan had known what his plans on Piloria were, but he'd wanted to be upfront with Storm. He didn't want secrets between them this time.

And he wanted a backup plan. There was always a chance

that one of them might not make it home from Piloria. This way, there were better odds that Lorcan would get what he needed for Arta.

And Arta would always be his priority.

She had to be.

TWENTY-FOUR

STORMCHASER

Three days later, Reban Don still hadn't made any attempt to talk to her. Not that she'd really expected him to. But it would have been nice if he'd tried. Then she could have had the pleasure of telling him to get lost.

She'd heard the Stipulators on board talking. Apparently, just before they'd left there had been a formal announcement that Silas Jung was the temporary Chief Stipulator for Ambulus City as well as Norden. There had been no mention of Reban at all. It had caused lots of questions that no one seemed inclined to answer.

The Stipulators who were guarding him were getting bored. There weren't exactly many places he could go on the ship. The first day they'd stood over him when he visited the servery to eat. By day three they were happy to stand at the other side of the room, eating their own food and ignoring Reban and the rest of the crew.

Storm couldn't eat when he was in the same room as her. She couldn't bear to even look at him. Just being in his presence made her so angry. So frustrated.

It didn't help that the rest of them seemed to have noticed. Leif had finally stopped being so frosty. As soon as Reban appeared he tried to engage Storm in conversation, always while keeping his eyes on Reban and the other Stipulators.

The rest of the new recruits all seemed to band together. The ones who'd worked in the labs had discarded their overalls and found bland-coloured tunics to wear. There were no big announcements. None of the hustle and bustle they'd experienced on the first journey over, and definitely no stopping to swim. One meeting with the megalodon was enough for the crew of the *Invincible*.

The temperature around them started to change as they neared Piloria. It was subtle at first. The overcoats they'd worn in Earthasia were casually discarded. For the females, hair was tied back and off their collars, while most of the guys wished they'd had a haircut before they boarded the ship.

The mood changed too. It was odd. Even more so for the people who'd experienced it before.

The mixture of excitement and fear meant that the never-ending rations weren't eaten with the usual fervour. The other recruits started to approach Storm, asking questions. Looking for hints. There was no competition this time, and Storm and the others knew what lay ahead, so she was happy to share a few cautionary tales.

On the last morning, Storm woke before anyone else. Jesa was quietly snoring, her hair a tangled mess around her face. The girl was about to meet her father. To come face-to-face with the man she'd held in a special place in her heart for the last nine years. What must that feel like?

Storm dressed quickly and quietly, walking along the deck, staring out at the horizon until she reached the servery.

There was only one person inside. Well, if you didn't count the Stipulators guarding him.

She could almost feel his eyes sear a hole in her back as she collected some fruit and cereal grains from the counter. She walked as far away as possible, finding a bench that would give her a good view when Piloria appeared on the horizon.

His bench scraped as he stood up, tossing his food onto a tray as he strolled across the servery towards her. The Stipulators didn't even bother following him.

He sat down opposite her as she continued to ignore him and glanced at the sea behind his head.

"There's no one here," he growled.

She kept eating, still not acknowledging his presence. "I think you'll find there is," she said pointedly.

Even though she wasn't watching him she could see him almost smirk. She hated that.

"There's no one *else* here, Stormchaser." He raised an eyebrow. "Or do you prefer Storm? You can talk to me."

She met his violet gaze with her own, trying not to flinch at the familiarity. This was the first time she'd truly looked at him since he'd been declared her father. "I don't *want* to talk

172

to you. I want to pretend you don't exist. Just like you've spent the last fifteen years doing with me."

He let out a huge sigh and glanced towards the entranceway. "If I'd acknowledged you, you'd be dead."

Her insides twisted. If she'd heard this a few weeks ago she would have thought it was rubbish. More lies. But she'd heard the comments in the parliament chamber. She'd heard the remarks by Jesa.

"I nearly was – on Piloria, the place you sent me to."

How dare he act as if she should be grateful that he'd abandoned her?

He turned his head and looked towards one of the portholes. "We're getting close," he said. "What can you tell me about Piloria?"

"Oh, so now you're interested." She couldn't stop the sarcasm, it just seemed to exude from every pore on her body.

He kept his voice steady. "I guess I'm ready to listen to the expert."

Not what she expected to hear. She looked up and met his gaze again as she frowned. She wasn't quite sure what to say in response.

She leaned back in her chair as she studied him. "It's not like anything you know," she said finally.

The way his eyebrow quirked annoyed her. The truth was, everything Reban did annoyed her. Reban. She couldn't call him her father. That seemed like a term of endearment – at least, everyone else she knew used it that way.

She leaned across the table towards him and narrowed her eyes. "Get used to not being in control, Reban. Get used to not knowing the minute – the second – that something could take your life. Get used to not sleeping properly, not knowing what lies over the next hill. Get used to being a target. Get used to thinking that the next time you go to relieve yourself something might be waiting for you in the bushes. There's no one here that will follow your orders – least of all me."

He stood up abruptly, sending the bench crashing to the floor behind him, pressing both hands down on the table in front of him.

She tensed. Expecting him to shout, expecting him to show some of the anger she'd seen in the past. But after a few seconds, and a few loud breaths, he looked down at her. For the briefest of seconds there was a hint of something in his eyes. Something she'd never seen before. Pain?

His voice was almost a whisper. "Sometimes I blink and I think you're her." As soon as he said the words he turned on his heel and left.

Storm couldn't breathe. The oxygen was trapped somewhere in her chest as her heart thudded an uncertain rhythm. She hated him. She hated him.

So why was she blinking back tears?

TWENTY-FIVE

LINCOLN

The first time he realized something wasn't quite right was as Piloria started to emerge in the distance. He'd grabbed fruit for breakfast, storing some other food in his backpack. No one had told them how long they were staying. It couldn't be more than a week. That was as long as it had taken them to reach all three nest sites last time around. But he'd hated the foil ration packs. He knew there was food on Piloria they could eat, he just wanted to have a few extra provisions.

Once he'd finished packing his bag, Lincoln walked out onto the deck and leaned on the rail. The early morning mist had lifted and the coastline was emerging before his eyes. It only took a matter of minutes for the others to join him.

Lincoln spoke first. "This doesn't look quite right."

Leif leaned forward as if to get a better look. "Maybe we're approaching it from a different direction this time?"

Lincoln shook his head. "No. No way. The coastline didn't

look like this. Remember, it was sandy beach all the way along, with the jungle right next to it? Look now" – he pointed – "those mountains? They weren't there. And this?" He gestured ahead to the natural bay of bright blue water. "We didn't see anything like that. It was just straight, sandy beach before. They unloaded that huge crate for Blaine further along it."

Jesa twitched at her father's name. "You mean we might not be near where my father is?" The anguish in her voice was palpable.

Storm had her backpack at her feet – she reached down and rifled in it. After a few seconds she pulled out a sheet of paper, unfolding it carefully. Lincoln looked over her shoulder as she scanned it, her finger tracing over the markings.

"This is it," she breathed.

"What?" asked Leif.

Storm seemed a little stunned. "Octavius. He gave me this. It's a map of the area we're about to land at. Look, there's the bay."

Lincoln frowned as he tried to merge the landscape in front of him with the map in Storm's hands. He'd never been good at this kind of thing.

Storm kept pointing at parts on the map. "Look, it was what I was asked to do – to map the area we'd covered. But Octavius gave me this part. The part that joins on to it. This is where we are."

The paper ruffled in the wind, nearly separating at the

delicate join of the two areas. Leif leaned forward, examining the careful sketches. Jesa just looked confused.

Leif frowned. "Who is Octavius? That's the second time you've said his name. And how on earth could he map part of Piloria? Has he been here?"

Storm bit her lip. She wasn't normally stuck for words. It was almost like she didn't know how to answer. "Octavius… works at the parliament. I was his…aide."

"You worked at parliament?" Leif looked astounded. "How come I've been on a ship with you for a week and you haven't mentioned this? I thought you worked with hay bales."

Storm shook her head. "I did. But when I got back they moved me. They figured out I'd been deliberately flunking all my tests in school. I got assigned to the parliament building."

Lincoln could tell Storm was uncomfortable.

Leif gave Storm a suspicious glare. "And what exactly does Octavius do?"

She licked her lips. "He…he kind of keeps the Chief Stipulators in order."

"What?" Leif shook his head. "And this is who you worked for?" He held up his hands. "How on earth did you end up here? How did any of us end up here? If you worked at the parliament, didn't you know people who could have got us out of this?"

Lincoln could tell she was struggling. He reached over and put his hand on Leif's arm. "I don't think it quite works like that."

Leif pulled his arm away sharply. "Really? Then you tell me how this works, Lincoln, because I don't even know where to begin. My head is still in Norden with my starving brothers and sisters."

There was no response to that pointed barb. It could have been aimed at either him or Storm with equal effect.

Lincoln stared at the bay in front of them. It was a perfectly hollowed-out semicircle in the white, crumbling cliffs. The water was clear and a brilliant shade of blue. There seemed to be coral-coloured stone just under the surface in places, with a whole host of small sea creatures darting around. The beach was small and the sand a little darker than he remembered. And it was quiet. Perfectly quiet.

This place didn't look like part of the dinosaur continent. This looked like some kind of magical place that children dreamed of.

Storm touched Leif's arm. "We're closer." She pointed to the map again. "This puts us here. Much closer to the nests." She looked up and pointed to the right. "The pterosaur nest should be just along the coastline. It's barely a half-day's walk from here."

Leif shook his head and said the words that Lincoln was currently thinking. "Then why didn't they drop us here the last time? Why leave us on that other beach with so much further to go?" He didn't even try to hide the anger in his voice. "Why make us go round that lake when we clearly didn't have to."

The lake. The place where Leif had lost one friend on the way over, and the other on the way back. Little wonder he was angry.

Storm seemed to hesitate over her words. "I have no idea. Maybe the other beach is the best pick-up point for Blaine. Or maybe that's the only place they have transporters."

Lincoln was scanning the beach. This spot was beautiful. Tranquil.

Silas's voice sounded behind them. "Get inside. It's time to prepare." As Lincoln turned, he saw the smug smile on Silas's face. "Let's spread the viruses and kill these dinosaurs."

It sent a tremor through him. A tremor he hadn't expected.

Maybe Storm was rubbing off on him?

TWENTY-SIX

STORMCHASER

From the second he started talking, it was clear Silas loved being the centre of attention. If she closed her eyes it was almost like listening to him in the parliament chamber again. She stared round at the rest of the people in the room and started counting. Fifteen, including herself, Leif, Lincoln and Jesa. And Reban, of course. He was standing at the side, muttering under his breath.

Silas swept around in his black cloak, using it like a theatrical prop. As if he wanted to emphasize the fact he still had his, while Reban did not.

There was a scientist in a white coat standing next to him. He had the same expression on his face that Lorcan Field always wore. The one where his body was present but his mind was obviously elsewhere, working on a million calculations.

Silas crossed his hands over his chest. "In a few minutes,

the Stipulators will take you ashore. This ship is too large to dock properly in the bay. Too many reefs. So you'll go in boats." He glanced towards the scientist next to him. "You'll work in teams and each team will get a set of the three viruses. Frolan here will tell you exactly how to disperse the viruses. Follow his instructions to the letter. There can be no mistakes." He wrinkled his nose disparagingly. "Sort yourself into three groups. Feel free to talk amongst yourselves. You can all go to the same site together, or to different ones. This is not a competition. This is a task. A task that must be completed. Each virus must be delivered to the watering hole nearest each nesting site. The ship will return in five days. Then you can come home, as long as you've succeeded in your mission" – he stared at them all – "and if you're still alive. The ship will arrive late afternoon. We won't wait." He waved his hand. "Frolan, tell them what to do."

Frolan seemed to spark into life as Silas put a hand on his shoulder. He was clutching something black to his chest. His arms released and the black parcel was revealed. It was some kind of sponge, with three glass vials inserted securely inside it.

"These are the viruses."

It seemed like everyone held their breath. All eyes were fixed on the coloured liquid sloshing in the tiny glass vials. One blue, one green and one red.

Frolan seemed excited. "Each one is labelled." He pushed his fingers into the sponge and pulled out the vial with blue liquid. "Each virus has to be delivered to the watering holes at each of the nest sites. It's up to you to identify where the watering holes are. You'll need to observe the dinosaurs and watch where they drink. Once they leave, all you have to do is pour this liquid into their watering hole. After that" – a large smile spread across his face – "we just need to wait and see what happens next. Once delivered the virus should pass between the dinosaurs" – he paused – "in a natural way."

He lifted a small silver carrier from the floor and pushed the black sponge inside it. "Blue for the pterosaurs, green for the velociraptors and red for T-rexes."

Leif was the first to speak. "The pterosaurs – they nest right next to the sea. Don't they just get their water supply from there? Does that mean we tip the virus into the sea?"

Frolan shook his head. "Oh no. They don't drink from the sea. Even pterosaurs don't drink salt water. They must have a clean watering hole somewhere nearby. You'll have to look for it."

Storm found her voice. "And all we have to do is pour the liquid into the watering hole? That's it?" It seemed too easy. Too simple. That was all it took to infect a dinosaur with a virus and take their life? It seemed almost unbelievable.

They wouldn't even need to get near the dinosaurs.

Part of her felt sick. Yes, she'd had a few thoughts about a safer Piloria. But did she really want to do this? Did she want to take part in killing the dinosaurs?

Her skin prickled with the enormity of it all. She was torn for selfish reasons, and ethical reasons.

Selfish, because they could do this task relatively quickly. The rest of the time could then be spent doing the other job for Lorcan Field – and for Arta. They could find the plants, and get the samples that were needed. Hopefully they could even find Blaine and persuade him to show them how he made the ointment.

But the whole ethical issue still made her guts churn. This wasn't *their* continent. She'd never wanted to steal the dinosaur eggs in the first place – never wanted the viruses to be created. But how safe could anyone ever be on Piloria if they didn't use them?

Silas still had a sneer on his face. "That's all you have to do, Knux. Or should that be 'Don'?"

She tried to still her flare of temper as the others in the room all glanced at each other. She hadn't told anyone outside her group that Reban Don was her father. Now, it seemed she wouldn't need to.

"What about weapons?" Reban's deep voice filled the small room.

Silas looked surprised. He didn't expect anyone to challenge him. His nose wrinkled and his mouth returned to its default position of a sneer.

"Weapons?"

"Yes, weapons." Reban strode forward. At some point he'd changed. He was wearing black now. A short-sleeved black top and trousers with multiple pockets. He was also wearing some kind of black waistcoat – it was covered in pockets too. Some of them seemed full already.

He tilted his chin and met Silas's gaze. It was clear that there was no love lost between these two men. "Weapons. You're sending us onto the dinosaur continent. You tell us" – he gestured to the silver carriers – "these vials are essential to help poison the dinosaurs. Yet you expect us to complete this mission without any weapons?"

Storm could see Silas trying to formulate a suitably cutting response. Last time they'd been sent to Piloria they'd been allowed to take old weapons from an assortment left behind. Not that they'd been much use. But Silas didn't know that.

Reban wasn't finished. He stepped closer to Silas until they were almost nose to nose. He lowered his voice. There was a hint of menace in it. "How much do you really want this to work, Silas? How much do your plans depend on it?"

Silence. She could swear a million insects had just started crawling over her bare arms. Why else would her skin prickle like that?

"Don't you want success to be assured?" It was almost like Reban was baiting Silas. What was it he knew that the rest of them didn't?

She could see the rage behind Silas's eyes. He didn't like anyone to challenge him. He certainly didn't like anyone to better him.

He spun around and gave a dismissive wave of his hand. "Open the weapons locker. Let them take what they need."

More silence. The Stipulators left in the room stared at each other in shock. One of them gave a nod and pulled a large key from his belt. "Over here," he muttered.

Reban was first. He was in the locker as soon as the door was opened and started handing out random things to those gathered behind him. Leif was given some kind of spear. Jesa a crossbow.

Lincoln got an axe. He gave an ironic smile as he held it up. "Well, this will slay a T-rex. I guess it's my lucky day."

For a few more seconds, Reban rummaged around the bottom of the locker, finally finding what he was looking for. It was a belt. A belt with knives sheathed all the way around it. "You take this," he said as he thrust it at Storm.

Her mouth dried. Knives. The weapon they'd had to use in the last part of the final Trial. Her mother had been a knife-throwing expert. It was something Storm had never really shared with anyone. But Reban had known. He'd used it in her favour then. He was using it in her favour now.

She said nothing. Just took the belt and fumbled as she tried to fasten it around her waist. It was bulky. Unwieldy. But she could get used to it.

When she looked up again she realized the room had filled with more Stipulators and crew. Of course. They'd just given the teams weapons. They wanted to ensure the weapons were only used on Piloria and only used against the dinosaurs. She looked around the room. The recruits were completely outnumbered.

She glanced towards the virus carriers now sitting on a bench.

"Get ready. You'll be leaving shortly," Silas told them. "Let's get this started. The sooner this continent is ours, the better."

Leif, Lincoln and Jesa turned towards Storm. Jesa licked her lips, clearly nervous. "Is this it? Are we ready?"

Leif folded his arms across his chest. "You seem to think it's a foregone conclusion we'll be working together." He shook his head. "I've been here before. Teammates should be trusted."

Storm stood straight. She was tired of all this. "You've made your point, Leif. But there are only so many times I can say I'm sorry." She put her hand on her chest. "And I *am* sorry. I'm sorry that in the few seconds after I won the competition I forgot to mention your family. I forgot to say they were *my* family. I was thinking on my feet. I was thinking about Rune and Kronar. I was thinking about the fact they'd lost their lives."

"You didn't seem to forget Lincoln's sister."

Storm threw up her hands. "Because she was right in front of me, looking like she could blow away in a wisp of wind." She shook her head. "I'm done saying sorry. I mean it, but I won't keep saying it. If you want to work with another team, go ahead. No one will stop you." She glanced sideways. "But before we start, Lincoln and I have to be honest with you both about something."

"That will be a first."

Lincoln looked at her in confusion.

But Storm kept going. "We have another reason for being here."

Leif frowned. "What could that be?"

Storm nodded towards the door. "Let's go outside."

The rest of the group followed her out into the passageway and she lowered her voice.

"We're looking for the plants that Blaine used to make the ointment he gave us last time. It helps the blistering plague. We need more for Arta – and for Rune's sister, Livia, and now his brother, Cornelius. He's started to show signs too."

"Cornelius has the plague?" The concern in Leif's voice was clear.

Storm nodded. "Yes."

Leif turned and stared out the porthole for a few seconds. As they waited for him, Jesa spoke. "This means that you'll be looking for my father? You'll be looking for Blaine." Her words were hopeful.

This time it was Lincoln who hesitated, clearly choosing his words carefully. "Of course we'll look for Blaine. It's just that...I'm not sure we'll be able to find his shack again. It was deep in the forest – well disguised."

"But you'll try?"

Lincoln gave the briefest nod. "Of course we'll try."

Leif made an exasperated noise and stalked over, picking up one of the silver carriers. "If we're doing this then let's do it. If Rune's brother and sister are sick then I will try and help." He glanced at the carrier. "And I have no problem killing a few dinosaurs along the way."

Storm shifted uncomfortably. The thing she'd been so opposed to before was now right in front of her. Killing the dinosaurs. But did she really want to face a T-rex or a raptor again?

Would these viruses even work? Lincoln hadn't seemed sure – he said they'd been made in haste. How did they know that these viruses would only kill the T-rexes or the raptors? She still had a horrible feeling the Stipulators wouldn't be above killing *all* the dinosaurs – not just the dangerous ones. Silas's words back in parliament hadn't exactly reassured her. What had he said – "rid us of the most dangerous dinosaurs – or *all* dinosaurs"?

She turned away. "I'll meet you out on deck. I'm just going to get my backpack."

It only took a few minutes. As she reached the rail she could see one of the boats about to be lowered to the clear blue water. It was amazing how the coastline along Piloria could look so different. The other beach had been much more rugged than this one.

The first group climbed into the boat with one of the Stipulators and a few members of crew. The second and third boats were ready to be lowered too. Storm walked over to the second, where Leif was already waiting. He gave her a sideways glance. "Let's get this over with, I'd planned on never seeing this place again."

Storm stared over at the golden beach framed with dark green jungle. It was clean. Inviting. She couldn't wait to get over there.

Her heart started fluttering in her chest. Piloria. The place that had haunted her dreams. Now it was within her reach. She'd wanted to come back here. The smell of the jungle was drifting over on the breeze. The richness, the depth, the flowers and the fruits. Her hands practically itched for it.

Lincoln appeared at her side with Jesa close behind. He murmured in Storm's ear. "I don't get it."

She frowned at him. "Don't get what?"

His bright green eyes were right in front of her and his brow had deep furrows. "How will they know if we've planted the viruses? We're back here in five days. Will there even be enough time to see if they've worked or not?"

Storm bit her lip. She still wasn't sure that she wanted to plant the viruses, let alone stick around to see if they worked. She shook her head. "I have no idea. Maybe they'll be waiting for Reban Don to report back to them. They're Stipulators. They'll have worked it out somehow."

Leif caught the tail end of their conversation and merely raised his eyebrows. As they got ready to climb into the boat there was a steady thudding of feet behind them. Storm turned around. Reban was practically on top of her, with his backpack slung over his shoulder.

"What do you want?" she snapped.

"I'm joining your group," he said matter-of-factly.

"No!" she said quickly. "No way."

Reban gestured towards the other groups. One already on the water, the other near the back of the ship. "Most of these other people have never been on Piloria. None of them have the knowledge that you do. I'm not like the rest of you. I'm not here for a few days. I'm here for life. I plan to learn as much as I can to stay alive."

Storm held her breath. Of course. He wouldn't be coming back to Earthasia. He was another Blaine. This was his punishment. This was his life from now on. Piloria. Whereas, as long as it was assured that she'd played her part and planted the viruses, she should still have a place on the ship home.

Right now even that made her angry. While others dreaded this place, she didn't. Oh, she was still terrified for her life. But what kind of life did they really have on Earthasia? No space, rationed food, limited energy.

She closed her eyes for a second and breathed. In, out, in, out. The aroma of Piloria was flooding through her, invading her senses. Was it her imagination or could she actually hear the insects chirping in the jungle?

Lincoln turned on Reban. "Storm doesn't want you here. Join another team."

"Don't tell me what to do." There was an edge to Reban's voice.

"We don't follow your orders now," said Lincoln. "None of us do. And as soon as we hit the soil on Piloria you might find yourself fighting for your life. Somehow I don't think any of us will try to help."

"I have to join a team. I've already told you why I'm joining yours. In a few days you'll be out of here. I won't. I plan on learning everything I can. You've been here before. I'm sticking with you all."

Leif waved his hand in amusement. "Just don't shout for me when you're T-rex bait," he said as he shouldered past and headed to the boat, the silver carrier clutched in his hand.

Storm hesitated. She wanted to fight with him about it. But there was something ingrained deep down inside her. She was so used to looking at Reban as Chief Stipulator, with everyone obeying his every word, that it was difficult for her to remove him from that position in her brain. She stalked past him. "Do what you like," she muttered as she climbed into the boat. She sat silently as the rest of the group joined her, with Reban pushing his way on board at the last possible moment as the boat was lowered slowly down to the clear blue water.

It would only take a few minutes to reach the shore. The bay was sheltered on either side. The large leaves of the jungle moved gently in the breeze.

The water around them was so clear. Storm couldn't help but lean down a little to let her fingers brush the warm water. She smiled, remembering how cold their part of the ocean was in comparison. It was almost as if they lived on entirely different planets.

A shoal of orange-coloured fish darted directly underneath them, heading towards the coral at the far side of the bay. The fish were tiny – too small to eat. A few moments later another shoal, this time grey and yellow, shot past. The first boat had already landed ashore, the third was in the water behind them. As the oars hit the sand beneath them, Leif jumped out first and started to drag the boat up onto the beach.

Storm stepped out, enjoying the feel of the water around her ankles, her boots in her hands. Why get them wet when she didn't need to?

There was a sharp intake of breath behind her. She turned just as Lincoln's body slammed into her, sending her onto the ground.

"Ooff!" The air rushed from her lungs as she hit the sand, one boot landing in the water and her backpack just missing the lapping ocean.

She sat bolt upright, ready to shout at him, then blinked as she realized the bay was changing colour. The pale blue water was filling with dark grey.

Quick-moving creatures, four times bigger than a human, were moving in a pack. They swam as if they were one, as if they were communicating with each other. They were clearly visible through the crystal water. Each had four paddle-like limbs and long sweeping tails that powered them through the sea. Their snouts occasionally poked above the surface, showing their long jaws.

Storm pushed herself to her feet. "What the—?"

No one spoke. The third boat was rowing through the water towards them, already cast off from the ship, but still a few minutes from the shore. The team on board looked panicked, their heads flicking from side to side as the pack of grey creatures moved rapidly in their direction.

"What are they?" said a voice next to her. Reban.

"I have no idea," she answered honestly.

"Are they plesiosaurs?" asked Lincoln.

She shook her head. "No. Look at them. They don't have a long neck. It's a distinct jaw and more of a snout. Their heads look—"

She never got to finish. The first creature banged sharply into the side of the third boat, rapidly followed by another. One of the team aboard had been standing upright, trying to get a better look at the creatures in the bay. He gave a yelp and fell backwards into the clear blue water. A few of the creatures moved towards him as the rest continued to ram the boat. It was persistent, coordinated behaviour.

"What are they doing?" Leif shook his head in astonishment.

The man in the water gave a few squeals as the pack surrounded him.

It was difficult to make out what was going on in the mass of flickering grey bodies and tails. "I think they're tylosauruses," said Lincoln hoarsely.

"What?" asked Storm. She could feel the anxiety in her chest.

"They're ramming him," Reban broke in as he took a few steps towards the water. "They're actually ramming him. Him and the boat."

Storm wrinkled her brow. "But why?" she stepped forward too, just as one final ram tipped the boat over and the rest of the team and crew toppled into the water. One of them was a Stipulator who had been guarding Reban. Storm let out an involuntary squeal.

Reban started striding out into the water but Lincoln grabbed his arm.

"Don't. Tylosauruses. They're marine predators. This isn't a mistake. This is how they kill."

Now that all the people were in the water, the pack seemed to move in the same motion. Ramming continually at the bodies in the water. The two Stipulators on shore were yelling. "Get out! Try and get ashore!"

Storm could see the conflict written all over Reban's face. She could tell he wanted to get in there, to try to drag the others to shore.

The first guy floated to the surface. It was clear he was unconscious, face down in the water. He would drown. The pack was concentrating on the others, ramming them all continually. This must be the way that they hunted. Once they had stunned their prey, they left them alone – obviously waiting for them to die.

It was systematic. And the water was so clear that everything was visible. The creatures had thick scaly skins, a bit like the tiny lizards back on Earthasia. Some were bigger than others – longer, their large bodies propelling them through the bay in only a few seconds. But it was clear their manoeuvrability was affected by the shallow edges of the bay.

One tylosaurus started circling the first guy. After a few seconds its jaw opened and snapped at his leg. A thin ribbon of red snaked out through the clear blue water, disappearing into the vast ocean just as quickly as it appeared.

The water was still full of grey. Six people now floated face down in the bay. Only one was left floating face up. Only one person still had a chance of survival. The Stipulator.

His black cloak floated around him, rippling in the water. The bodies were bobbing around, sometimes knocked by the waves created by the moving pack. The Stipulator's body was the only one edging a little closer to the shore.

The rest of the tylosauruses started circling the first body. Now that one had started feasting it seemed that the rest were equally engaged. Their jaws snapped at their prey and Leif hid his head in his hands. Things had been bad enough at the cloudy lake, now they could see virtually everything in detail. Storm winced and turned away.

Two of the other Finalists – Froan Jung and Tena Koll – were with the other team on the beach. They had their eyes averted already, not needing to watch what came next. But the rest of the group were dumbfounded. From the ship, the bay had looked tranquil and the green space of Piloria had called out to them, lulling them into some made-up fantasy. The reality was so different.

Reban moved from Storm's side, causing her to turn around. He was fast, going before anyone had a chance to stop him, his boots abandoned on the sand. He strode out thigh-deep in the water then dived underneath, lapping across the bay towards the unconscious Stipulator. Storm slapped her hand over her mouth to stifle her scream. She turned away, pressing her hands down on Leif's shoulders, who was kneeling on the sand in front of her. Leif looked up in astonishment. She couldn't watch.

Lincoln stepped in front of her and pulled her sideways towards him. "It's okay," he said quietly, "they're too busy."

He flinched and she gulped. The noise of flesh being torn from the bone ripped through the air. She couldn't breathe.

Storm turned again and looked out of the corner of her eye. Reban was moving so quietly through the water. His head wasn't even coming up for air, his hands just ploughing forward. He finally surfaced just as the black floating cloak was in reach. He yanked it towards him, using the cloak to reel in the other Stipulator.

Something happened. It was like a moment of recognition that someone in the water was not part of their pack. Reban must have sensed it instantly. His hands wrapped around the body of his colleague and he lay on his back, kicking madly.

The tylosauruses moved forward as one. The other Stipulators started shouting from the shore, "Come on! Come on!" and Storm couldn't help but join in. "Move, Reban. Move!"

It was madness really. There was no way he could hear anything with his head in the water and his legs powering so hard towards shore. The first tylosaurus caught him quickly, but it was cautious – almost as if it wasn't quite sure what this creature was. It gave him a sideways nudge. Reban didn't stop. His legs kept kicking furiously.

Lincoln glanced towards Leif. "Come on." He strode out into the water, ready to assist as soon as Reban was close enough.

Leif blinked, then moved. Storm couldn't believe it. After everything he'd experienced, after losing two friends, he still had the strength to stride out into the water towards another predator.

In a matter of seconds, both Lincoln and Leif were in up to their chests. The second nudge at Reban was more powerful, pushing him sideways. It took him a second to get back into the rhythm of his kicks. There was a moment of fury. These creatures were big and the rapidly approaching beach was impeding their movements.

The largest of the creatures raised itself up out of the water. Its long body was slim and muscular. Was it grey or green? Storm didn't have time to decide because its flattened tail slapped against the water, propelling it forward at lightning speed. For the briefest of seconds its smooth underside revealed its paddle-like limbs with lizard-type scales. But it was the mouth which took all her attention. The snout that had been used for battering its prey was hardly visible once it opened its jaws, exposing two rows of pointy, cone-shaped teeth.

The jaw snapped shut only a few millisectars from Reban's toes.

The geography of the bay was actually on the team's side. Because the creatures were so large and the bay relatively shallow, they couldn't turn easily or get too close to shore. Both Lincoln and Leif grabbed Reban's shoulders at the same time, allowing him to get his feet on the sand beneath him as they grappled for the unconscious Stipulator. But one of the tylosauruses was equally determined. Its head and jaw rose out of the water and snapped straight towards the Stipulator's body.

Storm couldn't help it. She was in the water too, her fear pushed aside by adrenaline. As Reban found his feet, his arm was still wrapped tightly around his colleague. The tylosaurus missed the Stipulator's leg, instead snagging part of the cloak in its mouth. Its jaw ground closed, yanking the Stipulator's body from Reban's grasp.

Reban let out a yell as Lincoln and Leif leaped forward in the water to grab at the body. Leif caught one arm, and Lincoln part of the collar of the cloak, both immediately leaning back towards the shore. The tylosaurus's jaw flicked from side to side with anger as it realized it hadn't really caught its prey. The motion sent a loud tearing sound through the air, as the black cloak was released from the Stipulator's body. The effect was instant.

Reban, Lincoln and Leif fell backwards, landing on their backsides in the shallow water just as the black cloak billowed up into the air like some kind of secret signal.

Storm jumped forward again and tugged the Stipulator back, just out of reach of the jaws of the tylosaurus. It was furious, impeded by the size of its body. It clearly wasn't like the deinosuchus. It had no ability to be on both land and water. For a few seconds it struggled as its body caught on the sandbank, before one large slap of its tail flipped it sideways and back into the bay.

The other two Stipulators ran over and dragged their unconscious colleague from the waves, up onto the beach. Leif, Lincoln and Reban were left panting on the sand.

The other team crowded around the Stipulators, trying

to help. Storm blinked. It had only been a few minutes and the clear, tranquil bay had turned into a hunting ground. She could hear the thud of her heart in her ears.

She turned and glanced at the ship. Most of the crew were staring in horror at the bay, watching the rest of the bodies floating in the water.

The angry tylosaurus moved with a flick of its tail, joining the rest of the pack. The pack that was circling the floating bodies.

Reban still hadn't caught his breath. He was panting heavily, but he pushed himself to his feet. "We don't need to watch this," he muttered. He glanced at Storm. "Can we get away from here?"

She was still shocked by what had just happened. It all seemed so unreal. So unexpected. Octavius had said this bay was safe. This was the place the ship normally docked for a week. She shook her head. "I don't know which way to go. We've never been here before. This isn't where we landed last time."

Reban frowned and strode over to the other Stipulators. "Why have we come to a different landing spot?"

One of them looked up at him blankly. The unconscious Stipulator was on the sand in front of him. But the man's chest was rising and falling. He was alive.

"We drop the candidates at one spot, then moor the boat here for the rest of the week. It's always been safe. There's never been any problem."

He glanced up at the bay and gulped. "I've swum in

this bay. We've caught fish here."

"Who told you to drop us here?" demanded Reban.

The two Stipulators glanced at each other. It didn't seem to matter that Reban was no longer Chief Stipulator. Now Silas wasn't around, they were apparently still a little in awe of the man who'd held that position.

After a few seconds one of them spoke. "Octavius," was all he said.

Storm could feel everyone look at her. Her teammates knew she'd worked for Octavius.

Reban persisted. "Why here? Why somewhere different?"

The Stipulator shrugged. "It made sense," he said.

Reban was clearly frustrated. He turned to Storm. "But why here? Why didn't he put you on a terrain you are familiar with? Surely that was the point of sending you here?"

"Some of us didn't get told the point," muttered Leif. "Some of us got dragged out of our beds in the middle of the night."

Storm shrugged. "Octavius – he gave me part of a map. He'd charted this coastline. We're closer here to the nests than we were before."

The other Stipulator looked up from where he was tending to his colleague. "I heard a rumour that Octavius said you weren't to go anywhere near that lake again."

Reban narrowed his gaze. "Who wasn't to go near that lake? Me?"

The Stipulator looked a little embarrassed. He lifted a slightly shaking hand. "No. Her."

Storm gulped as all eyes turned to her again. "I don't know. I don't know why."

Reban let out an exasperated sigh, striding off towards the green foliage next to the beach.

Lincoln shook his head as he watched, then glanced back to Storm.

Leif narrowed his eyes. "Where's he going? I thought he wanted us to help him. To teach him how to survive. Can't do that if he walks off."

The two Stipulators were still kneeling on the beach with their colleague. Froan and Tena from the other team had been helping, but now they stood up and looked around.

Storm turned to her other teammates. "Let's just leave the Stipulators here. They won't want to come with us." She glanced towards the two boats on the beach. "Hopefully they can find a safe way back to the ship."

She picked up her backpack from the beach, as Lincoln turned to Leif. "Have you got the carrier?"

In all the chaos no one had really thought about the reason they were there – the viruses.

Leif nodded and walked over towards a clump of bushes. He pulled the silver case from it and strode back over. He looked to Froan. "Do you still have yours?" Froan nodded and held up his identical case. "Then let's not waste any more time."

"We'll go to the raptors first," said Storm quickly.

Leif looked at her in confusion. "Why not the pterosaurs?"

The pterosaur nest was easiest to reach, but it was

nowhere near Blaine's shack. Nowhere near the leaves they wanted to collect. She spoke quickly. "We'll go there last. There's no point in us going to the same place at the same time. It would draw too much attention from the dinosaurs," she added quickly. That seemed simple enough. A group of ten people was sure to attract more attention.

The other team glanced at each other uncertainly before finally nodding in agreement.

"We'll go to the pterosaur nest first then," said Tena. "I guess we'll see you back here in a few days."

Storm pressed her lips together. Last time around two members of that team had barely made it back alive. Would their chances improve any with three new members? Would they actually manage to plant any of the viruses? It seemed unlikely.

Leif was watching Reban, who was standing a little distance away, waiting for them to move. He gave Storm and Lincoln a sideways glance and smiled. "Well, if we're taking along a new team member, I guess now we know how the Stipulators will find out if we plant the viruses."

There was a whole array of awkward glances.

And something else. Was it a feeling of dread? She'd seen how Reban had been treated in the parliament chamber. Surely he wouldn't still work for them? Octavius had mentioned he could report back on how the viruses worked. But would he also actually report back on whether they planted them or not? Would he actually report the fact his own daughter was reluctant, and cost her a place back home on the ship?

A few trickles of sweat ran down her back, reminding her exactly where they were. She didn't have time to worry about things like that. She and Lincoln had agreed why they were here.

Storm reached over and put her hand on Jesa's shoulder. Jesa hadn't said a single word since the attack. Her tanned skin was pale, her dark eyes wide.

Something clenched inside Storm. First time around this had been her. That first time, she'd seen the megalodon attack in the ocean, and then the deinosuchus at the lake. She knew exactly how Jesa was feeling right now.

"Welcome to Piloria," she said quietly. "Now let's move."

PART THREE

PILORIA

DAY ONE

TWENTY-SEVEN

LINCOLN

The jungle closed around them instantly: the insects alive and noisy, the bright bursts of colour from the forest floor, and the dark creeping vines around the trees. But the thing that put his senses on alert most was the smell.

Lincoln had forgotten this. The richness. The fullness of it.

Beside him, Jesa gagged and he smiled. It did take a little getting used to. He hadn't expected it to impact on him quite so fiercely.

After a few minutes of tramping, they reached a clearing. Reban was standing with his hands on his knees, sweat dripping from his face already. It was odd seeing him in clothes other than the Stipulator garb. The vest and waistcoat he now wore revealed muscles and definition Lincoln hadn't expected. Maybe Reban was fitter than Lincoln thought.

Piloria was much warmer than Earthasia, but it was as if

the jungle intensified the heat even more. Every breath was thick with moisture.

Storm barely even glanced at Reban on her way past – she was too busy staring at her map. "Come or don't come," she said blithely. "We won't wait for you."

There was a flicker of annoyance on Reban's face. But he picked up his discarded backpack and started to follow them through the jungle.

Lincoln ran his hands over the wide variety of leaves as they walked on. The range was huge. Every shade of green, from the palest moss to the brightest neon, some leaves prickly, lots smooth; from the size of a fingernail to the length of their thighs. The whole time he walked he inhaled deeply, as the ground squelched beneath his feet. Searching for the familiar scent – the strong evergreen leaves that were made into the ointment.

But it wasn't there. Not in this part of the jungle. Maybe the plant only grew in one particular place. He'd have to find out.

They trekked for more than an hour, leaves slapping constantly against his skin, until they finally emerged into the blistering sun.

This time there were no transporters waiting at the other side of the jungle.

This time there was no lake in the distance.

To their right, for as far as the eye could see, there was marsh.

Storm stepped up alongside him. "Interesting," she said. "Probably fewer dinosaurs too."

Lincoln pointed to the left. "But we have to go this way, to the raptor and T-rex nests."

Reban wandered a little ahead of them, staring at the unfamiliar terrain and out of their earshot.

"No," said Jesa sharply. "We need to find my father. I want to see him."

Lincoln turned to her. "We will. We need to find the plants. We need to find the cure for the blistering skin plague. Your father is the only person who knows how to make it. But" – he hesitated as he turned to Storm – "we may well pass the watering holes along the way. Is it really so wrong to try and plant the virus? Would it really be so bad to have fewer killer dinosaurs around?"

Storm's voice was the first to break the silence. "There are so many. I thought we'd met the worst of them the first time around. But then today, in the bay? I didn't even know those creatures existed. There's a whole continent of predators here. A whole continent that's evolved with no human interference. Is it really so right to start now?"

Leif spun around to face her, swinging the silver carrier. He couldn't hide the anger on his face and stepped right up to her. "Well, I'm going to interfere. I'm going to start as soon as I find the first watering hole. Do you think I want to hide up a tree from the raptors? Do you think I want to watch a T-rex rip someone's arm from its socket? No. I'll happily put this stuff in their watering holes. It might not work. Who knows? But if it does, I'll be glad. I'll be glad to have helped get rid of some of them." He gave an ironic laugh and held up his hands. "This place might actually be quite nice without them."

He turned and walked away. Lincoln could see the wave of emotions on Storm's face. Reban had rejoined them at the sound of Leif's raised voice and seemed almost amused by the whole situation, and Jesa had flinched when Leif mentioned the T-rex attack.

"Would you really refuse to kill the dinosaurs?" she asked Storm.

"Of course not," interrupted Reban. "That's why she's here. That's why you're all here."

Lincoln cringed. He knew exactly what kind of reaction that response would get.

Storm stepped up to Reban's face. "Always the Stipulator, eh? They dump you to die on the dinosaur continent and you still do their bidding. What's wrong, Reban? Don't you have a mind of your own? Can't you think for yourself?" She looked him up and down. "Just as well not everything is inherited."

"Maybe I just don't want to die," he said back. Sarcasm dripped from every word. "And what's a few dinosaurs between friends?"

Storm looked disparagingly over her shoulder. "You know, I don't like every dinosaur on this continent. Just like I don't like every person on Earthasia. Doesn't mean I should kill them though, does it?"

She left the words hanging in the air, tilting her chin and walking ahead, ignoring the others. Lincoln sighed and followed behind, falling into step beside Reban.

Reban's senses seemed to be on overload. Every rustle near them made him jump. "You get used to it," said Lincoln casually.

"Is that before or after you die?" shot back Reban.

"I hate to break it to you – but the dying thing? Here, it's all down to luck."

Reban glared at him. "How can it possibly be?"

Lincoln reached down and pulled up his trouser leg. "See this? T-rex bite. I was lucky it didn't get infected. It could have killed me." He gestured to his shoulder. "Same with the pterosaur wound on my shoulder."

Reban's steps slowed. "So what are you saying?"

There was something so antagonistic about the way he spoke. Even when he was asking a question.

"I'm saying that Storm and Leif were lucky to find a tree to climb when the raptors came after them. And any one of us could have been the victim on the lake. Any one of us could have been sitting in the spot that Rune was. You've spent your life making plans and rules for everyone. It's time to throw that out the window. Leave it behind. Life follows its own rules here."

Reban snorted. It was clear even though he'd said he wanted to learn, he didn't really mean it.

Lincoln felt Reban's searing gaze on him.

"What's the deal with the girl?"

"Storm? Or Jesa?"

"Jesa. Who is she?"

211

"She's Blaine's daughter. You know – the guy you all abandoned here nine years ago? She appeared at the dock out of nowhere. She wants to meet him. This was the only way."

Did he imagine it, or did Reban Don's footsteps just falter? "I don't imagine we'll have time for that," he said off-handedly.

Lincoln stopped walking. "Actually, we will." He wasn't afraid to challenge Reban Don. Reban stopped next to him and raised his eyebrows.

Lincoln continued, "Don't kid yourself about why we're here. You've asked us to test the viruses. But I work in the lab, and I don't believe they were ready to try this. It was too swift. Lorcan Field is telling you all what you want to hear. I'm here for another reason. So's Storm. And now, so is Leif."

Reban glared at him. "And what might that be?"

"The cure. The cure for the blistering plague. I need it for my sister. Storm wants it for her too. Leif wants it for Rune's sister and brother and Lorcan Field wants it for his daughter. If the only thing I do on this continent is find those darn leaves and take them home, I'll be happy."

Reban frowned. "And the leaves. How did you know about them?"

Lincoln shrugged. "Blaine showed us. He has a whole shack made of them. Apparently the smell masks human scent."

"Something else to know for my survival." Reban noticed Lincoln raising his eyebrows at the remark. "The odds aren't good on Piloria – or haven't you heard? And *I* didn't ask you to trial the viruses," he went on. "I'm not part of the government any more. I'm only interested in saving myself."

Lincoln kept walking. He didn't believe it. And he was suspicious of Reban's motives. Someone had to tell the Stipulators if they planted the viruses or not. He had the distinct impression that Reban Don might be a plant.

But Reban's eyes had been fixed on Storm as he said those last words. Lincoln couldn't help but smile. "Keep telling yourself that. Maybe at some point you'll believe it too."

TWENTY-EIGHT

STORMCHASER

The trek to the raptor nest site didn't take nearly as long as Storm thought it would. By the time night was falling, the nest was only an hour away. "How far afield do they travel?" asked Jesa. "Is it really safe to make camp here tonight?"

Storm laid out her bedroll. "Let's build a fire. We're far enough away."

Reban had hardly spoken, apart from the odd grunt. He'd filled his water bottle on four occasions already – he was obviously finding it difficult to get accustomed to the humidity on Piloria. He didn't seem quite sure what to make of the place.

Lincoln looked around. "At least we know where their watering hole is from last time. It shouldn't take us long to plant the virus." He sighed and put his hands on his hips. "We could even do it now."

"So we're doing it then?" Storm felt her anger flare. "No discussion?"

Lincoln looked up. "What is there to discuss? We were given a task to do. A dangerous task. But one we should be able to manage." He nodded towards Reban. "I have no idea how the Stipulators will know if we've done it or not, but the one thing I'm absolutely sure of is that I don't want to reach the bay with our ointment – our treatment for Arta, Cornelius and Livia – and be left behind because we haven't done what they've asked."

Storm swallowed. That possibility had played in her mind too. Watching the ship sail off in the distance without the cure would drive her insane.

Lincoln shrugged. "Like I've said before, I don't even think the viruses will work. I don't think they were ready."

"Isn't that more dangerous? Each strain is supposed to be specific to one kind of dinosaur." She felt a wave of panic. "Could they kill everything?"

Lincoln took a few seconds to answer. "Honestly? I don't know. But the truth is, I don't think they'll kill anything. It all just seemed so rushed." He ran his fingers through his hair. "I know what Lorcan's motivations were for saying the T-rex virus was finished. I have no idea about the other labs. The ones that made the raptor and pterosaur viruses." He looked up at Leif and Jesa. "But I guess we'll find out."

He walked over to Leif. "How about it?"

"In the dark?" Leif asked. "Are you crazy? We already know that they're fast and they're intelligent. For all we know they can see in the dark just as well as they can see in the daytime. What I definitely know for sure is that we can't. It would be a suicide mission. No thanks."

"We can wait for daylight," said Storm as she started to try to light a fire. She still wasn't convinced about any of this. She wanted a chance to mull things over. "There's no need to rush things."

"How soon do we reach my dad?" asked Jesa as she sat down at Storm's side.

Storm gave a half-smile. The irony of this killed her. Jesa was seeking her father out when Storm would gladly leave hers behind.

"We'll move as fast as we can. We're short on time and this was the best route. Once Leif" – she glanced over – "or Lincoln, has left the virus in the watering hole, we can start out straight away." The fire had caught now and was flickering in the dimming light.

Jesa nodded nervously. Her wild curls seemed even more exaggerated in the humid atmosphere and she started tugging at her hair. Storm dug into her bag and pulled out a piece of string. "Here. Tie it up. It gets too hot around here."

Jesa gave a smile and took the string, tying her loose curls up in a knot on top of her head. "I can't wait to see him," she said quietly, as she stared into the orange flames.

Storm said nothing as she pulled out some fruit from her backpack, then smiled as Lincoln did the same. They put the pile in the middle. "Everyone help yourself. After two days we either have to eat the ration packs or whatever we scavenge."

"You can eat the food here?" asked Jesa in wonder.

Leif and Lincoln smiled. It was obvious they remembered their own surprise at the discovery. Storm nodded, conscious that Reban was suddenly looking interested. "We found a whole variety of fruits the last time. Orange, purple and red. We'll show you if we find them again. They tasted good." She gave a laugh. "Though we might have overdone it. They gave us a little belly-ache the next day. But yes, you can find food here to live. Your father has done it for years."

Jesa's eyes narrowed as if she'd just thought of something. She turned to Reban. He was sitting on the very edge of their circle. As if he wasn't keen to be part of the conversation. "Reban." She said his name warily, as if she were just trying it out for size. He had been the Chief Stipulator for her city. Even being in the same place as him was intimidating. "You must have known my father. He would have been a Stipulator at the same time as you. Do you think he'll recognize you? Were you friends?"

Reban shifted uncomfortably on the wet grass. He looked as if he were searching for the right words. Storm recognized the signs. She'd done it herself with Jesa, when answering her questions about Blaine. "I wouldn't say we were exactly friends," said Reban. It was the first time she'd actually seen him look nervous in any way.

And that made her curious.

"What do you mean?" she asked.

Reban raised his eyebrows. She'd never really initiated a proper conversation with him before. She didn't really

217

want to. But there was only five of them now. It made him pretty hard to ignore. And it was only for another few days. Even she could last that long.

After that she'd be free and clear of Reban Don – probably for ever. He was banished, just like Blaine had been. And who knew if he'd learn to survive or not. Her stomach squeezed. She wasn't entirely sure how she felt about that.

Reban gave a sort of sigh. "Blaine and I didn't exactly see eye to eye on things. He was bright, smart. But he knew it." Reban glanced at Jesa. Storm could see he was picking his words carefully. "I'm quite sure the man I knew won't exist any more. It's been nine years. And a whole lifetime ago."

Leif gave a wry laugh. "You hated each other, didn't you?"

Reban leaned back on his hands. "Some people might say that."

Leif stood up, grabbed a piece of fruit and walked over to his bedroll. "I'm tired. And it seems like this place is every bit as bad as I remember." He gave an ironic kind of smile. "If Blaine is still in the same mood as he was the last time we saw him, then watch out," he said, nodding his head to Reban. "Because he'll kill you on sight."

DAY TWO

TWENTY-NINE

STORMCHASER

She was dreaming. For some reason she was back in the pale-grey room of the Shelter. Her tiny room was even smaller than she remembered and the walls seemed to be closing in around her. There was a constant banging at the door. One huge thud after another. It made her whole room shake. The walls still closing, the place getting claustrophobic. She couldn't move her arms and something was tangled around her legs. She was tied up. Tied up in something. Her breath caught in her throat. Panic spread in her chest.

A voice shouted at the door. "Storm! Storm!" The banging was even worse. Her whole room shook. Her bed was lifting off the ground.

"Storm!" This time the jolt was enough to make her eyes spring open. There were hands on her. Someone was picking her up. Daylight. Bright sun.

Thud. The whole ground shook. The trees next to them

visibly shuddered. Fear tore through her. Last time she'd felt the ground shake, a T-rex had been on its way.

But there was something else that shocked her. The person who had her in their arms was Reban Don.

Her view was suddenly obstructed by something grey. And huge. Reban was flung off his feet, sending Storm crashing to the ground. She didn't move, watching in horror as a massive foot made contact with her bed mat, crushing it completely.

A blanket. That's what was impeding her legs. She reached down to untangle it and set her feet free. If Reban hadn't picked her up and moved her, she would be dead now.

The enormous dinosaur continued to move. It was slow. Ambling forward, each footprint leaving a huge imprint in the ground.

"Stay down," hissed Lincoln.

He was hidden in the trees. Leif was nearby, with his arm around Jesa, who was crying and shaking. "Watch out for the tail!" yelled Lincoln.

Storm pressed her face against the ground just as a giant tail swept past. It was a momentous structure. With one slow-motion sweep it wiped out the trees Leif, Lincoln and Jesa were cowering in, ripping them from the ground as if they were pieces of paper. Dirt showered over them all.

Every muscle in Storm's body tensed as the huge tail swept only millisectars above her head. She cringed, remembering when Kronar had been struck by the tail of the T-rex. The sound of his bones crunching. The impact of him hitting the ground, and the gurgling sound of his lungs filling up with blood. But the T-rex tail was nothing compared to this. One swipe of this would kill you before you even hit the ground.

She choked back the dirt in her mouth as the tail swung slowly the other way, lifting her eyes fractionally to be sure the creature had continued to move.

Every step it took made the ground shake violently. When she was sure it was safe, Storm pushed herself up onto her hands and knees, coughing and spluttering the dirt from her mouth.

"Are you okay?" Lincoln was at her side in an instant. There was blood running down the side of his head.

She couldn't stop wheezing. She must have inhaled some of the dirt. She shook her head as she stayed on all fours for a few seconds, watching the dinosaur walking away from them.

"What is it?" she gasped as she watched its colossal frame.

Leif appeared at her other side and held out his hand to help her up. "It has to be a titanosaurus. What else is that size?" He shook his head as he watched it continue across the land. Every footprint that it left was huge – big enough for a human to lie down in. He turned to face her. "Don't you remember we saw footprints like that before? We just didn't know where they had come from."

Lincoln lifted his hand. "I guess we know now." He wrinkled his nose as he continued to stare. "Maybe it's a new kind. I didn't actually think they were *that* big. It's as big as a tower block."

"A tower block pushed on its side," murmured Leif as he continued to watch.

There was an angry yelp to her left and Storm turned in time to see Reban push himself to his feet while clutching one side of his chest. "Are you okay?" The words were out of her mouth before she even thought about them.

Jesa shot her a look as she moved to Lincoln's side and pressed something against his forehead.

Reban's face was pale, the veins under his skin clearly visible. "Knocked by a flying tree," he muttered. He looked stunned. He kept one arm on his ribs as he stepped over to where Storm had been lying. Her bedroll was compressed against the ground, thinner than a leaf. It lay perfectly inside an entire footprint.

Reban didn't speak. He just stood for a few seconds, obviously contemplating where they all were, what could have happened.

Storm's hands were shaking. She could have been killed. In an instant. Just like that. Because of a beast that wasn't even known to be ferocious. It was a plant eater.

They all stood and watched. The titanosaurus – if that's what it was – was in no hurry. It seemed to amble along. Occasionally it stopped to munch at the top of a tree that hadn't been felled by either its feet or its tail. It seemed oblivious to its surroundings and definitely had no concept of the destruction it was wreaking.

"Just think," breathed Jesa. "If we lived here – one of these could just walk through your compound in the middle

of the night. Wipe you all out. You might hear it coming –
but you'd never be able to stop it."

Storm flinched. It was crazy. But those kinds of thoughts
had filled her head at times. Not about being felled by a giant
dinosaur. But about what the human compounds might
eventually look like here.

In her mind, even if they managed to wipe out the most
predatory dinosaurs, the humans would still need somewhere
secure to stay. Her dreams had morphed the current
parliament building, built on the trees on Earthasia, into
something similar over here. A compound built on land, but
made entirely of trees, with a defence wall of trees circling
it. She hadn't figured on a titanosaurus, though. The creature
could flatten such a compound with a few sweeps of its tail.

Storm shook her head. "We should move. The titanosaurus
might wake up some less friendly creatures around here.
We can reach the watering hole this morning. Let's do it,"
she said, squeezing Jesa's hand. "Then we can look for
Blaine."

Her stomach gave a little flip-flop as she said the words.
She took a step towards Lincoln. "Is your head okay?"

He nodded and moved what he was pressing against his
head. "I think it's stopped. I must just have been caught by
one of the tree branches."

Storm paused, then turned back to Reban. "Are you ready
to go?" she asked tentatively. She winced as she glanced at
her bed mat, then walked over and rolled it back up. The
stress of the weight had crushed it, and parts of it cracked as

she rolled it, but she ignored this, attaching it to her backpack as before. "I might still need this," she said.

Reban was pale but he picked up his bag and slung it over his uninjured side. "Let's go."

Storm pointed to some hills in the distance. "It's this way," she said as she started striding in that direction.

She could hear the others fall in behind her.

"Hell of a wake-up call," Reban muttered.

THIRTY

LINCOLN

After its disastrous beginning, the day seemed to pan out much better. They crossed the open terrain easily. At one point, for as far as the eye could see, there was just rolling, green land. In the distance they spotted a herd of apatosauruses. "They don't look dangerous from this far away," murmured Jesa.

Lincoln smiled. "Generally, they're not. It's just the size thing. I think they're quiet creatures, peaceful. But we'd need to learn how to live with them."

He shifted on his feet. Had he just said that? It sounded like he was thinking about the long-term plans for humans settling on Piloria. He'd never even imagined leaving Earthasia before.

Jesa was clearly starting to get nervous. "My mum and Caleb will be so angry with me. I can only imagine the kind of things they'll be saying."

"And when you go home?"

She gave a sad smile. "They'll just have a thousand questions about Dad. They'll want to know how he is. If he's okay. What I can tell them about him." She shook her head. "The questions will be endless." She wiped away a tear that had sneaked down her cheek.

"What's wrong?"

"It's just…" She lowered her voice as she watched Storm, Reban and Leif walk on ahead. "I wish they were here too. It would mean so much to them. Just to talk to him. Just to touch him."

Lincoln nodded. "I get it. I do. It's hard being away from our families. But this task? It shouldn't take long. Then we can head towards the jungle where Blaine's shack is."

"Does he stay there all year around?"

"I…I don't know. I never asked him. I guess we just assumed that he did." He gave a half-laugh. "The first time I met him was in a cave, after running away from a T-rex."

He regretted the words as soon as they left his mouth. Jesa's reaction was instant – he could see the goosebumps appear on her arms. She ran her hands up and down them. Piloria wasn't cold. There were no brisk breezes. This was pure fear.

Her eyes were wide. "Do you think my father will still be here?"

His stomach clenched. He knew what the question really was. *Do you think my father is still alive?*

Lincoln took a deep breath. "He's already survived here

for nine years, Jesa. I think he'll have managed another couple of months."

Jesa gave a nod and kept walking. "Okay then," was the reply. Had he convinced her or not?

A short while later, Storm, who was walking ahead, gestured with her hand. "Get down," she hissed. They were approaching the brow of a hill.

Lincoln bent low, then crawled forward on his elbows until he was alongside her. "What is it?" he whispered.

"They're just over this hill," she mouthed.

He pulled back in surprise. "Isn't the watering hole still a bit away?"

She shrugged. "I thought so. Who knows how far they travel to hunt? One watering hole is as good as another."

Lincoln automatically lifted his tunic to his nose. He'd only been wearing it since yesterday. "What if they smell us?"

Storm squeezed her eyes closed for a second. "Let's hope the wind doesn't change, or they might." She looked from side to side. "There's no cover around here."

Lincoln looked around. She was right. No jungle. No bushes. Not even any rocks to hide behind. They'd passed a stream some time back, but that was it.

Keeping as low as he could, he edged a little closer to the brow of the hill.

Four velociraptors were drinking at a watering hole. It wasn't the watering hole he'd seen them at on his previous visit though. This stretch of water was murky, and surrounded by mud. One raptor was clearly the leader. It was bigger than the rest, its red crest more prominent. From here, it looked as if it was covered in thick brown skin, but Lincoln knew that wasn't the case. Up close, he had seen how the raptors were actually covered in feathers, with a few extra ones around their forearms.

The lead velociraptor stood proudly on its strong hind legs, with its snout in the air. Lincoln ducked down. "I think it's trying to find a scent," he whispered. "They must be looking for their next meal."

Leif kept his voice low. "Then what now? Do we hide here, hoping they'll go in another direction, or get up and run?"

Jesa looked terrified. From a titanosaurus to a group of velociraptors – it was hardly a great introduction to Piloria.

"The other watering hole was closer to the nest, wasn't it?" whispered Storm.

Leif nodded. "Definitely. I remember." He gave Lincoln a half-smile. "We passed it on our way back, after we jumped off the cliff."

Lincoln couldn't help but smile too. It was the first time Leif had even shown a glimmer of the friendship they'd had before. He nodded in agreement. "So maybe all these creatures have more than one watering hole? This could be a complete waste of time. We might put the virus here – and they never return."

Storm's eyes brightened a little. "Maybe that's actually for the best. As soon as they leave, let's dump the virus in the water and move on. We could get halfway to Blaine's shack tonight. Halfway to the leaves."

Lincoln shifted uncomfortably. Something was different about Storm. Only a few months ago she'd been so opposed to doing anything that might interfere with the dinosaurs' habitat. She hadn't wanted to steal the eggs. She'd been adamant they should leave the dinosaurs alone.

When she'd questioned him last night he thought it might end up in a stand-off. But now it seemed she'd accepted his belief that the virus wouldn't work. Part of him actually hoped it *would* work – but he couldn't risk saying that out loud.

"Let's just stay where we are for now. If we move, they might smell us. They're fast. I'm not sure we would win a race across an open plain."

The others nodded and pressed further down against the earth. Anything to stop their scent being picked up.

They didn't need to wait long. A few minutes later there was a high-pitched cawing noise.

Lincoln edged closer to the ridge. The noise came again at a different pitch. It sent chills through his body. He'd heard this before. He'd witnessed this before – even though he hadn't been entirely sure then. The velociraptors were *communicating* with each other.

He'd heard the Stipulators joking that these beasts had brains the size of a pebble. But they didn't know what *he* knew. He'd not only witnessed them communicating, he'd also witnessed their intelligent behaviour. He'd watched the velociraptors extinguish a fire by scraping at the earth and smothering it with dirt. Those pebble-sized brains were using all their functions.

"Don't move," he hissed to the others around him. He shuffled forward just enough so that he could see what the raptors were doing. Storm copied him.

The leader still had its nose in the air. It tipped its head back and let out the loudest caw yet. The other velociraptors copied it, moving in perfect synchrony.

There was a flicker in the corner of Lincoln's eye as a dark grey duckbill waddled into sight. Followed by another, and another. All heading in the direction of the watering hole. They were sniffing around the ground, oblivious to the danger.

Lincoln cringed. Duckbills. The very thing they'd trapped and used to lure the T-rex a couple of months ago.

In the blink of an eye, the raptors spread out, circling towards the duckbills. A moment later one of the duckbills noticed them, let out a noise and started running. But it seemed disorientated.

Its moment of panic alerted its companions. The other duckbills started grunting and running too. But the slow, thick-trunked creatures couldn't match the speed of the raptors. The first was despatched easily by the large sickle-shaped claw on the lead raptor's foot.

But instead of ensuring the kill was completed and starting to feast on the duckbill, the raptor ignored it – leaving it open on the ground. It followed the other raptors as they chased after the fleeing duckbills, heading over the hump of another hill.

Lincoln glanced at Storm. "What do you think?" He looked behind them. "Is there any way they can circle back and come up behind us?"

She thought for a few seconds. "I don't think so. This is our chance."

"You mean, this is *my* chance." Leif didn't hesitate. He flipped open the silver carrier, exposing the intact vials of red, blue and green. His fingers grasped at the green vial instantly, yanking it from the sponge it was cushioned in. He crouched low on the ground, his spear clutched in his other hand. "This is my job. My task. I want to do this. I want to be the one to infect them."

Storm flinched at the intensity of his words. Lincoln almost understood. This rage had been bubbling beneath the surface in Leif ever since their last visit. He was angry. Angry at the loss of his two friends. Angry at the dinosaurs.

Lincoln glanced over the ridge again. "It looks clear. But we've no guarantee it will stay that way. I think we should wait longer. Maybe they'll move on someplace else."

"But that someplace else could be over this ridge, where we have no hiding place – no protection."

"He's got a point." Reban's comment was unexpected. He'd hardly spoken at all during the morning's journey. He stood, stretching out his back muscles and picking up the weapon he'd chosen from the locker on the ship. It was double-ended. One end was like an axe, the other more like a sword. He nodded to Leif. "Let's do this. Let's get rid of some dinosaurs."

Before Lincoln could protest further, Leif had grabbed his spear and set off at a rapid pace down to the watering hole. Lincoln had forgotten how fast Leif could run, and what he hadn't expected was for Reban Don to almost match him. Reban was only a few steps behind.

Storm was right at Lincoln's side. "I have a bad feeling about this," she murmured.

Lincoln straightened, turning his head from side to side, watching for any change – any hint of the return of the raptors.

There was still noise in the distance. The squeal of the duckbills and the squawks and caws of the raptors. Lincoln looked around. Leif and Reban's backpacks were on the ground behind him. "Gather all their things. We want to be able to move in a hurry if we have to."

As he looked back, Leif had reached the watering hole. He held up the green vial. Even from here the bright green colour glinted in the sun. Leif fumbled, trying to remove the stopper. Reban stood at his back, checking in either direction.

Leif finally let out a cry of frustration and picked up a rock, smashing the vial and letting the shattered glass and its contents spill into the watering hole. Reban turned his head at the noise behind him, watching as Leif bent down for a second, rinsing his hands at the edge of the water before wiping them on his trousers.

Something inside Lincoln clenched. Had Leif got the

virus on himself? The Stipulators had never mentioned if it would affect humans. And, more foolishly, they'd never asked. They'd all just assumed it wouldn't. What if that assumption was wrong?

A squawk split through the air. Lincoln's head turned towards the noise at the same time as Reban's. The split second of Leif smashing the glass had distracted them. And that distraction might now cost them all their lives.

THIRTY-ONE

STORMCHASER

That was the thing about this place. Blink. And you missed it. Blink. And you could be dead.

She'd just bent down to pick up Leif's backpack when she heard the squawk. It was like being plunged into an icy pool. She'd heard those angry screeches before.

A raptor was racing back over the hump of the opposite hill, straight towards Leif and Reban. This raptor was the smallest of the group – barely the height of Storm. But its height didn't detract from the three claws it had on each forearm or the large sickle-shaped claw on each foot. *The killing claw.* That's how she'd come to think of it. These predatory animals used it with expertise.

Leif's face was instantly panicked. "Come on!" he yelled at Reban, as he grabbed his spear and started to run.

Reban glanced up towards the ridge of the hill where Storm and the rest of them were hiding. "GO!" he shouted.

Lincoln yanked the extra backpack out of her hand. "Move!" He took off across the open plain, with Jesa hard on his heels. But Storm couldn't move. She was frozen at the top of the hill in horror.

This should have been easy. They should have waited. They could have walked a bit, found somewhere to hide, then come back to plant the virus when the coast was clear.

Leif was already halfway back up the hill towards her. Reban seemed to be hesitating. The raptor moved quickly – faster than any human – and was in front of Reban within seconds.

Leif thudded past her, his eyes narrowing as she didn't move.

Reban had both hands on his weapon. The raptor raised its claws, swiping at Reban as he ducked from side to side. The forearms were just about avoidable. But the raptor's frustration was evident.

It lifted one leg, revealing the killing claw on its second digit. Its red crest bloomed in indignation at a creature attempting to fight back. It let out another squawk. Storm couldn't breathe. It was communicating. It was shouting for its group. Reban wouldn't stand a chance.

The first time it swiped with the killing claw, Reban caught the blow with the staff of his weapon, narrowly missing his hands. The second time the raptor lifted its leg to strike, Reban moved first. The underside of the raptor's belly was exposed. He thrust forward with one end of his weapon. The end that resembled a sword.

The next noise was one of strangulated surprise from the raptor.

Reban twisted the sword and Storm gagged. She couldn't believe he was still standing there. The raptor made another noise. A cry of distress.

Now she found her voice. "Move!" she yelled. "Leave it!" At the same second there was a yank on her arm so strong it felt like her arm was being pulled from its socket. Lincoln's face filled her view. "Storm. Move. Now."

Reban pulled back his sword as the raptor swayed, then started to run up the hill towards her.

Now she could move. Now she could run.

And she did. Thudding across the open plain with Lincoln's steps mirroring her own. She didn't turn back. She could only hear her own breathing. Her body naturally followed the curve in Lincoln's run as he moved to the right.

Every muscle burned. The air in her lungs could find a way in, but struggled to find a way back out. Her thigh muscles were on fire. These boots were finding blisters she didn't know she had. Sweat trickled down her forehead and back. But she couldn't slow down. Couldn't stop for a second.

There was an echo behind her. She wasn't quite sure what it was.

The plain seemed to stretch on for ever. But the terrain started to change a little. A few sparse bushes appeared. Some darker foliage in the distance.

Then all of a sudden Lincoln disappeared from her view. She didn't have time to process because the next moment she was falling, no, rolling, down hard and bumpy ground.

Brown. Green. More brown. Mud. Stones. Then *splash*. Face down in water.

She shook the moisture off her face and looked up. Leif and Jesa were crouched nearby, their eyes fixed above her, Lincoln just picking himself up. The backpacks were stored behind them and each had their weapons in their hands. Jesa's crossbow was visibly shaking.

The lukewarm water seeped through Storm's clothing. She shook her head again and tried to orientate herself. This was a stream. Definitely not a river. The flow was steady but small. She pushed herself up on all fours as Reban seemed to arch in the air above her. It seemed that he hadn't expected the sudden incline either.

She ducked back down as he landed with a crunch in the water next to her.

"Aargh," he groaned.

She held her breath and looked back up. The only noise was the trickling stream – the clear water dancing over the stones.

All faces were turned the same way. They waited. And waited.

After a few minutes, Lincoln's shoulders relaxed. He gave them all a nod. "I'm going for a look." He scrambled up the bank and peered over the top, sagging back against the crumbling bank with a smile. "Nothing. There's nothing there. They missed us."

The breath that she'd been holding seemed to leave her

body all at once, along with every ounce of energy. She didn't care that she was already wet. She just sagged back down onto the stream bed.

Leif bent his head next to her. "You're going to have to tell us why you were frozen there, later." His voice was barely audible. He lifted his head again as he prodded her with his finger. "Right, get up. You're ruining our drinking supply. This stream seems as good as any to refill our water bottles."

Lincoln slid down the rest of the bank, sending clumps of mud falling around them. "Sorry." He looked up and down the stream. "Once we've filled our water bottles we should probably take the chance to get cleaned up. Who knows when we'll get it again."

Reban was still lying on his back in the stream. Leif stood over him and held out his hand. "You okay?"

Reban made a noise and grabbed the outstretched hand, letting Leif pull him up. His backpack was totally flattened against his spine. He shrugged it off his shoulders. "Well, anything good in here is ruined. But hey, it broke my fall." His brow creased as he looked around. "Did someone bring the carrier?"

Jesa finally spoke. Her hands were still shaking as she clutched her crossbow. "I did." She pointed to the ground behind her.

Lincoln walked over and gestured to Leif's hands. "Did it get on you?"

Leif was already bending to fill his water bottle. He gave a wave. "Just a little. It's no big deal."

Storm stepped over and took his hand in hers, turning it one way then the other, as if to search for a trace of the virus. "You don't know that." Almost as soon as she said the words she dropped his hand, then felt horrified with herself. She resisted the temptation to rub her hand fiercely on her trousers.

It was too late. She'd touched him. If he had the virus, maybe she had it now too.

Reban stepped between them. "It will be fine. That thing kills dinosaurs, not humans."

It was odd. But even though he was saying it in a brash and no-nonsense kind of way, he gave Storm a sideways glance. Her stomach did a little flip. Reban was just as unsure as the rest of them.

Lincoln stepped closer to Reban. "What on earth made you stay and fight?"

Reban shrugged. "Honestly? I didn't think I could outrun it."

Storm couldn't help herself. She bent down in the stream and uncapped her bottle to refill it. But as soon as she had done that she started scrubbing her hands together, even picking up a smooth stone from the stream bed to help.

Raptors were fast. The truth was most humans would never be able to outrun them. But she had the strangest feeling that Reban hadn't actually been thinking about himself.

She lifted her gaze as she scrubbed at her hands. Lincoln was looking at Reban strangely, watching the way he was currently looking at Storm.

Her stomach clenched.

Reban hadn't really been worried about not outrunning the raptors.

He was just worried that *she* wouldn't outrun them.

THIRTY-TWO

LINCOLN

The second night was far easier than the first.

For Lincoln, it felt like some bizarre dream. By the time they'd tramped across the terrain and finally found a suitable place to camp, they'd all been exhausted. The burst of adrenaline earlier in the day seemed to have depleted their reserves. Reban had emptied his backpack of his remaining squashed food from the boat and shared it around. That, along with some berries found in nearby bushes, had been enough to replenish them.

Campfire chat had been nil. Reban wouldn't go into any details about the raptor – even though Lincoln had seen the blood on his weapon.

After they'd finished eating, Lincoln had lain down on his bedroll and stared up at the ink-black sky above. Every time he blinked, he saw what had happened today. Storm hadn't moved. For all she'd said she hated Reban, when he looked as though he might sacrifice himself, she'd been rooted to the spot. If Lincoln hadn't turned back and grabbed her, he wasn't sure if she would have ever moved.

He was almost sure that's why Reban had stayed to fight – to save Storm. In an ideal world, Lincoln would like to think that Reban had been giving them all time to flee. But he doubted Reban cared about the rest of them, and generosity had never seemed part of the Chief Stipulator's personality.

While chatting on their trek to the raptor nest, they'd mentioned a few times, in passing, that Leif and Lincoln were the fastest runners. Storm had won the final Trial because of her knife-throwing skills – not because of her speed. Reban would have known she was at risk.

Lincoln gave a wry smile. Both of them were continuing to pretend they didn't care about each other. But their actions were telling him something else.

And he still couldn't decide if Reban was a plant or not. He didn't say much, but when he did speak he didn't seem to have much love for the Stipulators. Could the man really still be working for them?

Lincoln looked up at the dark, perfectly clear night. It felt like if he reached his hand up, he could pluck the moon out of the sky. The sky in Ambulus City wasn't like this. It felt so much more closed in and shut off. A bit like the rest of the continent. If Lincoln held his arms out in the cave back home he could touch either side of the damp walls. The dank wetness filled his lungs every night. Getting into the sweating, claustrophobic lab the next morning was actually sometimes a relief.

Would the virus have any effect on the raptors at all? Could it actually kill them?

He shifted subconsciously on his bedroll. Some of his thoughts were making him uncomfortable. What would his mother and Arta think of this place? Arta would have the remedy for the blistering plague at her fingertips. For the first time in months her life wouldn't revolve around infected, bleeding lesions.

The stars shone brightly above. Beside him, Leif moaned a little in his sleep and turned over. Leif hated this place. Hated it, and its inhabitants, beyond measure.

But Lincoln wasn't quite so sure how he felt any more. If the viruses actually worked and the predators were taken out of the equation, wouldn't Piloria be a whole lot more attractive?

The climate was different. So was the plant life and the soil. Things actually grew here. Different things. Edible things. And they weren't rationed.

Blaine had survived here for nine years. Nine years with no running water or power. He'd adapted. He'd learned how to make systems that worked for him. Couldn't other people do the same?

There was a sniff beside him and he turned on his side. Storm was curled in a ball, rocking back and forward with her eyes closed.

"Hey," he whispered, touching her shoulder. "What's up?"

Her eyes opened and she sighed. "I don't know. I'm sore. I'm tired." She sucked in a deep breath. "I'm worried."

Lincoln had opened his mouth to offer instant reassurance, but he stopped. Storm was worried? She didn't do that. She didn't show any vulnerability. She liked the world to think she was invincible.

But she'd said those words out loud. To him. The guy who'd betrayed her for his family. Maybe they were finally getting back to an even keel.

"What are you worried about?" he asked gently.

She met his gaze. Under the moon's glow, her violet eyes were so like Reban's. "Dinosaurs. Blaine. And…the virus."

Lincoln frowned. "Okay, dinosaurs? Right there with you. Blaine?"

She glanced in the direction of sleeping Jesa. Jesa had huddled her bedroll next to Leif's so that he was within touching distance.

Storm kept her voice at a whisper. "You know what he was like the last time, Linc. What if he's worse? What if, even though we think he wants to see his family, after all this time he just can't cope? What if…he's bad to her?"

Lincoln's stomach coiled. "I didn't expect her to come," he admitted. "When they stopped me in the street…I just couldn't lie. They were desperate, Storm. They wanted news. What gave me the right to keep it from them?"

She nodded. "I know. But now…" She let her voice tail off.

Lincoln took a deep breath. "He's crazy. We both know

245

he's crazy. But is it just because he's been left by himself? Or is it because he's filled with grief about never seeing his family? Think about how long he'd treasured those sketches. Think about the way he looked at them."

Storm nodded and Lincoln instantly felt regret at his words. Her eyes glazed a little. She was thinking about her mother. He reached over and squeezed her shoulder. "It's my fault Jesa is here. I'll take responsibility. I'll look after her. If Blaine can't cope, I'll take her away."

Storm shook her head determinedly. "No, it's our responsibility. I just don't know how to prepare her. I don't think we can. I think we just have to wait and see how he is." She stopped for a second.

"What else?"

She blinked and pressed her lips together. It was almost like she didn't want to say the words.

"You didn't want us to find the eggs before. You didn't want them to get the DNA. Is this about the virus?"

She shook her head and an unexpected tear slid down her cheek. Lincoln was surprised. "Yes, and no. It is. But not the way you think."

Now he was really confused. "What do you mean?"

She held up her hand. It was shaking. "I should be angry about virus. I should have smashed those vials on the beach. But the whole time I'm here and looking over my shoulder, I'm wondering how much easier Piloria would be to live in without those dinosaurs. And now, instead of worrying about what we're doing, I'm worrying about *myself*.

246

How selfish is that?" She grimaced as she looked at her hand. "What if the virus doesn't only affect dinosaurs?"

Lincoln's first instinct was to shuffle backwards. But he tensed every muscle and refused to allow himself to do that. "You're sure Leif got it on his hands?"

She nodded. Tears were pooling in her eyes.

He swallowed and touched her shoulder again. "You're not selfish, Storm. Don't you think I've had the same thoughts about this place? Do you think I like working in the lab and living in the caves? If the dinosaurs weren't here, Piloria could be paradise. There. I've said it. I've said what the Stipulators have been saying all along. Does that make me a bad person?" He shook his head. "And the virus? Each lab worked on a specific virus for those specific dinosaurs. It shouldn't be able to harm us. We're an entirely different species."

He had left out the part about all the precautions the staff took in the lab. The fact they worked in separate air-pressurized rooms. The fact they all wore protective clothing and masks. He swallowed the lump in his throat.

"Don't worry. You're safe. I'm sure of it."

He wasn't. Of course he wasn't. But how could he say that?

But he'd put his trust in Lorcan. He had to believe that as a scientist, Lorcan would ensure his work didn't harm humans.

Storm blinked back her tears. He could tell she was angry that they'd been revealed. She kept parts of herself so hidden that Lincoln even wondered if she knew they existed.

She pulled her blanket up over her shoulder. "Night, Lincoln," she whispered.

Lincoln turned on his back and looked up at the stars again. "Night, Storm," he replied, as a shooting star sped across the dark sky.

He could get used to this.

DAY THREE

THIRTY-THREE

STORMCHASER

They were all tired. Sweat was running down every part of her. The jungle seemed to be closing in around them.

Storm turned for the hundredth time, trying to orientate herself. Every part of this jungle looked the same. Every trampled bush. Every broken twig. Every darn gigantic green leaf that smacked her in the face.

They'd been in here for hours.

Tramping first one way, then the other.

The trouble was, last time they'd come here Blaine had led them from the cave to his home – his home in the middle of the jungle. They were sure they were in the right piece of jungle, but they didn't know where to turn next. The only positive was that so far they hadn't met any predators.

"I think it's this way," said Leif, pointing to the left.

"I think it's this way," said Lincoln, pointing to the right. He reached up and touched the enormous trunk of the tree he was standing next to. "This seems familiar."

Reban let out a choked laugh. "Really?" He held up his hands. "All these trees look the same." He slapped the trunk nearest to him. "What makes this one different to the one next to you?"

The scratching noise was unexpected. It was quickly followed by a head and short beak poking out from a bush and scrabbling along the ground just in front of them.

Everyone froze, as the giant chicken-like creature emerged from the bushes. It was much bigger than the few scrawny remaining chickens back on Earthasia – almost half the size of a human. It had brown feathers on its thick body, short light-grey feathers on its elongated neck, a flash of red around the beak, oversized claws and prominent tail feathers.

It was closest to Leif. While Leif's body stayed frozen, his eyes widened and he glanced first at Storm and then Lincoln. It seemed as though they all remembered that apparently a dinosaur's sight could be partially based on movement. But they couldn't stay frozen for ever – not when they were so obviously exposed.

"What is it?" hissed Lincoln.

Everyone around Storm shrugged. "A giant chicken?" she mouthed. That's what it looked like to her. She was curious now. Something about it seemed a little familiar, but she couldn't place what.

Reban smiled, his voice low. "Dinner. Anything's better than the packs they gave us. Maybe we could try and catch it."

The creature seemed oblivious to them and started

scratching around the ground – the same way the chickens did back on Earthasia.

There was more rustling. More scraping. In the blink of an eye another appeared, then another and another. Within a few moments, around twelve of the creatures had emerged from the bushes.

Storm could hear the beat of her heart in her ears. She started to feel just a little uneasy. Her brain was still trying to fathom what she could remember from the book in Octavius's study. Very carefully, she turned her hands palm up, asking the silent question: *What do we do?*

One of the newly-emerged creatures butted its head against Reban's thigh. "Hey!" shouted Reban, an automatic response. Jesa let out a squeal.

It was almost like flicking a switch somewhere. It seemed the creatures – whatever they were – reacted to sound and hunted in packs.

Some surrounded Reban, the others surrounded Jesa.

Leif was quick – he picked up his spear just as one of the creature's claws slashed at Jesa's hand and she let out another squeal.

The creatures seemed to attack at once. Their wings were useless, but their claws fierce. Their short, stubby beaks ripped through Reban's trousers before he had a chance to even move.

His double-ended weapon came into contact with the first one at the same time as Leif thrust through the one closest to Jesa with his spear.

Both animals let out high-pitched squeals. Within a few seconds more emerged from the bushes, surrounding them on all sides.

Now Storm couldn't stay quiet. She pulled a knife from her belt and threw it without stopping to think – but her aim was accurate, catching one beast in the neck, a spurt of red blood covering the closest tree. She looked around frantically. "There's nowhere to go!" she yelled.

It was true. She saw the rest of the team look around frantically. It wasn't the size of the creatures, it was their number and the ferocity of their attack. Their claws were swiping with alarming precision. Blood had already stained Reban's trousers and was smeared along Jesa's arm.

Reban's eyes looked skyward. "Up!" he yelled. "We go up."

He jumped towards the nearest tree branch just as another three creatures tore at him with their angry beaks and hooking claws. He was right. There was no other way to go.

Storm grabbed at the tree behind her, as Leif speared another beast and bent down to give Jesa a boost up the nearest tree.

Lincoln charged, his axe above his head, swinging it wildly from side to side. Storm froze as she pulled herself up onto a branch. Why wasn't he climbing too?

Crunch. One creature's head went flying past her, swiped clean by Lincoln's axe.

Leif's eyes were wide. The creature's body, its claw raised to rake at Leif's head, shuddered and fell to the side. He gave the slightest shake. Lincoln had seen the danger before anyone else.

Reban had only climbed to the first branch on his tree – high enough to be out of target range, but low enough to continue swiping at the creatures with his weapon.

"Move!" screamed Lincoln to Leif, as he continued to brandish his axe.

Leif gulped and scrambled up the nearest tree. But Lincoln couldn't get clear of the pack to follow him.

Jesa was now balancing on a branch with her crossbow loaded. Storm could see blood dripping from her elbow but from the determined look on Jesa's face, no injury was going to stop her.

Jesa nodded at her and started firing. Storm followed her lead, aiming her knives at the squawking creatures below.

One. Two. Three.

Down they fell. It seemed that the animals could attack in force, but had little manoeuvrability. From their higher point in the trees, the team had the advantage.

Now that his friends were holding the creatures off, Lincoln leaped towards the nearest tree, swinging up to the first branch, then scrambling further up and sitting astride one of the stronger tree limbs.

After a few moments, the creatures realized they'd lost their closest prey and turned their focus on Reban sitting on his low branch, crowding around the bottom of his tree.

Reban didn't hesitate. The sword end of his weapon

swiped fearlessly, injuring one after another, blood spraying the jungle floor.

Storm looked down. Her knives were all gone. Hopefully she would have a chance to retrieve them.

"Jesa, are you okay?" she shouted over.

Jesa finally seemed to notice the blood dripping from her elbow. Her body shuddered as Leif leaned over to get better a look.

"Lincoln?"

He gave her a swift nod.

The words caught in her throat. "Reban?"

Reban took one final swipe at the last remaining creature below, missed, then laughed as it scrabbled off into the bushes.

He stood up on his branch, turning around to give them all a clear view of his torn trousers, part of his bare, ripped flesh on show. "Oh, they got me all right. But not as much as I got them."

Storm gulped and looked at the carnage on the forest floor. She counted. Twelve creatures lay dead – or almost dead – at their feet.

Jesa was visibly shaking. "What...what on earth are they?"

Leif pulled a cloth from his backpack and tried to catch the blood dripping from her arm. "Here, wrap this around it." He looked down and shook his head. "I have no idea what they are." He wrinkled his nose. "I just assumed they were plant eaters when they appeared."

"That'll teach us," muttered Lincoln. "Just because it's a chicken on Earthasia, doesn't mean it's a chicken here."

Reban pointed down. "The claws. Their hooks. You don't have those kind of weapons if you're a plant eater."

Storm tried to search her brain. "I've seen something like them." Her gaze connected with Reban. "In one of Octavius's books. This really old book full of sketches." She screwed up her nose. "Something like…therizinosaurids? There was a drawing and a name, but nothing else. I assume the author didn't know that much about them. What was his name? Magnus something…"

Reban shrugged. "Seems you got to see more of that book than I ever did."

She was surprised. Reban knew about Octavius's book? She didn't realize they had been that close.

Reban frowned as he tried to peer at his injuries, then glanced over at Jesa's elbow. "I think we should move." He pointed beneath him. "This is predator heaven. A T-rex banquet. Let's move before the smell of blood starts to permeate the forest."

The others nodded in agreement and started to scramble down from the trees. Storm winced as she retrieved her knives. Leif gave her a smile as he pulled one from the eye of one of the creatures and wiped it on the nearest tree leaf. "Remind me not to get you angry."

She shuddered as she placed it back in her belt. Instinct. That's what she'd acted on. What was this place doing to her?

Jesa was trying her best to be brave, but Storm could see

the tremor along her jaw line. She walked over and touched Jesa's arm. "You okay?" she asked quietly. "Let me take a look at that for you."

Jesa nodded, and Storm pulled back the cloth. "Ouch. I think that might need more than a little ointment. We need to find somewhere with clean water."

Leif walked over. "I know just the place," he said, putting his hands on his hips and looking around. "If only we knew where it was…"

Lincoln bent down. "Here." He pointed to a red mark on the tree. "I remember this. I'm not sure why. But I'm sure I saw it on the way to Blaine's shack."

Storm frowned. She didn't remember seeing anything at all. Blaine had moved through the jungle at such a rapid pace she'd struggled to keep up.

She touched the tree. There were no paths, just squishy undergrowth. "Okay, so you remember that. But how do you know which way?"

Lincoln frowned as he looked around them. "I'm sure the red mark was to my right as we passed it. So that means I think it's this way." He pointed forward.

Reban shook his head. "Well, lead on. That way is as good as any other."

Leif looked at the dinosaur bodies on the jungle floor. "We might as well. The sooner we get away from here the better."

They tramped on.

After a while, Storm stopped, and Reban walked straight

into the back of her. "Oof!" His head whipped from side to side. "What is it? Did you hear something?"

She couldn't help but smile. "No, but I smelled it."

Wrinkles formed across Reban's brow. He looked at her as if she were mad. "What?"

Storm held up her hands. "Guys. Stop a minute. Smell."

Jesa tilted her chin upwards and sniffed. So did Reban. But Storm watched Lincoln and Leif as they inhaled, waiting for the scent to hit their senses.

"Evergreen." They spoke in tandem.

Storm nodded. "It is, isn't it?"

Both of them nodded in agreement and looked around, trying to pick out any kind of sign among the trees.

"Someone want to tell me what's going on?" asked Reban.

Storm was still smiling. "This smell. It's the leaves that make the ointment. The cure for the plague. Blaine uses it to line his shack. He says the smell hides him from predators. They can't pick out the human scent because the scent from the leaves is so strong."

Reban breathed in too. Wrinkling his nose. "Okay. There is something. But what now?"

"Now, we follow our noses."

THIRTY-FOUR

LINCOLN

Within a matter of minutes, the scent was overwhelming. Lincoln held out his hands. "Stop!" He pointed just in front of them.

He could tell it took Reban's and Jesa's eyes a few seconds to adjust. The structure was almost invisible. Just a huge collage of thick leaves. It could be one enormous jungle plant that had taken over this part of the ground. But it wasn't. The leaves were intertwined around a structure of wood and fabric. It was hidden in plain sight.

Lincoln gave an anxious glance at Storm, conscious of the fact that neither of them had warned Jesa about what to expect when they found her father.

"Wait here," he said to Jesa as he walked around the other side of the shack, looking for the way in.

Leif and Storm were right at his back. When he found the entrance, he parted the fabric that hung there. "Blaine?

Are you there?"

Silence.

Lincoln walked in slowly, glancing around. Little had changed since the last time they were there. There was still a sheltered sleeping area, with a camp bed like the ones they had on the ship. Blaine had the equivalent of a noticeboard in one corner, covered in scraps of paper. A pad and some graphite sat on a tree stump in another corner, clearly prized from the last delivery. One kicked-in pair of sneakers was stacked against a wall. The new ones must be on his feet.

Storm rushed over and bent down, lifting up a blanket. One large bowl with water and three small clay pots. Exactly where he'd kept them before. One with some kind of yellow glue, one with red powder – hadn't he said it was spices? – and the third was the prize.

The third held the pungent green ointment that seemed to heal all wounds.

She held up the clay pot. "It looks like he just made some more," she said, her eyes sparkling with excitement.

"Jesa," she called. "Come in here! I'll clean up your arm."

There was a shout outside. "Who are you? What are you doing here? Why are you touching my home?" Followed by a loud squeal and a slap.

Lincoln ran outside. Reban was nowhere to be seen. But Jesa looked terrified.

Blaine's appearance hadn't improved any. His hair was still long and shaggy, streaked with grey. His beard was halfway down his chest. His clothes looked like a bunch of rags, stitched together roughly. The only thing that was relatively normal about him were the sneakers on his feet.

Jesa's eyes were wide. She was holding her hands to her face, while Blaine had a tight grip on one of her arms. There was a crumpled leaf at her feet – one that looked as if it had been tugged from the side of Blaine's shack.

"Leave her!" yelled Lincoln. "Let her go. She's with us!"

He could see the confusion on Blaine's face. Watched him take a few seconds to place Lincoln again.

Blaine let go of Jesa's arm as if she were something poisonous, and his face contorted. He shook his head fiercely. "No. No. It's not been a year yet. You shouldn't be here. No one should be here." He flung up his hands. "There's no room for all these people!"

Lincoln cringed and stepped between Blaine and Jesa.

"Don't worry. We won't be here for long. We just came to try something out on the dinosaurs."

"So soon?"

Lincoln nodded.

Blaine immediately looked suspicious. "What is it this time?"

Storm appeared from the shack. Her gaze narrowed slightly as she caught sight of the stunned Jesa. "It's a virus. They want us to plant it in the water supply to see if it affects the dinosaurs."

"A virus? Are they still pursuing those crazy thoughts? Why on earth do they think they can kill the most dangerous creatures on the planet with a virus?" Blaine shook his head

261

and walked away dismissively. "They're even bigger fools than before. Idiots. Imbeciles," he muttered.

Storm licked her lips and stepped forward, touching him on the shoulder. He gave her hand a glance of disgust. "But we have another reason for being here – two, in fact."

Blaine stepped backwards, trying to get out of her reach. "What?"

Storm kept her voice steady. "The ointment. The one you used on yourself. On Lincoln's wounds and on my feet. We took some back home. There's a plague on Earthasia. Do you remember it? The blistering plague. The ointment seems to help the condition. Can maybe even cure it. We need to find some of the plants and take them back. We need to grow them in Earthasia. And we need you to show us how to make the ointment."

Blaine shook his head. It was clear he didn't really believe what she was saying. "What plague? I've never heard of any plague." He started pacing around.

Leif appeared at Storm's shoulder. Blaine blinked. "You too?" He let out a rasp. "Why can't you all just go back to where you came from?"

There was a noise. Almost like a whimper. Jesa's eyes were still wide. When she slid her hands down she had a palm-shaped imprint on her face.

Lincoln felt rage build inside him. He stepped in front of Blaine. Piloria didn't belong to Blaine. He had no right to be like this. And if he wouldn't help them, Lincoln would rip off every leaf that was currently covering his shack, shove them into a bag and work out how to make the ointment himself. As he looked at Jesa's horrified face his anger intensified. This could never be the reunion she had in mind.

"You mean the place *you* came from too," he said, as he stepped in front of Blaine's line of vision. "Enough," he said, as he wrapped his hand around Blaine's wrist. "Come with me."

He didn't give Blaine a chance to argue. Leif and Storm stepped aside as Lincoln pulled Blaine sharply inside the shack. Blaine was indignant, he started to protest, "Wha—"

Lincoln cut him dead. "Don't." He walked over and tugged the graphite sketch from the wall, ignoring the fact that Blaine winced. "Your family. You wanted to know about your family." The paper felt as if it could disintegrate in his fingertips. Now he was looking at the sketch – even though it was nine years old – everything seemed so clear. The hint of curl in Jesa's hair. The almond shape of her eyes.

Blaine nodded as he took the delicate paper away from Lincoln and cradled it in his hands. "You know about my family?" he asked.

Lincoln breathed slowly. At this point Blaine looked quite pathetic. He gave him a sharp nod. "Yes. I do. I've met Kayna. I've met Caleb."

Blaine started to shake. "You have? They're alive? How are they? Are they okay? Are they in Ambulus City?" One question seemed to tumble out after another.

But Lincoln just shook his head. He stuck his head back out of the flap and gestured towards Jesa. She looked terrified but he gave her the most reassuring nod that he could and held out his hand towards her.

She was trembling. But after a few seconds, she slipped her hand into his. He pulled her inside.

Lincoln turned to face Blaine again. It was obvious he was agitated. His hands were fumbling in front of his chest. His mind was clearly on overdrive. He was mouthing the questions that were still streaming through his head.

Lincoln spoke clearly. "I told you I met Kayna. I told you I met Caleb."

Blaine nodded his eyes wide. Then something happened. Part of his brain must have clicked into gear. "But, what about…"

Lincoln gently slipped his arm around Jesa's back and edged her forward. "Blaine, this is Jesa. Your daughter. The person you just slapped." He watched as the words registered, then leaned forward and kept his voice low. "Touch her again and I'll kill you myself."

THIRTY-FIVE

STORMCHASER

The world moved in slow motion. Storm and Leif stepped back into the shack in time to see Blaine sway first one way, then another.

Leif took a step up behind him, holding his hands out as if to catch Blaine if he fell.

Jesa was still shaking. It was clear she was sick with nerves.

Blaine's mouth was open, his eyes wide. He didn't say a word. He just stared. Then finally, he took a tiny step forward, with one hand held up.

Storm could see Lincoln tighten his grip on Jesa's waist, offering her reassurance that she'd be okay. There was nothing threatening about Blaine's behaviour now. He was just stunned. Storm didn't know who was shaking more – Blaine or Jesa.

Blaine's hand came up to Jesa's cheek, Lincoln watching

him every step of the way. The tremble was extreme, affecting his whole body. He was trying to find words. As his hand cradled Jesa's cheek she let out a little whimper. "My... daughter." The words came out so hesitantly. It was almost as if Blaine didn't believe this was real.

Jesa's hand closed over Blaine's and she started to sob. "Dad? Daddy?"

Lincoln stepped back to allow Jesa to go forward into her father's embrace. Storm turned away, facing Leif. It seemed like a moment of intrusion. Father and daughter hadn't seen each other in more than nine years. She had the overwhelming sense that this wasn't something she should watch.

She stepped over to Leif and whispered, "Where's Reban?"

Leif shrugged. "I've no idea. He disappeared while we were in there with Blaine."

Lincoln walked over and joined them, his arms folded across his chest. His eyes kept darting back to Jesa and Blaine. "What now?"

"Your guess is as good as mine," said Storm.

Blaine started babbling. "What about Caleb? What about Kayna? Are you happy? Where do you work? Have you had any trouble from the Stipulators? How is Kaden?"

Jesa flinched at his final words. Kaden, the Stipulator who had been dragged from the house next door with his family. Storm hadn't forgotten any of the details of that story. Would Blaine even realize the same fate could have befallen his family too if they hadn't hidden?

Jesa still seemed stunned that she'd finally been reunited with her father. "We...we...should sit down," she said in the end.

Blaine nodded. "Of course, of course." At first Storm thought he'd stay inside the shack with her, but instead he took her back outside and guided her over to a very large tree trunk lying on its side. "Sit here," he said, as he settled on the log.

Jesa swallowed. Storm knew she was searching for the right words, and walked over, handing her a water bottle. She could only imagine how dry Jesa's throat would be right now.

Jesa gave a grateful nod and gulped down some water, keeping the bottle in her hands. "Mum...is fine. Well, she's fine now. When she hears about this?" Now Jesa's voice started to shake. "She won't believe it. She'll be so happy. She always believed that you could still be alive."

Blaine gave a nod. He seemed to be soaking up her words.

"Caleb? He's good. He's just started in one of the food plants. He says it's okay. A few of his friends from school started at the same time."

She paused and took a deep breath. "Kaden. I haven't seen him since I was small. We...we left. As soon as they took you, Mum made us pack up a bag and leave right away. We walked for days and ended up at Meridian City. It wasn't quite so cramped then and we managed to find somewhere and stay there for a few years. When we came back to Ambulus City, Mum tried to find Kaden and his family.

But…the neighbours told us that the Stipulators had come the next day – the one after you were taken – and kicked down the door." A tear slid down her cheek. "They said that Kaden and his family were dragged out into the street." She shook her head. "Nobody ever saw them again."

For Storm it was like a cold wind dancing over her skin. Jesa had mentioned this before. But now? Hearing her tell the tale to her father? It seemed to give the story new context. A level of understanding that Storm hadn't felt before. If Reban had been discovered, would Storm and her mother have been in the same position?

She watched as Blaine put his hands over Jesa's. "I'm sorry," he said. "I'm sorry that I caused this." He started to rock back and forward a little. "This is my fault. I kept your mother secret. I kept you all secret. It was the only way to try and keep you safe." He stopped for a moment and seemed to fixate on the trees in front of him. "But if I'd wanted to keep you truly safe I would have stayed away. I wouldn't have visited. I *shouldn't* have visited."

"But then we would have never known you," Jesa said quickly. "It was hard enough when you were taken away. But to have never known you?" She shook her head. "No. No. That's not what Caleb and I would have wanted."

She pulled her hands away from her father's and leaned forward, resting her elbows on her knees and tangling her fingers through her curls. "Caleb will be so angry with me. So angry. I know he would have wanted to be here. But I just thought it was too risky. When I heard that Lincoln had told

Mum and Caleb about you I was mad. How dare they speak to Lincoln without me? Then, when I got the note asking if we wanted to send a message?" She shook her head again. "A message wasn't good enough. It just wasn't. So I packed my bag and headed down to the dock."

Blaine sat back. He glanced first at Lincoln and then at Jesa. "Kayna – your mum? She doesn't know you're here? She doesn't know that you've come?"

Jesa let out a wry laugh. "Oh, she'll know by now. But she would never have let me come here. Never in a million years."

Blaine shifted uncomfortably and Storm smiled. It was almost like Blaine was contemplating whether he should actually be telling Jesa off or not. Storm watched as he stared down at his patchwork clothes. He shifted a little further along the log, one hand coming up and patting his shaggy hair. He was becoming self-conscious. The only way Blaine would have seen his appearance over the years must have been as a reflection in water. Was he even aware how he really looked? Or how he smelled?

He stood up, taking tiny steps back and forward. Storm felt Lincoln tense next to her. They'd seen Blaine's agitated behaviour before. It was almost like he had a pressure valve. Too many people, too many questions just seemed to set him off.

Jesa was totally unaware of this. She pointed at his sneakers. "Lincoln said you ask for these every year. What else do you ask for? What else do they give you?" She frowned a little. "Do you get any new clothes?"

There was a noise. A crack. A twig breaking in the jungle. Everyone was on their feet instantly.

Leaves rustled, then parted, as Reban walked back through the bushes, examining a piece of fruit he held in his hand. He didn't even look up.

There was a split second when nothing happened. Then Blaine's eyes widened. There was a frown. A few seconds of recognition. Then fury erupted across his face.

Before anyone had a chance to do anything, Blaine let out a blood-curdling yell and launched himself at Reban.

"Don! You—" The word was lost as Blaine landed on Reban, knocking him to the jungle floor. There was a punch. Then another. The sound of flesh impacting on flesh. A groan from Reban as Blaine pushed himself back to his feet and started kicking furiously at the man on the ground.

Lincoln's and Leif's mouths were hanging open. It took a few seconds before they nodded at each other and jumped forward. Jesa was horrified. Storm was dumbstruck.

It took both Lincoln and Leif to pull Blaine off. By then, Reban seemed to have got his wits about him. His hands were up to protect his face and his legs were contracted, trying to shield his abdomen from the fierce kicks.

Lincoln was stronger than he looked. The muscles around his neck were rigid as he dragged Blaine back. "Stop it! Stop it now! What do you think you're doing?"

Blaine's face had been replaced by a mask of fury. His eyes were glittering and dark. He spat as he spoke. "Him! Get him off my land! Get him off my continent!" He turned to face Reban again, hissing, "You did this! You did this to me and my family. You've stolen the last nine years of my life! And now you come here? I'm going to *kill* you." He wrestled in Lincoln's and Leif's arms as he raised his voice. "I'm going to kill you!"

Storm had thought him crazy before. But she'd never seen him like this. Never seen him quite so mad.

Reban was lying on the ground in stunned silence. Whatever he'd had in his hand had vanished. He propped himself up on one elbow and gave a few coughs. His expression was cold. "Blaine Thredell. Lucky me." He started to dust himself off. "I see time hasn't nourished your soul." He got to his feet. "Or made you any more rational."

Reban's black trousers and top were now smeared with mud. But somehow, it just made him look even more menacing. He stepped forward and nodded to Lincoln and Leif. "Let him go. He wants to fight? Let's fight." From his stance, Reban looked ready this time.

Lincoln shot Storm a look before letting Blaine's arm go. But instead of swinging a punch, Blaine seemed to think a little harder. He stepped forward until he was millisectars away from Reban's face. "You sent me here. You sent me here to die. When I survived? You refused to let me come back to Earthasia. You refused to send me news about my family."

Reban snorted. "I did all that? Just me? Or was it parliament? A parliament of your peers. A parliament that banished me here, just like they did you."

271

Blaine frowned. The recognition seemed to sink in. "Why are you here?"

Reban gave an ironic smile and opened his arms wide. "Haven't you heard? Piloria is my new home."

Blaine started shaking his head. "No. No, it can't be. You can't stay here. You can't live here!" He leaned forward, hissing in Reban's face. "I won't help you. I won't. You'll be dinner for the T-rexes within a few days."

Reban shouldered past him. "Watch out, Blaine. People will think you're mad. Remember your daughter is here."

Blaine gave a jolt. He threw Jesa a quick glance. His fists were still clenched at his side. Storm had no idea what was going on. Was it really Reban who had sent Blaine here? Either way, she couldn't stand the horrified expression on Jesa's face.

Storm nodded at Lincoln and tilted her head towards Leif, her eyes telling him to bring Jesa. "Jesa needs her arm cleaned. We were attacked in the jungle earlier. Giant chickens. Or something like that. She could do with some ointment."

Blaine seemed to snap into action. "Of course, come here."

He guided Jesa inside and over to his pots, and lifted some rags, dipping them into clean water. If Blaine noticed the clay pots were already uncovered he didn't mention it. He worked methodically and gently, cleaning her wound, applying some ointment and a few of the wide leaves, then wrapping a strip of cloth around it all.

Storm walked over as he finished and touched Blaine's shoulder. "The leaves, Blaine. Can you show us where you get the leaves, and how to make the ointment?" She pointed to Lincoln. "Lincoln's sister is really sick. Just the tiniest bit of ointment healed part of her arm. But we don't have any more."

"My ointment?" Blaine gave a nonchalant shrug as she nodded. "Told you it was good." He tapped the top of his leg where his scar lay.

"Will you show us how to make it?"

Blaine gave a nod. He turned to Lincoln as he picked up the green ointment. "I just made some. But we can make some more. It's not hard."

He walked over to a sack in the corner and started pulling leaves from it. He had a larger clay pot and some heavy stones to one side. The bottom of the stones were stained with the bright green colour of the ointment.

Blaine went outside for a minute and came back in holding some yellow strands. They looked like the vines that were wrapped around some of the trees nearby. He threw them into the bowl, then picked up an old cup full of clear liquid from the corner of the room. He looked at it proudly. "I made them give me some cups. This is the last one." He frowned. "Maybe I should ask for some more. I should make a note of that."

Storm kneeled down next to him and gestured to Lincoln to do the same. This was what they were here for. This was why they'd come.

Blaine carefully poured some of the liquid from the cup into the clay pot. "What is it?" asked Storm.

Blaine looked pleased with himself. "Oh, it's just water. But it's been boiled so that I know it's clean. I'm careful."

He smiled as he pounded the ingredients together, smushing the leaves and vines with one of the stones smeared with green. Lincoln was watching the whole process carefully but kept glancing at Storm. He pointed to the remnants of yellow vine. "We need this too," he mouthed.

Storm nodded and smiled. "So, are you able to show us where we can find the evergreen leaves? We'd really like to take a few of the plants home with us, to see if they can grow on Earthasia."

Blaine shook his head. "No point. They won't grow there." He said it so quickly she wondered what she was missing.

"Why not?"

Blaine held up his hands. "They need heat. One year it was a bit colder. The evergreen all withered and died. It didn't bloom again for months. Not until the climate was warm again."

He stared off into space, rubbing one hand on his arm. "It was cold then. I had to make blankets. I had to wear all the clothes I had."

Storm took a deep breath and willed herself not to glance at Jesa. Sometimes Blaine seemed quite mad. She assumed it was because he'd been by himself for nine years, with only a crate left annually on the beach with supplies. She closed her eyes for a second.

Back home, living in an atmosphere with so many people was stifling. There were rations for food and energy. No proper health care for everyone. Walkways so busy it was hard to get by.

Piloria was completely at the other end of the spectrum. What would living here be like? To realize you were unlikely to see another living soul for years at a time? To constantly be on the watch for predators? To know that there were no buildings, no noise – just jungle or greenness for as far as the eye could see?

Lots of Storm's dreams had been like this. Visions of her running over the wide green plains of Piloria. When she'd returned to Earthasia the tightly stacked buildings had made her shudder.

But were those dreams all just a fantasy? Maybe the truth was, if she lived here, she'd end up just as strange as Blaine.

Lincoln nudged her. "Okay?" There was concern written on his face and she gave herself a shake as she nodded in response.

Blaine had gone back to pounding the contents of the larger clay pot together with the stone he held in his hand. Storm kept watching. It seemed a simple enough process. By the time the paste was created there was no trace of the yellow vines left, just the heavy greenness from the leaves. The ointment was thick and pungent. Blaine's movements were rhythmic – it was almost hypnotic watching him.

He sat back and wiped his hands on his ragged trousers. "That's it."

"That's it?" Both Storm and Lincoln spoke in unison. They were surprised it was so easy.

Blaine got back to his feet. He waved to them. At first they thought he was turning around to speak to Jesa. But he actually walked past her as if he'd forgotten who she was. "If you want plants, come now."

Lincoln pulled a face at Storm and grabbed the backpacks.

Blaine led the two of them through the jungle, the rich evergreen scent enveloping them more with every step. There almost wasn't a way through; the thick trees had no space between them. The evergreen plants seemed to envelop everything. Blaine simply bent down and started ripping the leaves from the plants and stuffing them into his sack, looking up every now and then to rip a few random yellow strands from the vines surrounding the tree trunks.

Lincoln dropped to his knees and started digging in the jungle floor with his hands. "Blaine – we want to take a few plants home. Can you help me try and get this?"

Blaine frowned but nodded. "You can take them, but I doubt they'll grow," he said. It was the second time he'd mentioned that and she could see Lincoln bristle at those words. But he didn't say anything. What could he say? Climate was one thing that they couldn't control.

Blaine bent down to help Lincoln. Storm started following the strands of yellow vine that were coiled around the nearest tree. Tracing the origin of the plant wasn't easy. Its starting point was nowhere near the tree and she had to crawl some way before she finally found the roots of the vine.

As they collected more leaves and dug up the plants, Blaine started to seem more connected. "You mentioned a virus. Do they really think it will kill the dinosaurs?"

Lincoln gently lifted a plant out of the ground, cradling the roots in one hand. He shrugged. "They hope it will. We planted one of the viruses at the watering hole for the raptors before we came here."

Blaine looked confused. "What do you mean 'one of the viruses'? You have more than one?"

Storm nodded. "They gave us one for the raptors, one for the T-rexes and one for the pterosaurs." She paused for a second. "Maybe we don't have to use the other two though." She glanced at Lincoln. "We could just tell them that we did. I know you were worried about them finding out if we didn't do it, but how could they? We don't even know how long the viruses are supposed to take to work."

Blaine seemed shocked. "Wait. You have a virus that could kill the T-rexes and you're not going to bother?"

Lincoln looked directly at Storm and narrowed his gaze slightly. "We still don't know how the Stipulators will find out if we use the viruses or not. I don't want to risk the chance of us being refused passage home. Not now we've found the leaves and can make the ointment."

Storm sat up a little straighter. Of course. Lincoln was still only thinking about Arta. Just like she should be. But she couldn't help hating the idea of releasing these viruses.

"Where is it?" Blaine stood up and started pacing. "I need it. I need it!" He pulled up his trouser leg, revealing part of his scar. "Do you think I want them around after they did this to me? Why wouldn't you put the virus in the watering hole?" His head kept flicking from side to side. "Who has it? Are you scared? Give it to me. I'll do it! I'll poison them. Even one less T-rex would be an improvement."

Storm licked her lips as she gingerly carried the vine plant over to Lincoln's backpack. Blaine was getting worked up again.

"Lincoln works in the lab, he's not even sure if the virus will really work. They rushed everything."

"Let's go." Blaine started walking in the direction from which they'd come. It was clear the conversation was over. Storm looked at Lincoln in panic. They didn't really know the way back to the shack from here. If they didn't follow him now they could get lost. She grabbed the sack on the ground – Blaine seemed to have forgotten about it.

Lincoln looked annoyed. "We need to get more samples. We can't leave yet."

Storm shook her head. "We can find a way to come back later." Blaine was already disappearing from her line of sight. "Let's go."

Lincoln shook his head, but he stood and closed the backpack. "There's only one reason I'm here and this is it. I won't go home without what I need."

She could see the little tic in his tight jaw.

Something inside her squeezed. She understood. She knew Arta. She liked her. No, more than that, she cared about her. Storm had seen the suffering of the blistering

278

plague and hated the fact that back on Earthasia there was really nothing she could do to help.

She gave a nod of her head as she started after Blaine. "Don't panic, Linc. We have time. We'll find a way to get back here. I promise."

Her stomach gave another uncomfortable twinge. Who was she to promise him anything?

She only hoped she wouldn't be proved a liar.

THIRTY-SIX

LINCOLN

Lincoln looked around, trying to contain his anger as he searched for signs of broken twigs or branches. "Just how fast does this guy walk?" he snapped at Storm.

She sighed and stared at the jungle around them. She was seeing exactly the same as him. Trees, trees and more trees.

"This way," she said, moving off in one direction.

He shook his head and gave a smile. He could tell she wasn't sure and was only pretending. He adjusted the backpack on his shoulder. "Why not."

In the end, it took them over an hour to get back to the shack. It seemed that their previous visit had given them a moderate amount of tracking skills. When they arrived, sweaty and bedraggled, Leif was standing in a corner with his arms folded and Reban was looking amused by it all.

Jesa rushed over. "Where have you been?"

Lincoln gave an exasperated sigh. "We got a bit lost. Your

dad took off too quickly for us to follow him." He narrowed his gaze as he realized Blaine was nowhere in sight. "Where's he gone?"

Jesa pointed to the shack. "He's in there. He's looking at the viruses in the carrier case."

Lincoln turned to Leif. "Leif? What's going on?"

Leif gritted his teeth. "He took them off me. He's adamant that he's the best person to plant the virus at the T-rex watering hole."

Storm spoke first. "So we're planting it then? I thought we hadn't agreed that yet."

Leif scowled. "No. *You* hadn't agreed that. The rest of us are happy to get on with it."

Lincoln glanced in Reban's direction. He still didn't trust him. He still suspected Reban might be spying on them. "My priority is the ointment and a passage home. If I have to plant the viruses to guarantee a place on the ship then I'll do it."

Storm let out an exasperated sigh.

Lincoln touched her arm. "Do you really want to be face-to-face with a T-rex? Look what happened to Galen."

"Who's Galen?" asked Jesa.

The rest of them glanced at each other. Reban frowned. He clearly remembered Galen too. Lincoln turned to Jesa. "Galen was one of the Finalists who came to Piloria last time. He was very…competitive. And ruthless. Not someone we would call a friend. At the last nest site, he seemed more interested in doing me damage than actually capturing the T-rex egg. He ended up cornered by a T-rex."

Jesa's face paled a little. "What happened?"

Lincoln bit his bottom lip. Maybe it wasn't the best tale to tell when they were just about to go and plant a virus at the T-rex watering hole. "He got his arm ripped off."

Jesa swayed and Storm stepped over beside her. She gave Lincoln a glare, then changed the subject rapidly. "No one knows the dinosaur behaviour better than Blaine. Maybe he can help keep us all safe."

Reban gave a brief shake of his head. "I don't care who plants the virus, just as long as someone does it. The fewer T-rexes on this continent the better. Some people here have the privilege of going home. The rest of us don't."

Storm shifted on her feet. Of course. Reban had to stay. Lincoln looked at him suspiciously. He literally only had the clothes he was standing in – how many belongings had he been forced to leave behind on Earthasia? Or would he be returning to them after all?

Blaine came back out from the shack, cradling the carrier.

"How far to the T-rex watering hole?" Lincoln asked Blaine.

Last time around they'd come here from the cave. He wasn't quite sure how long it would take them to reach the watering hole from Blaine's shack. Blaine finally looked up from the carrier. He seemed fascinated by the red and blue viruses. He kept tilting the carrier up and down, letting the glass from the vials catch the light. Every time Blaine appeared to be a little bit sane he did something crazy again.

"Half a day," he said quickly. "We won't leave until

morning." He gave a shake of his head. "Too many predators at night."

Lincoln felt an involuntary chill. The jungle was warm and on a few occasions he'd found himself swept away by thoughts of what it might actually be like to stay here. But words like those brought the harsh reality back home.

On Piloria, no one was safe. Not ever. Not for a second. To get comfortable was to die. Blaine's words were a stark reminder.

Blaine looked around – as if he finally realized they might be staying with him overnight. There was a visible second of panic, followed by another anguished glance towards Jesa. How did you learn to be father to a teenage girl overnight?

Reban was standing on the sidelines watching with those cool, violet eyes. For the first time, Lincoln felt a twinge of sympathy for him. He had no relationship with Storm. He'd missed out on almost sixteen years of her life.

Lincoln gave a sigh. "Well, I guess we better bunk down for the night." His stomach clenched and his leg gave an involuntary itch. "Tomorrow it's the T-rexes."

He unrolled his mat and sagged down onto it. All he really cared about was the plants. Now he had a few specimens he had to keep them safe. The last thing he wanted to do was go anywhere *near* the T-rexes.

But if he wanted to keep Blaine onside, to help them gather more plants and get out of here alive, and ensure a ride home, it seemed it would be essential.

It looked like Lincoln had no choice.

THIRTY-SEVEN

STORMCHASER

"Happy birthday, Stormchaser."

She jerked her head up at Reban's words. "What?"

He was sitting next to the campfire with his legs pulled up, watching the flames crackle and burn. The rest of the camp was sleeping, but she'd spent the last few hours staring up at the dark sky.

He nodded. "Today is day 274 of this year. It's your birthday – the day you were born. Happy sixteenth."

Words jammed in her throat. "How do you know?"

He gave her an ironic look. "Well, I didn't. But you wrote down your day of birth when you applied for the Trials. After you returned from Piloria and won the final Trial, and once I had suspicions – I looked."

Storm pushed herself up. She was a little stunned. "So until that point, until the Trials, you had no idea I existed?"

He sighed but gave a shake of his head. "The first time

I saw you was when you delivered that message at the parliament. You gave me chills. You're just like your mother. I mentioned how similar you were."

"To who?"

Reban licked his lips and gave her a steady stare. It was almost like he was trying to discern if she were ready for the news.

"You mentioned me to who?" she asked again.

Reban kept his voice low. His face was lit by the flickering flames. It was the first time she'd seen anything other than a harsh expression on his face. This time there was something else. Against the orange and yellow flames he looked almost...rueful.

"I spoke to Octavius." The words were so quiet she thought she hadn't heard correctly.

"Octavius?"

His violet eyes met hers. Something washed over her. A feeling. A realization. A tiny little part of something she knew, but hadn't quite acknowledged.

She caught her breath. "Octavius mentioned my mother's name. But I never told him. At the time, I thought he must just have checked my records."

"What records?" said Reban. "Your birth was never recorded. I know because I checked."

"It wasn't?" Storm was stunned. She knew some births weren't recorded on Earthasia. She'd just never expected one of them was hers. But then again, if her father was actually a Stipulator it was no surprise that her mother hadn't wanted a birth record.

Her voice shook. "Why did you speak to Octavius? He's the Captain Regent. He was the one person who could really get you into trouble."

Reban sucked in a deep breath and picked up a stick, poking at the fire with it. "Would he?" He was staring at the fire as if it held the answers to the universe.

It didn't sound like a real question. There was something strange in his tone.

She shifted on the ground. She just couldn't get her head around any of this. All of it seemed so unreal.

"Why would you talk to Octavius Arange instead of anyone else?"

Reban drew his gaze away from the fire. His violet eyes were bright in this light. Almost shining like the moon in the sky above. His voice was steady. "Octavius had a vested interest in things."

"What's that supposed to mean?" Storm was getting angry now. "What 'things'?"

Reban gave a sigh. "Octavius was related to Dalia," he replied, looking a little hesitant. "Your mother."

Storm was stunned. She shook her head. "What? No. No. He would have said something. He would have told me."

Reban poked at the fire again as he shook his head too. "No, he wouldn't." The glance he gave her was one of pity. "Do you really think Octavius requested you as his aide out of nowhere?"

Storm was still stunned. "But…but if he knew Dalia, he must have known about me. Why didn't I ever meet him?"

Reban gave a little shrug. "Dalia was Octavius's niece. They'd been out of touch for a number of years. Octavius never knew that Dalia had a daughter."

"We stayed in Ambulus City and Octavius never knew we were there?"

Reban rolled his eyes. "*I* never knew you were there. Remember how many millions of people live in Ambulus City?"

Storm shook her head. She still couldn't really understand all this. "Then…how did Octavius find out?"

"I told you. He found out because of me. He hadn't made the connection when he first saw you – when you delivered the message to parliament. Remember he hadn't seen Dalia in years, and" – Reban let out a wry laugh – "and your eyes, obviously, were the same colour as mine, not hers."

Reban's voice got more serious. "But after Piloria. After you nearly got sent to the mines – after the final Trial – I spoke to him about you. But neither of us really knew. We just suspected. After you'd told me your mother was dead – I had to tell Octavius that too."

Storm's skin prickled. "Was he upset?"

Reban pulled up his legs and ran his fingers through his hair. "Of course he was upset. Things became so complicated. Dalia had told me she was related to Octavius. It made her wary of me. Dalia and Octavius didn't always see eye to eye. She didn't like Stipulators. But Octavius was still protective of her, and in a way she seemed to resent it. She was too much of a free spirit."

It was the way he said the words. In such a throwaway fashion. As if he really knew her mother. Knew how she functioned. Knew how she thought about things. Something twisted deep inside Storm. She hated that. She hated that someone else had known her mother so well, and yet, hadn't played any part in their life. Jealousy flooded through her.

"She was right to be wary of Stipulators."

Reban nodded and gave her a sideways glance. "I know that. Dalia never told me she was pregnant. She knew the risks. For you, for her and for me."

"What would you have done if she had told you?"

The words were out there and she couldn't bring them back. She was cringing inside.

There was silence. Too much silence. Too long a silence.

"I don't know," Reban finally answered.

It was like something in her curled up and died. Anger flared inside her. "What kind of an answer is that?" She jumped to her feet and started to pace around. "I mean, what kind of a Stipulator were you anyway? You knew you weren't supposed to get involved. You knew you weren't supposed to have a family. You put me and my mother at risk." She threw up her hands. "And Octavius? What did he think of all this? You got his niece pregnant. We could have ended up in the mines. You could have condemned us all to death. In fact, you nearly did! You got me sent here twice. Do I really get to go home? No one's actually told me that yet. The Stipulators' families normally disappear for good." Panic started to sweep over her. She hadn't really thought about this. She hadn't thought this through at all. "What if, when I get back to Earthasia, they send me to the mines anyway?" In her head she'd imagined getting home and going straight back to the house with Rune's and Kronar's brothers and sisters. All the tiny hairs stood up on her arms. The fact her reality might actually be the mines filled her with dread.

Reban's face paled. "Octavius won't let that happen. He won't. Never." He shook his head. "In the chamber he was thinking on his feet. No one expected what Silas did. Octavius hoped that sending you here would give him time to sort things out back home. Put plans in place for an alternative end to all this. Just think, coming back from here twice makes you a double hero – how could they send you to the mines then?"

Storm put her hands on her hips as she continued to pace. "What about my friends?" she hissed. "They got sent here too. They don't have my life. What are their guarantees when they get home? Lincoln, Leif, they didn't deserve this."

Reban shook his head. "You're right, they didn't. But this was always going to happen. They would always have wanted to test the viruses. It made sense to send you all back."

She spun around and bent down, her face right up against his. "Made sense to everyone but us." She prodded a finger into his chest. "You sent me here the first time. You sent me to Piloria, knowing I could be your daughter. And if you hadn't done that, I wouldn't be here now."

His forehead completely wrinkled. "No, I didn't. I told you. I didn't know you could be my daughter till the final Trial, when you told me up on the stage. Up until that point you were just a girl who looked like Dalia. I wondered if you were related to her – a niece, a cousin. Until you told me your mother's name, and I checked how old you were, it was never even a possibility in my mind."

She frowned again. Did she believe him? She wasn't sure. "But right from the beginning, you were never that nice to me – or to Lincoln."

Reban sighed and ran his hand through his hair. "Because something seemed off. Maybe I had some kind of intuition." He glanced over at Lincoln. "He's more interested in you than you know, by the way."

She felt heat rush into her cheeks. "And why is that your business?"

Reban stayed calm, but he didn't answer. He held up his hand. "Stop it. You'll wake the rest of them up." He looked around. It was dark now; they were surrounded by jungle. He leaned back on his hands, stretching his legs out in front of him. Her flare of anger didn't seem to faze him.

He stared out into the darkness. "This place. Piloria. It's not what I expected."

She nearly choked. "What on earth did you think it would be like? It's the dinosaur continent!"

He nodded. "I know. But...I'd never really thought about it in detail." He held up his hands. "It only ever featured in the recesses of my mind. Not in reality. It was all just some faraway place. A place that needed to be conquered."

Her footsteps faltered as she stopped pacing. "And now?"

He met her gaze again. "And now, well, whether I like it or not, it's going to be home." He kept his gaze steady. "But not for you. Octavius will ensure your safety once you get back. You're already the people's champion for stealing the eggs. If the world finds out that you've poisoned the dinosaurs too? Silas won't be able to touch you. No way. He couldn't face the wrath of the public if he sent the person who'd found the dinosaur DNA, then returned to the continent to poison them, to the mines. They'd probably kill him."

Something pricked in her brain. "There's a major flaw in your plan," she said drily.

"What's that?"

She sat back down next to him. "We're here to test the viruses, but what if they don't work?"

Reban held up his hands. "Then I guess I'll have to get used to dodging raptors and T-rexes."

Storm pulled her knees up to her chest. "You won't ever be able to rest," she said.

"I know that. I also imagine that my life expectancy has just plummeted. Probably just by sharing the same continent as Blaine, let alone any of the dinosaurs."

Storm glanced back towards the shack. "What is it with him? He unnerved me the last time I was here. It's like he's just not good around…people."

Reban nodded. "He's never been good around people. I'm not quite sure how he ended up a Stipulator but he was certainly never going to be a Chief. He used to have flare-ups before. I don't think this is new. I think he just used to contain it better. Or maybe Kayna helped him contain it. On a continent of dinosaurs, why contain anything? Over the years the reports have always come back from the ship's crew that he's mad."

"That seems like such a cruel word."

Reban gave her a thoughtful stare. "It probably is. Another thing I haven't thought about much. He's survived here for nine years. You have to give him credit for that. I'm sure I can manage to find somewhere to hide like he has. It's a big enough continent. There's so much to explore. I don't have to live in his part of the world."

Her hands started to shake a little. "Then you're happy? You're happy to stay here?"

He smiled. "I have no choice. I knew that the moment they turned on me in parliament. It was done."

Her gaze narrowed. "I never thought you'd give up so easily."

He snorted. "Give up? I'm just getting started." One eyebrow arched and the tone of his voice softened. "Sometimes you sound so like her. She used to do that, you know."

Every tiny hair on her arms stood on end. Her voice was shaky. "What?"

There it was again. That feeling. Her memories of her mother were fading as she grew older. It upset her. Sometimes she would lie in bed at night and try her hardest to remember whatever she could. Flashes and fragments would appear. Her mother in the woods when they still existed. Her mother throwing knives at a target. Her mother spinning around, her long dark hair fanning out as she turned.

At night her mother used to tell her stories. Mainly about made-up magical creatures, or birds or butterflies. Storm used to love those stories. There had been one about a big blue bird with blue and yellow feathers. Dorba? Zorba? Her mother had told her it over and over again. But the stories? They were fading faster than normal. Like sand slipping through her fingers on the beach of Piloria.

But now here was Reban, with memories of his own. Ones that she had no part of. Was it so wrong that, even though it made her jealous, she was so desperate to hear them?

"She used to challenge me," said Reban. "Every time I saw her. Every time I was with her." He gave her another glance. "You have her drive. Her determination." He laughed. "Her obstinate behaviour." He sighed. "Her intelligence. She hid hers too. She hated being indoors. She would never have worked in the lab or the manufacturing plant."

It was the oddest sensation. Part of her was raw but part of her was flooded with emotion. "How did you meet?"

He stared at her for a few seconds. She didn't really know where the question had come from. It just seemed to bubble up from inside her.

"We met in the forest." He shook his head. His voice had a sad tone, but it was the expression on his face that was mesmerizing. It was almost as if he could see Dalia in his head as he spoke. "A knife whistled past my ear. It barely missed me. Another millisectar and she would have killed me. I shouted. I raged. And when I found her, she was standing in her long black dress, with her brown hair shining in the sun and her hands on her hips. She looked at me as though I shouldn't be there. As if *I* were invading *her* privacy. I'd never met anyone as stubborn as she was." He gave a soft smile, almost as if the thought had jolted him back to the present day. He looked at Storm again. "At least not until now."

Tears pricked at the back of her eyes. He spoke about her mother with such affection. "I still hate you," she whispered.

He gave an appreciative nod. "I wouldn't expect anything else."

Something bubbled inside her. "Why? Why did you stay at the watering hole? Why did you give us all a chance to get away? The raptors are vicious. They hunt in packs. And they're fast. They could easily have outnumbered you."

He took a few moments to answer. She could almost feel her heart swelling in her chest. Part of her was sure that he'd stayed to ensure she got away. At least, that's what she *felt* had happened. But maybe she was just imagining it?

"They could have. But now I know. Now I've seen the raptors in action."

She felt a prickle of amusement. "That's not an answer to my question."

His gaze was locked with hers. "No. It isn't."

It seemed that both of them had issues acknowledging their feelings for the other. She was almost certain he'd been trying to protect her, but she couldn't ask him outright. And he didn't seem to be able to say the words.

She'd told him straight that she hated him. He'd accepted those words easily.

But she wasn't so sure that they were true.

"Lincoln," she said bluntly.

"What about Lincoln?"

"Right from the first Trials, you didn't seem to like him. I'm still not sure you do. What is it about him?"

Reban shrugged. "I didn't trust him. I knew he had some kind of agenda. I just didn't know what it was." He sighed and gave her a sideways glance. "Now I know it was his family. It's not such a bad trait. Is it?"

The words hung in the air between them.

"And now?" she asked.

He licked his lips but didn't meet her eyes. "Now, he's a teenage boy, and maybe I don't like how he looks at a teenage girl."

Something washed over her. That whole uncomfortable feeling that teenagers the world over must feel when a parent shows concern. She wasn't used to it. She didn't even know how to respond. She could shout and tell him it was none of his business – that's how she would normally react – but all of this just felt overwhelming. She actually just wanted a little time to process everything. To work out how she felt, without worrying about anyone else.

"I'm tired," she lied. "I'm going to sleep. It's the T-rexes in the morning. We better be ready."

Reban gave her a nod. "I guess we better."

And he sat there. Staring into the flickering flames as she fell asleep.

DAY FOUR

THIRTY-EIGHT

LINCOLN

Blaine seemed to wake with a remarkably clear head. Everyone else had slept outside the shack, sheltered by the jungle canopy with a small fire burning. "When do you leave Piloria?" he asked Lincoln.

Lincoln shook his head and rubbed his eyes. "Tomorrow."

Blaine dumped some fruits in a pile before them all as the rest started to wake. "Eat," he said with unusual motivation. He glanced back at Lincoln. "You should take your biggest supply of plants at the last possible minute. Then they have a better chance of being viable when you reach Earthasia."

Lincoln nodded. It made sense. He wanted the specimens to be in as perfect a condition as possible.

As they trekked to the T-rex watering hole, Blaine managed to engage Jesa in conversation. Lincoln and Leif stayed close by, both watching Jesa carefully. It was strange how they both seemed to feel responsible for her. But Blaine's conversation was mainly questions, asking about his family's house, jobs and schooling. Other questions about people he used to know meant nothing to Leif or Lincoln.

Lincoln was watching both Storm and Leif closely too – looking for a sign that the virus had affected them in any way. But both of them seemed fine. Maybe his fears were unjustified, and the virus really wouldn't work – or at least would have no impact on humans.

Leif wasn't quite so tense as he'd been. "How bad is Rune's sister? And what about his brother, he's sick too?" he asked.

Lincoln shook his head. "Storm said Cornelius wasn't too bad, but Livia – the first layer of her skin has started to blister. It started on her torso but has spread up her neck. She's nowhere near as bad as Arta though. If she was, Storm would have insisted she was hospitalized."

Leif gave a nod. "And Arta?"

Lincoln let out a long, slow breath. "I'm only here for the plants. We didn't get enough yesterday. We have to collect more. Blaine said to take the plants as late as possible so they have the best chance of still being alive when we reach Earthasia. I'm trying to keep him sweet. He seems interested in the viruses now. That's the only reason I'm going along with this."

"Arta's that bad?"

Lincoln gave a sorry smile. His question-dodging hadn't been lost on Leif. He just gave the briefest nod. "How is your family back in Norden?"

Leif's jaw tightened. He automatically ran his hands up

the outside of his arms. "It seems to be colder. We can't keep the house warm at all. The coal doesn't burn as well as before, and even when it does burn it just fills the house with smoke. My parents get thinner every day." He sighed. "But no one has the blistering plague. We're wondering if we should move. Ambulus City is warmer, apparently. Even though there's nowhere to stay." He stared at the horizon as they tramped forward. "I just wonder how much energy we waste trying to stay warm."

Lincoln frowned. "When you say it's colder, what do you mean?"

He knew Norden was cold anyway. It had much more snowfall than Ambulus City. But he didn't know quite how much.

Leif shifted his backpack. "A few years ago we had snow five months out of twelve. This year there has been snow for seven months so far. When I got home after the Trials it was still snowing. When they dragged me out of my house for this trip, it was straight into a snowdrift."

Lincoln looked around at the bright green landscape stretching before them. There were large hills in the background, covered with darker green, and a stretch of marshland off to the left. "Somehow I think this place has never seen snow," he murmured.

Leif nodded. "I doubt it. But could you stand the heat? The moisture? Sometimes it seems so thick I can barely breathe."

It was odd. Were they both actually contemplating living

on Piloria at some point, despite everything they'd been through? But strange as it seemed, it didn't stop Lincoln continuing. "Yeah, but somehow it doesn't seem so bad near the beach, or the coastline."

Leif shook his head. "But would you want to be there? That bay looked so tranquil – until it filled with tylosauruses. And what about the pterosaurs?"

"Or the megalodon. You'd never know when it was lurking."

"At least it can't walk on land." Leif looked thoughtful. "I wonder if there are any creatures that can walk out of the sea?"

Lincoln swallowed slowly. He knew exactly what Leif was thinking. The deinosuchus lived in the lake but came onto the shore to attack. It was the creature that had killed Rune and played a part in Kronar's death.

"We should change the map that Storm has. We should draw pictures of where all the dinosaurs are. Make it more relevant for anyone who might come here."

Leif raised his eyebrows. "You're assuming we're getting out of here alive."

Lincoln gave a determined nod. "I'm counting on it. I'm taking those plants home." He shot a sideways glance at Leif. "And if I don't get them home, I'm counting on one of you to do it for me." He held up his fist.

Leif looked at it for the briefest of seconds, then held his up too and bumped it against Lincoln's. "Count on it. We've got out of here once. We can do it again."

Lincoln kept in his reply. He wasn't forgiven. Leif would never really forgive his betrayal. But they'd reached some kind of truce and that was enough for him.

THIRTY-NINE

STORMCHASER

Her head felt fuzzy. It was either the fruits she'd eaten this morning, or the lack of sleep from the night before. She'd buried her head in her blankets after her conversation with Reban, even though her brain had been wide awake.

By the time she finally fell asleep, the sky was already changing from dark blue to violet – a sign that the sun was on its way up.

The hatred was slowly but surely edging its way out of her. He hadn't known she existed. He hadn't known Dalia had a daughter. At least, that's what he said.

As for Octavius – why hadn't he told her he knew her mother? That he was her uncle. In a way, she guessed he had. He'd hinted at knowing Dalia Knux, but Storm had been much too nervous to ask him what he meant. Now she just wanted to go back to that office and sit down and have an actual conversation with him. Octavius Arange, the Captain Regent – and Storm's great-uncle.

How well had he known her mother? How much time had he spent with her? What had she been like as a young woman? Was she anything like Storm? A few people had mentioned their physical similarities, but only Reban had mentioned her temperament. And maybe he was just saying that to try to win Storm around.

She watched as Blaine led the way ahead. Part of the terrain had been open. Part of the trek had been past a marsh. Last time around she was sure they'd found some boots there – remnants of other Finalists who'd vanished without a trace. Hadn't someone on the other team said they'd been stuck in the marsh for a few days? Watching as creatures devoured their teammates.

It didn't even bear thinking about.

Finally, Blaine turned and raised his finger to his lips. They all crouched down, crawling forward to a viewing point over the watering hole.

It was deserted. The water was murky-looking, as if it had recently been disturbed. The surrounding area was muddy. They could practically see the footprints. But there was no sign of any T-rexes.

They sat in silence for a while. Scanning the surrounding landscape, looking for any possible glimpse of the T-rexes. Listening to every tiny sound carried by the wind and, more importantly, catching any scent in the air. The T-rexes were vile. The smell when she had last encountered one had been overwhelming – the stench of rotting meat seemed to emanate from their very pores.

Leif flicked open the carrier, pulling out the bright-red vial. The virus for the T-rexes. Storm's stomach somersaulted.

The T-rexes were terrifying. Part of her hated herself right now, but another part wouldn't be sorry if this virus worked.

She leaned down and put her head in her hands for a second. In so many ways they were magnificent creatures. Stunning. But inhabiting the same continent as them?

Maybe she should start wearing black. Maybe she secretly had the mentality of a Stipulator. After all, her father was one, maybe they weren't so dissimilar after all?

"Give me it," said Blaine. "The coast is clear. I'll do this one. I have a vested interest in not seeing another T-rex."

Leif looked a little hesitant. "Are you sure?"

Blaine gave a slightly creepy smile. *Vengeance.* The word shot through her in an instant. She almost understood it.

Leif handed over the glass vial. "The top is tricky. I struggled to get it off last time," he said. "I ended up just smashing it."

Blaine was still smiling. "I think I'll manage."

He went to leave, but Jesa grabbed hold of his arm. He turned back. She was struggling to find the words. "Be careful," she finally said, her voice shaking.

And, in the blink of an eye, Blaine shot over towards the watering hole.

It all happened so quickly. One moment they were

watching Blaine. The next, they were watching something else entirely.

From over to the right, a few other people shot out of the trees, running as fast as they could. Storm's heart missed a few beats. "It's the other team!" She couldn't help the surge of guilt that swept through her. She hadn't even given them a second thought so far. But here they were. They must have visited the pterosaur site, and now reached the T-rex one. Froan and Tena, two of the other previous Finalists, were on that team.

There was a moment of confusion. The other team were all clad in dark green. It was obvious they didn't recognize Blaine, nor him them. Two of them stopped sprinting, glancing behind them to their counterparts. Blaine turned back to their group. "More?" he shouted angrily.

Storm waved her hand. Gesturing Blaine on, but letting the other team see her too. At least then they would realize Blaine was actually with them.

Blaine lifted the vial and smashed it off one of the rocks at the watering hole, the red liquid vanishing instantly. At the same time there was a blurring to the left.

"Oh no," breathed Storm. "Raptors."

Lincoln's voice was right in her ear. "They're too big to be raptors."

Five creatures had appeared, streaking from the forest. Like raptors and T-rexes they were theropods, running on their strong back legs with their front legs raised in mid-air.

From the ridge of the hill, they all practically had a

bird's-eye view. They were far enough away to be safe, but close enough to see everything unfold.

"What's that on their heads?" asked Leif.

Storm screwed up her nose. The creatures had what looked like a pair of rounded crests on their skulls and some bunched skin around their necks. "I have no idea," she breathed. "I've never seen anything like this before."

The creatures seemed naturally curious. They were looking first one way towards Blaine, then towards the other group.

"They'll go for my dad!" Jesa's voice was high-pitched. She jumped from her crouching position to her feet.

"What on earth are they doing at the T-rex watering hole? Are they crazy?" asked Lincoln.

"Just as crazy as us apparently," said Leif as he pulled Jesa back down.

Blaine hadn't moved. He'd stayed crouched down at the edge of the watering hole. The other group started to panic.

Reban's voice was low. "Those are dilophosauruses. At least I think they are. Give it a minute."

"How do you know that?" Storm didn't even turn her head towards him. She couldn't look away right now. She had to keep her eyes on Blaine and the others.

"I know someone who wrote a book about dinosaurs."

Storm had a wave of understanding. The book in Octavius's library.

Now she did flick her head around. "Magnus…Don?"

He nodded. "My uncle, unfortunately."

Something burned inside her. Curiosity. She wanted to ask questions. But it was hardly the time. She looked back down.

Froan was running back towards the trees. But another dilophosaurus appeared from them. Where had it come from? It was slightly smaller than the others – around the same height as Froan – and it was obvious for a few seconds that Froan contemplated his chances against this unfamiliar dinosaur.

That's when everything changed. The smaller dilophosaurus seemed to move into defence mode. It opened its mouth and let out a strange noise, the skin around its neck opening out like a bright red frill, and something shot from its mouth.

"Aargh!" Froan lifted his hands to his face. His scream was deep, and another noise filled the air.

He pulled his hands back from his face. Even from here, Storm could see that his skin was sliding, hissing from his face.

Storm was horrified. She turned to the others. "What is it? Acid?"

All the other creatures turned in the direction of the attack. Now Blaine moved. But instead of running up the hill towards them, he darted in the other direction. The direction of the caves they'd hidden in before, when they'd first met him.

"Where's he going? And where's the rest of that team?" asked Jesa, wide-eyed with shock. All but one of Froan's teammates had vanished while the dilophosauruses were distracted.

"They must have scarpered. I think we should go too, but not down there," said Reban quietly.

"I think you're right," said Leif. He grabbed Jesa's elbow. "We can catch up with Blaine later."

"What? No!" Her voice was louder than it should be. One of the dilophosauruses lifted its crested head, turning in their direction.

Froan's remaining teammate below was hesitating near the trees – Tena Koll had been a Finalist with them and obviously had some loyalty to Froan. But the rest of the dilophosauruses were circling him now. He was holding his hands out in front of him, screaming for someone to help.

Tena hesitated just too long. Another dilophosaurus turned towards her, its bright-red neck frill on display as it opened its mouth and sprayed her with acid. She crumpled to the ground with a squeal, her hands over face. It was the second time Storm's feet had been frozen to the ground.

She didn't want to watch the attack but she couldn't seem to move. The largest dilophosaurus took the first bite, snapping at Froan's outstretched hand. He yelped and pulled it back. But it was too late. Simultaneously, the rest of them pounced.

Storm's group were too far away to help. Even if she tried to throw her knives they would never reach the dilophosauruses. She glanced at Jesa – who looked far too shocked to pull out her crossbow. Running down to help would only give the attacking dinosaurs more prey.

Tena was on the ground. It didn't matter that she couldn't see anything. She had to be listening in horror as Froan's blood-curdling screams filled the air along with the sound of ripping flesh.

One of the dilophosauruses was still looking towards them on the hill.

Reban grabbed Storm roughly. "Move!" he yelled, taking her hand and yanking her in the direction that Lincoln, Jesa and Leif were already running in. He ran much quicker than she expected – her feet could barely keep pace with him, her arm nearly pulled from its socket.

She couldn't breathe as she ran. Her eyes were still seeing the horror that had just unfolded in front of her.

The others were a good way in front, heading towards a thick patch of jungle.

As soon as she hit the jungle she dropped her hand from Reban's. As she rushed through the dark-green leaves, the jungle seemed to envelop them, hide them from any pursuers. The only trouble was that it also hid Leif, Jesa and Lincoln from them.

Storm kept pushing forward, slapping the thick leaves away from her face. The foliage was dense. The bright sunlight barely managed to filter through the canopy above. After a few minutes, Reban stopped and tugged at her arm. "Stop," he murmured.

She kept trying to push on, but he got more insistent. "Stop!"

Her footsteps halted. "What?"

He put his fingers to his lips. "Listen."

She stopped instantly. Had he heard something? Were the dilophosauruses coming after them?

Reban crouched down on the jungle floor and gestured for her to do the same. Sweat was running down the side of his face, she could feel the heat emanating from him. Every breath was laboured, hers as well as his, as they listened closely for any jungle sounds.

At first it was the rustle of the bushes, the crack of the twigs, then there was a murmur. Reban tilted his head to the right. "This way," he mouthed.

He moved forward, still crouching, watching where he placed his feet. But it was impossible to move silently through the jungle. After a few seconds, the murmur got louder – it was voices.

Storm's face broke into a smile of relief. They pushed their way through, but as the foliage was thick, Storm missed what Lincoln was doing and fell straight over him, tumbling to the ground.

Almost instantly the smell overwhelmed her. She coughed and spluttered. "Wow."

Lincoln's bright green eyes met hers. His hands were covered in dirt as he scrabbled on the forest floor.

Storm shook some twigs from her hair. "What are you doing?"

He frowned at her. "What do you think I'm doing? Can't you smell it? It's more of these plants. I'm digging up a few to put in the backpacks." He nodded his head to the left.

"Leif's grabbing some of the yellow vines over there." Leif was scrabbling to her left, frantically yanking some of the vines and stuffing them into his backpack.

Even after what they'd just witnessed Lincoln never seemed to lose his focus – never seemed to forget what his priority was.

Storm looked up at the yellow vines wrapped around the nearby tree trunks. "Isn't it weird," she asked, "that these two plants seem to grow near each other?"

"Luck," said Lincoln. "That's what I call it. First bit of luck we've had around here." He lifted a plant from the ground, cradling its roots as he put it into the backpack.

There was a loud crack behind them. Reban turned around, his eyes wide. There was a strange snort.

A few seconds later a small duckbill crashed between them all.

"Move!" yelled Lincoln instantly, as he picked up the backpack and started chasing after the creature.

Storm was on his heels in an instant. There was only one reason the duckbill would be running like that. It was being chased.

Jesa and Leif were to her right, Lincoln straight ahead and Reban practically on her shoulder. The thuds behind told her all she needed to know. The dilophosauruses they thought they'd lost were in the jungle with them.

Did they track by sight? By smell? She had no idea. Nor had she any clue how fast they could run.

Leif gave a shout as Jesa followed. "This way," he called,

banking sharply further to the right. There was no time to think, no time to argue. Lincoln kept pace with him. The leaves slapped into Storm's face, twigs and branches scratching her arms and legs, tearing at her clothes as she forced her way through.

There was a short, sharp squeal. Then she ran straight into a wall.

Except the wall was Lincoln.

He was teetering at the edge of a crumbling cliff.

There was a splash below, the sound of something scrabbling around. The duckbill.

Leif had stopped dead too, Jesa and Reban next to him.

Storm stuck her head around the side of Lincoln's back. "Uh oh." She grabbed hold of his shoulder. It was a straight fall down into a pale-green lake far, far below.

Leif looked as though he might be sick. They weren't just high. This seemed higher than the cliffs that the pterosaurs nested on.

They had no idea what was in that lake and there was surely no way they could jump that far safely.

Lincoln turned to Reban. "What now?"

The crashing noise continued behind them. The dilophosauruses weren't far away. There was nowhere else to go. Storm looked around frantically. No ropes. No vines they could climb down. It looked as if part of the jungle had just plummeted downwards at some point.

"No," said Leif, his eyes fixed on the pale-green lake. He spun back around. "No way, I can't."

His face was deathly pale. But Jesa had no idea what was going on.

Storm gulped and leaned forward again. This lake wasn't murky like the other one. The water was relatively clear. What she wasn't sure of was whether it was deep enough. The duckbill was still scrabbling around in the water, its four little legs working overtime to try and get it to shore.

Nothing had attacked it. Surely that meant there was nothing lurking in the lake?

The crashing grew louder, there was no time to think. Jesa moved before anyone else. She took one glance behind her, put her hand on Leif's chest and didn't give him a chance to respond. "Now," she said as she pushed him backwards, falling off the edge with him.

"Go," said Reban as he watched the thrashing bushes.

Storm turned, ready to jump. But there was a caw at her back. She whipped around to see that the dilophosaurus was there already. She gaped in horror as it opened its mouth.

But she didn't get a chance to react. Reban moved, but Lincoln was quicker. He stepped in front of her, allowing his back to take the brunt of the spray, and pushing her with one hand as he jumped. She fell backwards.

It seemed to last for ever. There had been no chance to catch her breath. No chance to fix her hand on the backpack.

The cool, green water pushed the remaining breath from her lungs. She was conscious of a splash next to her, then another almost on top of her.

The momentum of the fall carried her down, down, until she hit the bed of the lake.

Her legs pulled up from the sharp, brittle stones. It took a second to get her bearings before she pushed with her boots, trying to get back to the surface. But the weight of her boots was heavier than she expected. She broke up into the air, but was already being dragged back down again. A second later she choked as her tunic pulled around her neck. Someone had grabbed it from behind.

She started to struggle, flailing her arms and legs. "Hold still," growled Reban. There was a loud cawing noise above them.

She looked upwards. The dilophosaurus was standing right at the edge, dirt crumbling beneath its clawed feet. Its bright-red frill was on display and she could see the drops shooting from its mouth. It was furious. Furious at losing its prey.

Lincoln. She looked anxiously around the lake as Reban dragged her to the side. Lincoln was lying quite still, floating on his back. Jesa and Leif were sitting on the shingles at the other side of the green pool, obviously still trying to catch their breath.

Her feet hit the lake bed as they neared the water's edge and she stood up immediately, coughing another few times as she tried to clear her lungs. "Lincoln!" she gasped as soon as she caught her breath.

His hands were moving slowly at his sides. It seemed as though he were keeping himself afloat, even though he looked as if he were in some kind of trance.

Reban let out a sigh and shouted over to Leif, "Get the bags," as he dived back in and headed towards Lincoln.

Leif hesitated at the side of the water. Jesa frowned next to him, opening her mouth as if to ask what was wrong, then catching Storm's eye. Storm shook her head, then watched as Jesa jumped back in to retrieve the two backpacks floating on the surface.

Reban pulled Lincoln to shore a few seconds later. Lincoln's eyes were almost glazed over and as Storm bent to help drag him in, he winced and let out a yell.

She gulped as she locked gazes with Reban. As soon as they sat Lincoln forward in the shallow water she could see exactly what was wrong. Part of his tunic had evaporated. Burned by acid. The water must have helped, as the fabric was loose and not stuck to the skin. But the water didn't hide the angry red welts that almost sizzled beneath her eyes. She squirmed. If Lincoln hadn't stepped in front of her, the acid would have hit her face.

She kneeled down in the water next to him. "Lincoln, are you all right? Are you in pain?"

After a few seconds he blinked, then grimaced as he moved his shoulders. "It…it's okay," he said through gritted teeth.

The dilophosaurus let out another caw of frustration above them, then disappeared back into the jungle.

Storm breathed a sigh of relief as Leif and Jesa walked around to join them. "Lincoln, how are you?" asked Jesa, her eyes widening once she saw the welts on his back. "What happened?"

Storm shook her head. "It was aiming at me. Lincoln stepped in." She took a deep breath. "Thank you." The words almost stuck in her throat. It wasn't something she said easily. It wasn't something she often had to say at all. Most of the time there weren't a lot of people around to thank for anything.

For the briefest second, Reban caught her eye then glanced away. Her stomach rolled. She hadn't thanked him when he'd stayed behind to delay the raptors. But somehow that felt even more difficult. She just knew those words would have been even harder to say.

Lincoln pushed himself up, wincing again. It was obvious every movement was painful. "We should try to get back to Blaine's shack. He has ointment. We could use some of that."

Jesa pulled a face. "Wait a moment." She wrestled in one of the bags and pulled out a now slightly soggy pot. "We could use this."

Storm couldn't hide her surprise. "When did you steal that?"

Jesa shrugged. "I didn't *steal* it. It's my dad's. I'm sure that means at least part of it is mine. Anyway, I heard you talking, saying you needed the ointment for your families. Dad can make some more. I'm sure he won't mind."

Leif tried to hide the smile on his face. He was obviously sharing the same thoughts as Storm. Neither of them were sure that Blaine wouldn't mind.

But that didn't stop Storm taking the pot and dipping her fingers into the ointment. It was wet. Some of the lake water had collected on top, but she just brushed it off. The liquid hadn't diluted the ointment at all. It smelled as pungent as ever.

She gestured to Lincoln. "Turn around, the sooner we get some of this on those wounds the better."

He was still staring at the ledge above. "What's the chance of the dilophosaurus coming down here?"

Leif shuddered. He made no attempt to hide it. He was still staring at the lake. "I'm more worried about something coming out of the water."

Jesa started to open her mouth, but Storm put her hand on her arm. "We had a bad experience somewhere else."

"Somewhere other than the bay?"

Storm nodded. "Oh yeah." She stared at the water. She doubted there was anything in there. If there was, it had missed the perfect opportunity for six meals. "Maybe we should make a move anyway?" She dabbed the last few bits of ointment on Lincoln's back. "But I have no idea where we are right now. How do we get back to Blaine's shack from here?"

They all looked around. Leif pointed left. "Shouldn't it be in that direction?"

Reban cleared his throat. "Do we want to go there, or do we go on to the pterosaurs?" He paused for a second. "Or… do we go and see how the other team is doing?"

Storm stared at him in shock. Was that compassion?

Was he actually concerned about the other team? Did he feel guilty for leaving like she did?

"Do you think my dad will be back at the shack?" Jesa's voice sounded a bit high-pitched.

Leif appeared at her side. "If it's safe, he'll be there. Don't worry, he's much better at this than all of us."

Lincoln was peering into his backpack and trying to drain out some of the water. "Plants look okay," he murmured.

But Reban hadn't finished. "Where were the T-rexes? Why were dilophosauruses at their watering hole?" He stepped away and put his hands on his hips. "Aren't the T-rexes the kings around here? Seems strange for some other lesser dinosaurs to be hanging around," he mused.

Jesa wrinkled her nose. "But surely all dinosaurs have to drink? Maybe we just timed it wrong. Maybe the dilophosauruses wait until the coast is clear and then drink?"

Reban narrowed his gaze. "Does that mean we've just wasted the virus? We've ruined the chance to kill the T-rexes? How long does the virus last in the water?"

Storm's skin chilled again. Just when Reban almost surprised her, he seemed to revert right back to character. He was worried about himself. He was worried about the T-rexes still being alive. He didn't really care about anyone else.

She picked up her dripping backpack. "Let's move anyway. I don't want to stay here in case the dilophosaurus decides to come looking for us."

"Then where?" asked Leif again. "If I'm voting, I want

to head back to the coast. Back to the bay where we'll get picked up."

Silence.

No one had really thought of that. No one had mentioned the fact they'd need to get on board one of those boats again to get back to the ship.

What if they were attacked again?

Leif looked pale. He seemed to read all their unspoken thoughts. "Okay, let's try to find our way back to Blaine's then."

No one argued. Everyone just picked up their backpacks, all except Lincoln – Reban gave him a nod and slung his backpack over his other shoulder. "Got it." He stopped and stared at Storm as the edges of his lips turned upwards. "After you."

She tossed her damp hair over her shoulder and looked at the surrounding scrubland. Blaine's shack. She didn't have a single clue which direction to take, but didn't really want to admit it. So she tilted her chin and started to stride confidently through some wilting bushes.

This way was as good as any other.

FORTY

LINCOLN

He'd spent the last few hours trying not to concentrate on the pain in his back. The welts hurt more than he cared to admit. He'd changed his top, which meant that now he had fabric rubbing against the sensitive, damaged skin.

He wanted to take the top off and walk bare-skinned. But somehow that didn't seem quite right. It would almost look as if he wanted them all to see the wounds, so it was best he kept them hidden.

But being out of his mind with pain meant that he'd missed a few other vital things. Like where on earth they actually were.

They'd been tramping across this terrain for ages. At first, they'd seemed to go uphill and then down again. They'd crossed a river he hadn't recognized, seen a titanosaurus in the distance, followed by a huge flock of duckbills. They'd wandered through small patches of jungle, all to no avail.

"What did you do with that map?" Lincoln nudged Storm.

She screwed up her face. "It got a bit damp. I'm not sure how much use it would be."

Reban was walking alongside her. Lincoln had noticed she'd changed her pace a few times as if trying to shake him off, but Reban seemed determined to stay by his daughter's side. Was he trying to keep her safe after the latest attack?

"How did you know they were dilophosauruses?" Lincoln asked out of the blue.

Storm's footsteps faltered.

Reban answered easily. "I know someone who wrote a book about dinosaurs."

"What book?" asked Lincoln.

"It's called *The Continent of Monsters*."

Lincoln couldn't hide his interest.

"*The Continent of Monsters* by Magnus Don," Storm said slowly.

Lincoln turned to face her. "What? How do you know that?" He glanced between Storm and Reban. They'd both seen the same book? Hardly anyone saw books. The only paper books left were the ones in school and they were all standard textbooks. Did Storm have a chance to look at real books some place? Now, he was definitely curious.

Reban looked at Storm with interest. "Didn't you study it?"

She looked annoyed. "I didn't have much time. I didn't realize about the name until now. You said he was a relation?"

"Your great-uncle. He died around twenty years ago."

Lincoln tried not to smile. Storm and Reban had only had a few conversations since they'd arrived on Piloria. But this was the first time he'd really heard Reban have a family-type discussion with Storm. Had he actually managed to wrap his head around the fact that Storm was his daughter?

She was clearly annoyed for some reason. "How on earth did he manage to write a book about" – she held out her hands and wrinkled her nose – "here…" Her voice tailed off.

Reban took a few moments to answer. "Magnus was a Chief Stipulator, like me. He was my mother's brother." He ran his hands through his thick dark hair. "He wasn't the nicest person in the world. He could be cruel at times."

Could this relationship be any more complicated? Suddenly Lincoln was glad for his quiet family life – despite the illness.

Reban glanced around him. "There have been a few expeditions here over the years – even before we started hunting for food. Several of the Stipulators charted some of the dinosaurs. But there are just so many. Blaine was asked to try to chart some more for us."

He nodded at Storm. "I strongly suspect part of the whole reason Octavius called you to parliament was to help him update some of his books."

"He told you that?"

Reban laughed. "No. He told me nothing. The first time I knew you were in parliament was when you came and gave me the message. It's a big place, you know. Lots of people."

Storm pressed her lips together. Her voice was tight.

"That *is* why I was there. He wanted to know everything about Piloria. As much as I could tell him."

"Well, it's useful information. For all of us."

"Only if you're coming here," Storm said quickly.

Lincoln's skin prickled. Had Reban Don known he was coming here? Had Octavius been gathering information to help him? Could Leif's allegations about him being a plant have some truth after all?

FORTY-ONE

STORMCHASER

Storm watched Reban closely. "So, you studied the book?"

He gave a small smile. "When Octavius let me. He guarded it fiercely. Books are his thing. You might have noticed."

She knew exactly what he was saying. Reban had done this a few times. No one could describe him as gushing, but now and then, there was a glimmer of something beyond the condescending image of the black-cloaked Chief Stipulator. Something more human.

Being on Piloria should have stripped him completely bare. Yet he still had an air of authority about him. An assurance in everything he did, even though he'd never been here before. Perhaps it was from studying that book – even though it was outdated. In some ways, he seemed better equipped than she did.

Now she wished she had taken the chance to look more

at *The Continent of Monsters*. If she'd spent any longer working for Octavius, if she'd had any idea she was coming back here, then she would have. Especially if she'd known it was written by her great-uncle! Another relative she knew nothing about. "What was Magnus like?"

It was the first time she'd really enquired about his side of the family. Reban let out a laugh. "He was the most terrifying man I ever met. Ferocious. I guess that's what happens when you've spent time with dinosaurs." He gave her a sideways glance. "You might have a bit of that yourself." Then he shook his head. "Anyway, he never, ever spoke about Piloria. I didn't find out about the book until much later."

Storm gave a nod as she kept walking. "What about Octavius?"

"What about Octavius?"

She tried not to smile. "What does Octavius think of you? After all, you got his niece pregnant and put her at risk."

Reban sighed. "I like Octavius. I respect Octavius. But we've never really seen eye to eye. Sometimes I wonder if he somehow knew about Dalia being pregnant and suspected it was me. I'm not sure though. She just disappeared. I think he was as in the dark as the rest of us."

"Didn't you try to find her? Didn't you look?"

Reban threw up his hands. "Of course I did! But there was only so much I could do. Needle in a haystack doesn't even come close. Millions of people stay in Ambulus City and we have no proper records of them all. If someone wants to stay hidden, they can."

"Well Kaden didn't, or Blaine."

Reban shook his head. "But they were Stipulators. They were easy, recognizable people. It's not hard to get a Stipulator followed, and the truth is, Blaine and Kaden were sloppy. They should have taken much better care to protect their families. Love made them careless."

It seemed like such a horrible thing to say. Lincoln shot her a look and glanced in the direction of Jesa – who was walking ahead of them, deep in conversation with Leif – obviously hoping she couldn't overhear. It was like a warning glance, telling Storm to keep her temper.

Storm gritted her teeth to stop herself yelling. "Well, we all know love didn't make you sloppy."

His steps slowed. "It might have." He gave a smile. A private kind of smile. "Before Dalia vanished…her mood, her temperament had changed – probably because she knew she was pregnant. She didn't want to be around me any more. At the time I didn't know why, but Dalia was such a strong-minded woman. When she vanished I had to respect her decision. She wouldn't have wanted me to go chasing after her. Once she'd made her mind up about something – that was it. I respected her. Even though she never told me about you, I still do."

Storm pressed her lips together. Oh, to have five minutes with her mother again. To ask her the questions that she would now. To ask her about Octavius and Reban. To find out what she thought about them – to find out what she would think about Storm now. She hated that there was no opportunity to do that.

She blinked back tears and concentrated on the landscape ahead. They were heading for yet another patch of jungle. This one looked identical to the other three they'd thought might hold Blaine's shack. It turned out having been on Piloria before wasn't always as much of a help as it should be.

She was beginning to understand the terrain a little better though. The trickling streams, the hills, the distant mountains. It was so vast that there were parts which had never been explored. The desert. The marshes – but she'd no wish to be near those. There was a valley that the diplodocuses seemed to favour. It was beautiful. They seemed such docile creatures. Sociable and parental. And if they couldn't kill her with one swish of their tails she might actually think that would be a good place to set up camp.

There was a crop of trees ahead with fruit hanging from some of the branches. She reached up to grab one, rubbing it against her leg. It was an unusual shape, not round like an apple, it was almost like someone had pulled one end of the fruit to make it longer. She bit into it, and gave a yelp as the juice ran down her chin. The others were watching her, waiting to see what she made of the latest find.

She almost choked on how sweet it was. She laughed. "Fill up your backpacks. I could eat these all day."

They all grabbed some, then tramped on through the jungle, still trying to find Blaine's shack.

"This place does look more familiar," murmured Leif. He ran his hands across the bark of some of the trees.

"I think I smell something," said Reban.

Right on cue they all lifted their noses in the air and sniffed. But this time the smell wasn't evergreen. Instinctively Lincoln lifted the axe in his hand. There was something in the air. A hint. A tang.

Their voices fell silent. Now they all watched where they put their feet, trying not to crunch twigs too loudly, or to let branches crack as they pushed their way through.

The smell was getting stronger. There was a horrible familiarity about it.

And they all recognized it. The smell of death.

Every hair on Storm's body stood on end. Jesa might not have known the smell straight away, but it didn't take long for recognition to hit. She didn't make a sound, but Storm watched a single tear of fear trickle down her cheek.

Please don't let it be Blaine. Please don't let it be Blaine.

It wasn't as if people didn't die on Earthasia – the blistering plague took care of that. But because the city was so populated, no death went unnoticed for long and bodies were disposed of fast. Piloria was almost at the other end of the spectrum; add in the higher temperature…and the smell of death quickly became putrid.

They were practically tiptoeing now. On one hand, it might make more sense to turn around and head in the opposite direction. On the other – they all knew they had to find out what the source of the smell was.

If it was one of the other team members, they would have to send the news home to the family.

Storm pressed her lips together and willed the rising bile

away from the back of her throat. The last thing she wanted to do right now was be sick.

Lincoln shot a glance at Leif and they both wordlessly took the lead. Her heart swelled a little in her chest: both of them were trying to protect Jesa. Reban seemed to understand what they were doing, and he moved directly in front of Jesa too, as if to block her view from anything that might lie ahead.

The thick jungle seemed to thin a little around them. The stench was stronger every second, rancid. Storm closed her eyes. She couldn't take this. If a human body was causing this smell, the sight would be too distressing for words.

Lincoln waved with his hand, gesturing for the rest of them stop.

He and Leif moved forward again, disappearing out of view.

By now, Storm had her hand over her mouth and nose. She gagged. She couldn't help it.

Reban gave a little jolt, as if something had just occurred to him, then the frown disappeared from his face and he strode forward, following Leif and Lincoln.

A few seconds later there was a shout. "All clear. Come on."

Storm's heart gave a leap. It wasn't Blaine! Jesa's shoulders slumped in relief, but her footsteps were still tentative.

Storm pushed forward, sweeping the remaining dark-green leaves away with her free hand, and stepped out into a sort of clearing.

Her eyes immediately started watering. The sight was

disgusting. On the ground in front of them was the swollen, bloated corpse of a velociraptor. Its head was at a peculiar angle, its mouth and eyes open.

Jesa vomited all over her boots.

Reban walked around it slowly in a circle.

Leif just shook his head. "Man, that stinks."

Storm kept her hand firmly over her mouth.

"Let's go," said Lincoln.

Reban held his hand up. "Wait."

"Why?" Storm gagged again. She couldn't bear to be around this any longer.

Reban obviously didn't have a normal sense of smell. He didn't have his hand over his nose like the rest of them. He had his hands on his hips. "How did it die?" he asked.

"Something killed it," said Lincoln quickly.

"No." Reban shook his head.

Storm stopped looking away and shot a glance back at the bloated corpse. The grey skin was stretched with what looked like trapped air. Some kind of insects had taken root in the mouth and eyes. But there was no huge open wound. No visible signs of a predatory attack. There were some slighter wounds around the legs – but they looked as if they'd been made by some smaller creatures, and probably after the raptor had died.

Storm's eyes widened. "Do you think it was the virus? The watering hole? That was only a day ago."

They all exchanged glances. Reban held up his hands. "I'm not sure what else could have caused it to die." He wiped some sweat from his head. "From the temperature, I would think that things will smell bad pretty quickly around here." He looked around. "Trouble is, I've no idea where we are in relation to the watering hole."

"Can we just move?" choked Jesa. "This smell is terrible."

Reban nodded in agreement. "We should probably move. If we can smell this, other predators can smell it. It will attract scavengers. We should be careful."

The stench was bringing tears to Storm's eyes. "Yes, let's go." She went in the direction that Reban pointed, because she had no idea where they were anyway.

Reban fell into step beside her. Lincoln led the way, watching carefully as they trekked through the jungle.

Storm glanced sideways at Reban. Her stomach churned. "Do you really think it was the poison?"

Reban met her gaze. "I hope so."

"You do?" It came out much more squeakily than she wanted.

He nodded. "Of course. If the virus really works, then Piloria will be a safer place for me, and for Blaine." He lowered his voice. "If he's still around."

She felt sick. "'Can it really have taken hold so quickly?"

Reban shrugged. "There was no other sign. That raptor hadn't been attacked by another dinosaur. Unless it just fell over on its own, there is a chance that the virus did its work."

Storm stopped walking and sucked in a deep breath. "Do you really think that will make Piloria a safer place? What if

332

the virus kills them too quickly and doesn't get a chance to spread? Those can't be the only raptors on the continent. Same with the T-rexes and the pterosaurs." She flung up her hands. "If the viruses only kill a handful of dinosaurs, what difference will that really make?"

Just then, Lincoln increased his pace ahead of them. "Come on," he shouted.

Storm began to jog, the evergreen smell starting to surround her. That's what Lincoln had noticed. They might be near Blaine's hideaway after all.

After that, it didn't take long to find the shack. Jesa ran ahead, pushing her way inside. "Dad!" Her exclamation sent a wave of relief through Storm's body.

They crowded in behind Jesa. "You're okay?" Leif asked.

Blaine was sitting on the floor of the shack, mixing up some new ointment. "Of course I'm okay. I've been dodging these dinosaurs for years." He gave a wave of his hand. "I wondered where you'd all got to."

The hurt was written all over Jesa's face. She put her hand over her mouth and pushed her way back out of the shack. Storm dropped her backpack on the floor and followed Jesa out.

Jesa was sitting on the log outside, shaking her head. Storm sat down beside her. She didn't talk, she just reached over and squeezed Jesa's hand.

She kept a hold of it as she finally spoke. "I should have warned you. I wasn't sure how much you remembered about your dad."

Jesa frowned. "Should have warned me about what? That one second I would be the most important thing on the planet, the next he would just ignore me?"

Jesa's words made Storm cringe. "I only met him for a few days. He seemed passionate about getting a message to or from your mother and his family. But…" She paused as she tried to find a way to say it. "He wasn't that good around people. We weren't exactly sure why. He kind of hinted he didn't want us around and that he was glad when we were leaving."

"But what does that mean?" A tear rolled down Jesa's cheek.

Storm shook her head. "I don't know. I asked Reban—"

"You mean, your dad?" Jesa looked annoyed now. "You never call him that. Why don't you ever call him your dad? You know that he is."

Storm kept shaking her head. "But I can't call him that. It doesn't seem right. I hardly know him."

"And whose fault is that?"

"What's that supposed to mean?"

Jesa held up her hands. "He wants to talk to you – I can tell. He saved you from the raptors. And you had two of them saving you from the dilophosaurus. He watches you all the time. Sometimes, when he knows you're not paying attention, he gives this…this kind of proud smile. As if you're doing and saying exactly what he'd expect you to."

Storm stood up and waved her hand. "You have no idea what you're talking about. This isn't about me, it's about you."

But Jesa shook her head. She stood up too, so they were virtually nose to nose, and pointed towards the shack. "I had a whole host of dreams about what my father would be like. Is it his fault he doesn't live up to them?" She shook her head and put her hand on her heart. "It's enough I've met him again. It's enough I can go home and tell my mum and Caleb that he misses them, that he loves them and he still has a picture of us all that he's drawn. They don't need to know the rest. They don't need to know he's agitated. They don't need to know he seems to have a cut-off point. I don't understand it – how could I expect *them* to?"

Tears were falling down Jesa's face, and Storm reached out to her and wrapped her arms around her neck. "I'm sorry," she whispered. "I'm sorry I didn't prepare you better for this. I just didn't know what to say. I wasn't sure he'd still be the same. I don't know...I just thought, once he actually met you—"

"His whole personality would change?" Jesa smiled as she pulled back and wiped the tears from her face. "I was too young before to know what he was really like. And we only ever saw him for short periods of time. I guess I didn't really understand. I guess all memories of my father were wrapped up in the mystery of him being a Stipulator and being taken away from us."

Her warm brown eyes met Storm's. She pressed her lips together, taking a second to collect her thoughts. "But you have a whole other chance."

"What?"

335

Jesa nodded. "I don't want to be blunt, but I still have my mother and my brother, even after I leave Dad here. You don't. Reban is all the family you've got left."

Octavius's face swarmed into her mind. Her great-uncle. But Jesa didn't know about him. "And?"

Jesa held up her hands. "Then you have about one day left to get to know your dad. We'll be heading back to the pterosaur nest tomorrow, and then along the coast to meet the ship. You barely have any time left at all. Stop being so stubborn! Talk to him. Find out more about him."

Storm put her hands on her hips. Jesa was setting every one of her nerves on edge. "I have spoken to him."

Jesa rolled her eyes and gave a quirky smile. "Maybe a little. But you're still holding back, I can tell." She sighed and pushed her curls out of her face. "I'm going to go back in there and try to get my father to remember I'm actually here. I'm going to see if I can persuade him to write a note to my mother. That would mean the world to her." She tilted her chin. "He only has to put up with us for a short spell. Whether he likes it or not, he'll have to suck it up."

Storm gave a smile as Jesa turned on her heel with an angry toss of her mad curls.

Sometimes Jesa reminded Storm of herself.

DAY FIVE

FORTY-TWO

LINCOLN

He couldn't sleep. It didn't help that he could hear constant murmurs coming from Blaine in the shack about "too many people". And even though his whole back was covered in ointment, every part of it still stung. The acid spray was almost as painful as a T-rex bite.

Lincoln had so many plans in his head. Once he got back to Earthasia, he would talk to Lorcan about growing these plants. The lab managed all growing of food, because the soil was so devoid of nutrients due to overuse. It didn't matter that the plants probably needed a warmer and more humid environment – Lorcan could help create that. Lincoln had some plant specimens already. If he could collect a few more and keep them safe during the transport back on the ship, he was sure they could grow the plants and make the ointment back on Earthasia.

In the meantime, he'd spent most of the night following

Blaine's instructions and making as much of the ointment as he could. It was a fail-safe. If something happened to the plants he would still have enough ointment for Arta, for Lorcan's daughter and for Rune's brother and sister. While the others slept, he used the time to fill their backpacks with ointment. This way, if something happened to him, one of them could still get the cure home.

Leif woke early in the morning. He disappeared for a few minutes to wash in the nearby stream then sat down next to the fire, taking some scraps of paper from his backpack. He smiled when he spotted the stash of ointment. "Getting us ready?" he asked.

Lincoln nodded. "We don't have much time here. Makes no sense to waste it."

He wrinkled his brow as Leif pulled out some graphite and started to sketch. "What are you doing? I didn't know you could draw."

Leif shrugged. "That's because I didn't tell you. Anyway, paper is hard to come by. I'm just making use of what there is."

Lincoln leaned over to glance at Leif's work. His fingers moved swiftly, the graphite quickly capturing the outline of a face. In only a few minutes, he had sketched the contours, the light and shade, the tiny lines, the strands of hair, the ragged, earth-worn look.

"You're sketching Blaine? Why?" Lincoln was surprised. It wasn't quite what he expected. Leif had captured so much of Blaine's essence – but although he'd outlined the almond shape of Blaine's eyes, he'd left the detail until last.

Leif sighed and put down the graphite.

"What's up?" said Lincoln quietly. "You're almost done."

"How true do I make it?" Leif had a troubled expression on his face.

"What do you mean?"

Leif held up the graphite. "The eyes. They are the most important part. People say that the eyes capture the soul, and I think they're right."

"So why haven't you finished?"

Leif pulled a face. "You know that look that Blaine gets in his eyes. That mad, far-off look. Is that what I want to give Jesa to show to her mother and brother? Do I really want to capture the true Blaine?"

Lincoln shook his head straight away. "No. Not at all." He looked back at what Leif had already drawn. He examined it a little closer. It wasn't quite as accurate as he'd first thought. "I think you've already answered that question." He gave a smile as he pointed. "The hair isn't quite as wild as it is in real life, and you've made his clothes look a little more normal – less patchwork, less dishevelled. I guess you already knew what you were doing."

Leif gave a conciliatory nod and quickly finished the eyes. They were accurate but there was no spark, no essence to them, they were quite flat.

But now Lincoln understood why. "It's good," he said. "But there's something else."

Leif looked up as he set the paper on the log next to them. "What?"

"You didn't see Kayna or Caleb, Jesa's mum and brother, and I can't describe them well enough for you to draw. But you could capture Jesa. You could give Blaine an up-to-date picture of his daughter. Do you have any paper left?"

"I have one piece." Leif pulled it from his backpack. It was slightly crumpled and he took a few moments to flatten it. This time when he lifted the graphite, his hands flew. It only took him a few minutes to capture Jesa. Her wild curls, the laughter in her almond-shaped eyes, the determined tilt of her chin. Lincoln gave Leif a suspicious smile. "Wow, it's perfect. It's absolutely Jesa. Every bit of her."

Leif gave an appreciative nod. "Good. Hopefully Blaine will like it." He wandered a little further away to collect some fruit.

Around them the others started to wake. Reban groaned, spending a few minutes stretching out his back. Storm sat straight upright, her eyes going immediately to the entrance of the shack.

"Has Blaine appeared?" she whispered.

Lincoln shook his head. She reached forward and picked up the pieces of paper. "What's this? Oh, wow. Who did these?"

Lincoln nodded towards Leif. "He did. Seems he's been keeping his talents secret."

A strange smile came across Storm's face as she looked at the sketch of Jesa. "Looks like that's not all he's been keeping secret."

Something twisted inside Lincoln. This was the kind of chat he used to have with Storm.

He'd missed it. Someone to talk to. Someone to confide in. Someone to worry about who wasn't actually part of his family.

Someone to worry about who he *chose* to worry about. He wasn't obligated to look out for Storm, but he couldn't help it.

Her dark-brown hair was swept up in a band on top of her head. Her skin seemed to suck up the sun. When they'd started out from Earthasia she'd been pale from working in the parliament all day. Now she had the honey-coloured skin she'd had the first time he'd met her. Skin that showed she worked out in the fields. A few days on the ship and on Piloria had tanned her skin once again. She suited it. It looked better on her.

He swallowed back all the feelings he was having. "That's good for Leif. He's been so angry. Angry with me, and with you. If he feels a connection to Jesa, that's good. Good for her too. The journey home will be hard. She'll be leaving her dad behind."

It took a few seconds for him to realize what he'd said. The impact of his words seemed to wash over Storm's face. She turned away quickly. Lincoln knew he should be cringing. But somehow he wasn't. The words didn't feel so out of place.

His words hadn't been aimed at Storm. But if they made her think, then that was fine.

Lincoln still didn't trust Reban. He just couldn't. The man who slept beside them at night was still the angry man who'd looked at him with distaste and then sent them all to Piloria, knowing the odds were stacked against them.

It wasn't that Lincoln wouldn't have come. First time around he'd wanted to come, he'd *fought* to come – anything to win health care for Arta.

He'd wanted Reban to select him. He'd wanted to be here. But the Stipulators had known far more about Piloria than they'd ever told the Finalists. What was it – laziness? Indifference? – that had sent them here so unprepared? The truth was the Finalists were seen as disposable. And Reban might be Storm's father, but he'd known all this the first time he'd sent them here. He knew how hopeless their task was, how dangerous. How could Lincoln possibly forgive him, or trust him?

He watched as Storm walked over and picked up a piece of fruit lying near the campfire and bit into it. Her backpack was already over her shoulder. "Are we going soon?" she asked the others. Reban picked up his backpack and stood next to her.

Leif and Jesa were sitting together, talking over the sketches. Jesa put the sketch of her father into her backpack and lifted the other hesitantly. "Give me a second." She disappeared into the shack.

It only took a few moments. By the time she reappeared she looked a little easier. Blaine had obviously taken the sketch of her and he appeared behind her.

"Let's go to the pterosaur nests," he said. "We'll go around the edges of the marsh. It will be quicker. Once you reach the nests, it's only another few hours' travel back along the coast to Blue Bay."

Lincoln shuddered. Blue Bay. Of course, the name was obvious. The first time they'd seen the bay they'd been struck by the bright blue, clear water. But now? When he imagined the bay it was filled with dark-grey bodies and red-streaked water. He'd never have the tranquil picture in his mind again.

"Anywhere else we can collect some more plants?" asked Lincoln.

Blaine looked a bit disinterested. "Probably."

"I'm not sure about the marshes," said Storm quickly. "One of the other Finalists got trapped there for days. He said there were horrible creatures in there."

Blaine waved his hand. "Of course there are. It's a marsh. What do you expect? But we don't need to worry."

Lincoln picked up his backpack and looked around. Chances were this would be the last time any of them would be at Blaine's shack. It was the oddest feeling.

It was everything it should be. Well hidden, protected from the dinosaurs. Probably one of the safest places on Piloria. But he didn't want to stay any longer, and if he never saw it again? That would be fine. He needed to get back to his sister.

Blaine walked on ahead and Lincoln lingered a little. Once the others were all walking he did exactly what he had to – he stripped the leaves from the side of Blaine's shack and stuffed them in his backpack – the more evergreens he had the better.

He wasn't going to forget why he was here.

FORTY-THREE

STORMCHASER

This was the last day. The last day before they went home. And what was home anyway?

What would she say to Octavius when she got back? Part of her was angry at him. He could have told her at any point that they were related. But he hadn't. He had kept it secret.

He could have told her things about her mother. Just like Reban could have. But it was almost as if Reban and Octavius didn't want to share their memories – as if holding on to them would keep Dalia as only theirs.

What was it with her family and secrets? And why did they all seem to be kept from her?

It wasn't fair.

She narrowed her eyes as they tramped through the jungle again. This way was a little clearer than others. Almost as if Blaine had used it so much that a path had been worn.

Maybe that wasn't such a good thing? What if other creatures used the path too?

Hopefully they'd be back on the ship soon. Then, seven days after that, she'd be back in Ambulus City.

Back in the world of grey, built-up, crammed towers. No green. No space. And her stomach gave a little flip. Maybe no Milo either. She hadn't seen the plesiosaur at the loch since she'd come back from Piloria the first time. She'd spotted Milo in the sea – in fact Milo had helped her with the final Trial – but since then? Nothing.

Her heart gave a pitter-patter. The house. The house she'd won. Filled with Kronar's and Rune's unruly brothers and sisters. It was official. She was rubbish at being the responsible one. The one who tried to take care of everyone else. Most people wouldn't believe her, but she felt safer on the continent of dinosaurs than she did in the house full of kids.

They emerged from the jungle into blistering sun and damp air. Of course. They were near the marsh. It was so humid here that even breathing in was difficult.

"Stay away from the edges," Blaine warned them. "Especially the reeds. Walk at least a body's length away from the edges of the marsh. But keep an eye on the trees. Sometimes raptors shelter in there." Storm's hand tightened around one of her knives. It was clear the others felt the same: Jesa had her crossbow out, Leif his spear, Lincoln his axe, and Reban kept both hands on his double-ended weapon.

The journey around the marsh took a few hours. Every

now and then there would be a noise, a grunt from the bubbling mud. Once, Storm thought she saw a pair of eyes staring at her from the surface.

"What do you think's in there?" murmured Lincoln as they walked past.

She shuddered. She couldn't help it. "I don't know. Do you think it's a deinosuchus again?"

Lincoln flinched. "Please no." They'd already seen a deinosuchus launch itself from the loch and kill one of their friends. "Could they survive in mud? The loch, it was water, not mud."

He grabbed hold of her elbow and moved closer to the trees. "Better safe than sorry."

Storm raised her eyebrows. "And if there are raptors hiding in the trees?"

He gave her a smile. "We have previous experience with raptors. You have knives, I have an axe. We can last at least" – he raised an eyebrow – "maybe ten seconds?"

She nudged him with her shoulder. "With that attitude, we'll be fine." She kicked at some of the dried mud they were walking on. "Do you think the virus really worked?"

Lincoln pulled a face. "I don't know. I honestly didn't think it would. Everything seemed so rushed. I just felt that Lorcan's mind really wasn't on it. Maybe the head scientists at the other labs were more switched on? But – put it this way – I wouldn't bet my life on it."

"Do you think the other group got the pterosaurs?"

"Do you think any of the other group are still alive?"

As she ran her hands through her hair, the band holding it snapped. "Darn it!" She took a couple of steps towards the reeds and made a grab for one – just as something reared out of the swamp.

She didn't even have time to think. The familiar grey-green body of the deinosuchus, with its monstrous jaws and rows of teeth, filled her vision. Last time she'd seen that jaw it had been wrapped around the T-rex's neck.

Lincoln didn't hesitate, he yanked Storm back as he jumped forward, swinging his axe at the creature's jaw.

Storm hit the ground with a thud. She scrambled, turning around and trying to get back up on her feet. She'd seen how quickly a deinosuchus could move. "Move, Lincoln!" came a scream to the right.

The creature shook its head, shaking off the axe partly embedded in its snout, blood pouring from the wound. Reban grabbed Storm from behind, hauling her to her feet by her tunic. There was a thrash of its powerful tail. This thing was a monster. Ten times longer than a human. And far too close to Lincoln.

She fumbled for her knives, but before she even had time to pull one from its sheath something else flew through the air. An arrow.

The shot was clean and true. It landed straight in the deinosuchus's eye.

There was a spurt of something, the creature thrashed from side to side, and then it disappeared back under the mud.

Storm turned around, her mouth open. Lincoln was the

348

same. Jesa had one knee on the ground, one arm completely straight holding the crossbow, while the other arm was bent from the release. Her face was deadly pale.

Leif was behind her. He put his arm on her shoulder. "You did it. You did it, Jesa. You did it."

Blaine walked around her, putting his hands on the crossbow to make her lower it. Her arms were shaking.

Jesa struggled to get a breath to speak. "I didn't have time to think." She shook her head as Leif helped her up. "I'd already loaded it. I just fired."

"And you don't know how happy that makes me," said Lincoln, as he crossed the ground towards her. He reached over and touched her arm. "Thank you, Jesa."

Storm's heart was racing in her chest. This was her fault. All her fault. She'd bent to grab a reed to tie her hair – and Lincoln could have died.

She pushed past Reban, who was gripping his weapon as if he might be about to kill someone. "I'm sorry," she said quickly. "I wasn't thinking. I...I just wanted something to tie back my hair." She knew exactly how pathetic that sounded. She shook her head and felt tears swim into her eyes.

Blaine shot her a look of disgust and walked over to the trees, plucking part of a thin vine from a trunk. "Here," he sneered, as he handed it over.

She could sense Reban bristle on her left side, and Lincoln on her right. She gave a slight shake of her head. They didn't need any more fighting. They only had to last a few more hours, then they could head back to Earthasia.

But what about her? Would there be a place on the ship for her? She hadn't voiced her fears out loud to anyone except Reban, but that didn't mean that they weren't still there. And the second question was, did she really want to get on the ship?

Jesa had put her crossbow away. Leif was walking alongside her, talking quietly. Blaine had already strolled off in disgust.

Storm stared at the vine in her hand, then took a deep breath and twisted it around her hair. She gave both Reban and Lincoln a nod.

"Let's go, guys." She glanced over her shoulder. "The sooner we get away from here, the better."

FORTY-FOUR

LINCOLN

Something seemed off.

They crossed the flatlands easily. Too easily. There were barely any grazing dinosaurs in the distance.

Although they'd been at the pterosaur nests before, they'd never gone too far inland. Inland from here was different from the other parts of Piloria that they'd explored. The green scrubland changed quickly to dark earth, followed by sand. Yellow sand that seemed to stretch on for ever.

Everything about this was odd. Standing at the edge of a coastline and seeing desert, with only the bushes and flatlands behind them, just didn't seem right. But, then again, nothing about Piloria was normal.

When he spun back around he wasn't sure whether seeing the dark-blue ocean stretch in front of them was a blessing or a curse. It could be either.

But the dark-grey cliffs were definitely familiar. Leif stood with his hands on his hips and looked from side to side. It seemed quiet. There was only one pterosaur, circling much further out to sea. "Okay, so we know where the pterosaur nests are. But where on earth do they get their water from?"

Blaine was standing just a little bit away.

"Blaine?" Lincoln shouted. "Do you know where the pterosaurs get their water from?"

He looked at them blankly and shrugged.

"I guess not," said Lincoln as he kept walking. "Okay, everyone, look for the nearest freshwater pool."

"Who says pterosaurs drink fresh water? Maybe they're different? Maybe they drink seawater?" Storm sounded angry and she looked tired. "I still don't know about this," she muttered. "The pterosaurs aren't nearly as much of a threat as the raptors."

Lincoln gave her half a smile. That was easy for her to say, when her shoulder hadn't been raked by one. He still wasn't quite sure how he felt about using the virus either, but the one thing he was certain of was he needed to ensure his place on that ship home. "Keep looking, slacker. We're not done yet."

The search took longer than anyone expected.

After a while, Reban gave a shout. "Over here!"

By now they'd moved away from the cliffs and coastline. The watering hole was close to a large patch of bushes and trees, one of the last before the land gave way to desert.

Jesa frowned. "How do we know this is the one that the pterosaurs use?"

Reban smiled. "We don't. We wait."

"Why don't we just dump the final vial of virus and leave? Does it really matter if it's their watering hole or not?" Leif opened the silver carrier and took out the bright-blue glass vial. He held it up. It glimmered in the bright sunlight.

The attack came out of nowhere. They hadn't even noticed the creature in the air above them.

There was a squawk. A noise. And the hard flap of wings. The huge pterosaur blurred Lincoln's line of vision just as Leif let out a yell.

Lincoln was caught so off-guard he reached for the axe he didn't have any more. The pterosaur's huge claws fixed on Leif. One on his backpack, the other on his shoulder. And the creature wasn't finished. It flapped its enormous wings, keeping everyone back. Leif continued to yell. Lincoln winced as he heard the claws crunch against the bone in Leif's shoulder.

Reban jumped forward, lashing out with his double-ended weapon. But the sharp beat of the pterosaur's wings carried too much momentum. Reban couldn't get near the body of the bird.

Storm's first knife fell to the ground, swept away by the strong wings. Lincoln lunged forward, trying anything to reach Leif, but the thudding wingbeats swept him clean off his feet.

Leif's legs crumpled under him, the pain too much. And Lincoln didn't think any more. With even more determination, he leaped again.

This time, its wingbeats weren't enough to deflect his weight – just put him off target a little. Instead of landing straight on the pterosaur's back, he landed sideways across the creature's body. But the action was enough to dislodge the pterosaur from Leif's shoulder.

There was a sucking noise. The sound of tearing flesh. Leif swore as Lincoln was thrown to the ground. The pterosaur soared into the air with an angry hiss. But something wasn't quite right.

The flight path of the pterosaur wasn't smooth. If Lincoln didn't know better he'd think it was drunk, or unwell. It seemed to stutter and stop, every few seconds plummeting towards the ground, then flapping its wings madly to rise into the sunlight.

Storm and Jesa were on the ground. Storm was pressing tightly on Leif's shoulder and her hands were already covered in blood. "Get me something – anything to put over this," she said through gritted teeth to Reban.

He moved quickly, disappearing into the bushes. Blaine's head flicked from side to side. There were deep lines in his brow.

"What's wrong?" asked Lincoln.

Blaine didn't answer, just lifted his head, almost as if he were trying to catch a scent in the air.

Lincoln bent down next to Storm. He nodded at Leif. "How's he doing?"

Blood was still seeping out from under Storm's palms. "Ask me in a minute." She looked up at Blaine. "What on earth is he doing? Why isn't he helping?"

Leif stopped squirming under Storm's hands, making a gasping noise and sagging on the ground.

Jesa squealed. "Is he dead?"

Lincoln gulped and pressed his fingers to Leif's neck. He shook his head. "No. I think he's just passed out with the pain. We need to get him patched up. It can't be good losing this much blood." He glanced towards the bushes. "Where's Reban?"

Just as he said the words, Reban emerged from the bushes. "Sorry," he muttered. "Had to look about, I couldn't find leaves big enough." He had a few large, fringed palms in his hands.

The blood-curdling scream came out of nowhere. Another blur. Something came hurtling through the bushes towards them. Lincoln automatically crouched over Leif, trying to protect him. Jesa yelled and jumped to her feet, fumbling for her crossbow. Storm seemed frozen. Reban didn't even get a chance to turn around. The thick tree-branch hit him on the back of his head, sending blood spurting around them. His body crumpled to the ground.

Storm's eyes widened. Every muscle in her body seemed rigid, her mouth open in shock. It took a few seconds before she clicked into defensive mode.

For the briefest of moments, Lincoln didn't move either. "Galen?"

He couldn't believe it. Galen was dead. At least, he should be. Last time they'd seen him was a couple of months ago when his arm had been bitten off by the T-rex. They'd all assumed he'd died.

Galen's clothes were dirty and tattered, his eyes wild. Once clean-shaven, he now had a bedraggled beard. Where his arm used to be was a stump. A dirty, ragged wound. The stench was overwhelming.

In his remaining arm he held a thick tree-branch, which he was using as a club. He jumped towards Blaine, swinging madly, catching him on the side of the head. Blaine swayed, then fell.

Galen dropped the club and spun around, pulling a short axe from his waistband. He leaped towards Storm. "You left me!" he screamed. "You all left me!"

Lincoln kicked out at Galen's arm as he brought the axe down towards Storm. Galen's grip was strong, but the kick threw him off balance. He staggered to the side as Lincoln grabbed at Storm to pull her away.

But the fact he'd missed them just made Galen angrier. He swung madly, just as Blaine was getting back to his feet.

The axe caught Blaine by surprise, slicing the air at the side of his cheek.

Everything seemed to happen simultaneously, in the blink of an eye.

Blaine's hand came up automatically, grabbing for Galen's body just as the axe came back again and impacted the back of his head.

Storm's knife flew through the air with precision, landing squarely in Galen's eye. There was barely time for any noise.

"Dad!" yelped Jesa.

Lincoln couldn't breathe. Galen's swing had stopped dead, surprising even him. He lifted his hand, leaving the axe where it was as Blaine slumped forward. Then in slow motion, Galen fell backwards onto the ground.

Storm was frozen, still leaning forward, her hand open from releasing the knife. Lincoln looked from side to side, unsure of where to go first. Storm? Reban, knocked out from the blow to his head? Blaine with the axe in his skull? Motionless Galen? Stricken Jesa? Or Leif, still unconscious and bleeding?

Reban gave a judder. His leg twitched and he rolled onto his side.

Jesa collapsed next to her father. "Dad? Dad? Are you okay? It's Jesa." Her hands reached forward to touch him, then she pulled back, whimpering. How did you touch a body with an axe embedded in the head?

Galen wasn't moving. Lincoln really wanted to go to Storm, but Leif was looking whiter by the second. He did what he should. He ignored Galen, but checked for a pulse in Blaine. Of course, it was absent.

One glance at sobbing Jesa told him he should leave her right now. He scrabbled on the ground and found the broad leaves that Reban had been carrying, grabbing them and pressing them firmly to Leif's wound. He kept one hand there, grabbing his backpack with the other and pulling out one of the pots of ointment they'd acquired from Blaine's shack. He stuck his fingers straight in the pot, pulling out a huge gloop of green. He lifted one leaf for a second and slapped the green ointment on it. Leif gave a groan as Lincoln tried to bind the leaves in place on his shoulder with some vines. Storm moved over beside him. Her eyes were wide. She pressed her fingers to the vine so Lincoln could tie a knot.

"You okay?" he whispered.

"I think I killed him." Her voice was shaking. "I think I just killed someone."

Lincoln tied off the vine and put his hand over hers. Her fingers were freezing. He leaned forward, talking low in her ear. "Storm, you did what you had to." He glanced towards the two bodies still on the ground. Galen's uninjured eye was wide open. It was clear he would never breathe again. Even if he hadn't been dead, Lincoln knew he wouldn't have done anything to help him.

Lincoln drew in a breath. "You might just have saved us, Storm."

Part of him wanted to stay with Storm, but Jesa was hunched over the body of her father. The man who'd given them the potential cure for Lincoln's sister.

Lincoln gave Storm's hand one last squeeze as he moved over and put an arm around Jesa. "Help your...Reban, Storm. Make sure he's okay."

Jesa was shaking. Her whole body. Lincoln squeezed his eyes shut for a second as Blaine's blood started to pool on the ground in front of them. He tightened his grip on Jesa as he stood up, pulling her to her feet and turning her away from the sight of her father's body, back towards the bushes.

Reban pushed himself upwards. He still seemed semi-stunned. He rubbed his head and looked around. "What happened?"

His eyes fixed on the two bodies on the ground. His head whipped around, stopping as soon as he saw Storm taking a few steps towards him.

It was like slow motion. Lincoln imagined he could see every single cell in Reban's body sigh in relief before his angry mask slipped back into place. He pointed at Galen and shook his head. "Who is this? Why on earth would he attack us?"

"It's Galen," Lincoln sighed. "Or, at least, it was."

Reban wrinkled his nose as the stench of Galen's old wound drifted towards him. "Galen? The Finalist? I thought he was dead."

"So did we," murmured Storm as she glanced around. She moved over to Jesa and put her hand on her arm. "Jesa, I'm so, so sorry."

Jesa gave another sob and buried her head in her hands. Lincoln left her with Storm and went back to Leif, who was coming around.

He'd only just bent forward to help Leif up when there was a roar.

A familiar roar that sent a chill down his spine. "Move!" he yelled, sliding an arm under Leif and dragging him to his feet.

Reban grabbed both Storm and Jesa and started running. The rugged coastline offered no safe haven and the noise was coming from the trees behind them. Which left them running in the one direction they'd never gone before – towards the desert. The remnants of green were quickly replaced by prickly dead branches.

There was a thud behind them. Reban looked back, his eyes widening as he saw the T-rex erupt from the trees.

Lincoln was moving as fast as he could, but Leif was still dazed and weak from the pterosaur attack. He'd lost a lot of blood. Leif couldn't run, his feet just stumbled along next to Lincoln's.

Lincoln kept glancing behind him. "How did it find us?" yelled Reban as he ran. He was moving so quickly that Storm and Jesa could barely keep up.

Lincoln's mind raced. He was thinking the same thing.

"The smell!" shouted Storm. "It must have been tracking Galen."

Of course. Galen's wound had stunk. The T-rex had proved its senses to them before. It was incredible that Galen had managed to evade it all this time.

Lincoln looked back again. The T-rex had paused next to the two bodies. It was nudging Galen's body with its nose. Thank goodness. Leif was slowing him down more than he wanted to think about.

Reban stumbled slightly in front of him, pulling Storm sideways and shoving into Jesa with his other shoulder. "Right!" he shouted.

Lincoln had no idea why. But he didn't have time to think about it. He just veered right. "Leif, come on. Try to help."

They kept running, stumbling forward. Running on sand wasn't easy. Sweat started to pour down Lincoln's face. It was odd, even though they weren't far from the coastline, as soon as they'd hit the desert, this whole terrain felt different. The heat around the jungle was humid, the heat here was starting to change. It was drier. More acidic.

Lincoln scanned the horizon. Sand dunes, with the occasional spurt of tiny green, or bare branches. Maybe he was missing something? True, he had most of Leif's body weight on him. But where was the shelter? Where were they heading?

"Reban?" he spluttered out with the little breath he had left. "Where are we going?"

Reban's head barely turned. He just kept running, dragging Storm and Jesa alongside him.

Lincoln's mind started to race. They should have headed to the coastline. They should have tried to double back to the jungle – at least then they'd have some coverage.

"Anywhere!" came the unhelpful shout from Reban.

It was the noise he heard first. That horrible thudding. That horrible, familiar sound. He held on to Leif tighter, pulling him along, their feet practically tangling with each other.

He wouldn't look back. He couldn't. He didn't want to know. He'd seen the inevitability. He knew exactly what a T-rex could do.

There was a roar. More like a bellow. The thudding was getting louder, the noise closing in around them.

Sweat poured down his back and face. He tried to adjust

Leif's position, but his arm was aching from continually propping him up. He tripped. Both of them fell sprawling onto the ground.

Reban turned around, so did Storm. Lincoln could see the horror on her face.

He scrambled to try to pick up Leif. But Leif's body was like a dead weight. Leif was still groaning. Still not completely with it.

The smell surrounded him. The signature stench of the Tyrannosaurus rex. That rancid, putrid smell of decaying flesh. For a split second he had a thought – was it animal or human flesh?

"Move, Lincoln!" screamed Storm. She was struggling, but Reban was holding on to her arm tightly, refusing to let her come back.

There was another noise. Different.

Now he had to turn.

For a few seconds, he didn't understand what he was seeing.

The T-rex was on the sand, it was only a few sectars away. Another few paces and it would reach him and Leif.

But it wasn't moving forward. Its tail was thrashing from side to side, as was its head.

Its feet seemed rooted in the sand. Stuck there.

But no, not stuck. Sinking.

The T-rex opened its mouth and roared, letting forth an even stronger gut-wrenching odour.

"Move." Reban's voice was low in his ear as the older man

slid his arms under Leif and pulled him to his feet. Reban slung Leif's arm around his shoulder and dragged him along.

Lincoln walked backwards slowly, still facing the T-rex. "What…what's going on?" he asked.

Reban shot him a smile. "Quicksand, I think. Let's just move before we find out first-hand."

Storm and Jesa were at his side now. They all stumbled backwards, open-mouthed.

The T-rex was panicking. The more it thrashed, the more it sank. Its thick hind legs had now disappeared into the sand. The powerful tail was vanishing before their eyes.

The sight was mesmerizing. Lincoln kept glancing down at his feet, checking the ground they were on was actually firm. He turned to Reban. "How did you know?"

Reban shrugged. "I'd heard about the dry quicksand here. I literally felt it shift under my feet. That's when I told you to go right."

Storm stared at him. It was the strangest expression. "The book?" she asked.

Their gazes seemed to connect. A kind of acknowledgement. Lincoln smiled. They couldn't see the similarities that he could. They couldn't see how alike they were. Storm was too busy pushing Reban away to notice how connected they really were.

Reban gave the briefest nod. "The book."

"Maybe not all parts need updating," she added quietly.

The T-rex wasn't giving up without a fight. Its body was now firmly encased in the sand. Its front arms clawed at the ground around it. It roared. It bellowed.

Storm touched Lincoln's arm. "Maybe we should move? What if its calls attract other T-rexes? We don't want to end up trapped."

Jesa was still glancing in the direction from which they'd come. Lincoln cringed. He'd no idea if the T-rex had taken a bite out of either Blaine or Galen.

The T-rex lifted its head in the air, giving one last roar as the sand closed in all around it and it disappeared from view. It was so final.

They all took a deep breath.

"I want to go back," said Jesa. "I want to bury my father. I want to say goodbye."

Reban shifted position and gave Leif back to Lincoln, then leaned forward and took Jesa's arm. His voice was authoritative. He sounded like a Chief Stipulator again. "No. I'll do that. I'll bury your father. I promise you. It's time to get back to the bay. You should hurry, the ship will be there soon."

Lincoln glanced at Jesa's face then at Reban. "You know what, it will be easier if we help." He gestured at Reban. "You might struggle on your own." He pressed his lips together for a second, then glanced at Storm as he said the next words. "Let's give Jesa a moment to say goodbye to her dad."

But it wasn't really Jesa he was thinking about, as Reban took her by the arm and led her away.

It was Storm.

FORTY-FIVE

STORMCHASER

It was amazing how fast you could dig when you had to. Leif wasn't fit to help at all, so she, Reban and Lincoln quickly dug out the grave for Blaine's broken body in a spot away from where Galen still lay.

As they laid Blaine to rest in the ground, Jesa sobbed openly, leaning forward and touching his forehead. "I'm sorry, Dad. I'm so, so sorry. I'm going to tell Mum and Caleb about you. How you survived out here. How brave you were. How resourceful." She glanced at Storm and Lincoln with wide eyes. "And how you might be the person who helps create a cure for the blistering plague."

Leif had his arm wrapped around Jesa. Storm wasn't sure who was holding who up, but it didn't really matter.

What did matter was the horrible feeling that was sweeping over her. How would she feel right now if it was Reban they were burying? How would she feel if he'd laid down his life to save one of them?

Lincoln's fingers brushed against hers. "We would never have survived here without him," she murmured.

Lincoln nodded. "I know." He leaned forward and put his hand on Jesa's shoulder. "You'll never know just how much I appreciate what your father has done." He gave a half-smile. "He's shown that people can survive on Piloria. There is a chance for us here." He glanced at Reban, obviously contemplating if he would be as resilient as Blaine had been. "And hopefully a chance for those left at home too."

Lincoln spoke a little louder. "Just remember, Jesa, how much he loved his family. He kept the pictures of you all on his wall. He wanted to send messages home. He never stopped thinking about you."

Jesa nodded as her tears dripped onto her father's tattered clothes. From here, for the first time, with his head wound hidden, he did actually look peaceful. Storm signalled to Lincoln. They had to make tracks or they would miss the ship. He nodded and they started to slide earth back into the grave, followed by a range of stones on top.

When they'd finally finished, Jesa had stopped crying. She lifted her chin, and put her arm around Leif's waist. "Thank you," she said quietly. Then added, "Now, let's get off this damn continent."

FORTY-SIX

STORMCHASER

They all seemed to drift back along the beach towards the bay. No pterosaurs came near them, but one lay dead on the beach. Either it had washed up, or it had just died there.

There was no smell. The death was recent.

"Do you think it was us?" Storm asked.

"Not really," answered Leif. "I'm not even sure if the last virus ended up in the watering hole – I dropped it when the pterosaur attacked me."

"Maybe we didn't need to plant the virus there," said Lincoln. "Maybe the other team had already done it."

They stood in silence for a few seconds. Reban tilted his head to the side. "How intelligent do you think these creatures really are?"

Storm frowned. "What do you mean?"

He held up his hands. "I mean, why did the pterosaur attack us in the first place? Do they have any memory capacity? Would they remember if other humans tampered with their watering hole? Would they associate that with the deaths of some pterosaurs?" He shook his head. "Are dinosaurs more intelligent than we've been led to believe?"

Lincoln looked at him steadily. "I guess, over the next few months, you'll find out."

Every hair on her arms stood on end. Hours. That's all they had left.

She couldn't look at Reban right now. Blaine had survived here for nine years. It was possible. But Blaine had been different. He'd learned how to do new things. He'd learned how to adapt. Did Reban Don, Chief Stipulator, have that capacity?

Jesa's hands were still trembling. She'd lost her father. Storm bent down and picked up some sand and watched for a few seconds as it trickled through her fingers. Yellow sand. Not like the sand back on Earthasia. That was darker.

She stood and pressed her hands into her hips, arching her back to stretch it, and taking a few moments to stare back across the terrain.

Grey cliffs, green land, dense jungles and the uncharted desert. She could look in every direction and see a different scene. In Ambulus City, everywhere she looked she would see grey, tall buildings. The only exceptions were the parliament building and the loch. But there were plans for the loch. Working in parliament meant she found out things she didn't always want to know.

The ground surrounding the loch had been tested. It had

been designated "safe". Which meant in the next few weeks, building around the loch would start. It would soon be surrounded by grey buildings too. What would Milo think? Maybe it was best that he seemed to have already disappeared from the loch.

Lincoln put his hand on her back. "Storm? You okay?" He handed Leif back to Reban and hung back to stay with her.

She looked up. How much had he changed since she knew him? The determination was still there in his bright green eyes, but had they lost a little of their spark? His shaggy blond hair was a little shorter now and his skin paler.

She knew he would never stop fighting for his sister. And she admired that. Arta was worth fighting for. All the people with the blistering plague deserved a chance of treatment – a chance of survival.

She gave him a tired smile. "I'm fine." She took a deep breath and glanced at the backpack. "Do you really think this will work?"

His answer was swift. "It's got to. Or this will all have been a wasted journey."

The air coming off the ocean was brisk. Storm ran her hands up and down her arms. "We might have got the plants. The leaves, the samples – but I don't trust Silas Jung." She shook her head. "I don't trust him at all. He's not interested in curing the plague. In fact, I think he might be really against it." She held up her hands. "The last thing he wants is more people."

Lincoln shook his head. "Don't worry. I have plans. I'm

not going to tell Silas about the plants. Lorcan Field is going to work on this. We have areas where we grow plants in the labs. No one will notice if we plant something else. We can do this without telling anyone. Silas will be so excited about the viruses that he won't think about anything else."

She pressed her lips together for a second. "Do you really think people will come here?"

Lincoln nodded. "What choice is there? And if people are told we can kill the most dangerous dinosaurs, they might actually want to come here."

Storm stopped walking, guilt washing over her. "So how do we actually *know* that the viruses worked, and the deaths aren't just some weird coincidence?"

Lincoln shrugged. "We're not here long enough to really find out. We saw one dead raptor, one dead pterosaur and one angry one. As for the T-rexes, who knows? Maybe they've changed watering hole? Maybe we put the virus in the wrong place – or maybe it just doesn't work for the T-rexes."

Storm opened her mouth to reply and then stopped herself. She could already glimpse Blue Bay in the distance. Once they got there, it would be time to board the ship.

"Do you think any of the other team will be at the bay?"

Lincoln sighed. "The dilophosauruses seemed vicious, and organized. A dangerous combination. I hope some of them made it. But I just don't know." He turned around and started walking backwards. "Galen? Who'd have thought? I was sure he was dead, I mean, remember? His arm getting torn off by the T-rex?"

Storm nodded. "That sight is permanently seared into my brain. But look at what happened to Blaine, he had a terrible injury too. He survived." She realized what she'd said and shuddered. Something sparked in her head. "Don't you remember Blaine muttering a few times about too many people? I thought he just meant us, but now I think he knew about Galen."

Lincoln raised his eyebrows. "Can't imagine Blaine rolled out a welcome for him. But surely he would have given Galen some of the ointment?" He wrinkled his nose. "That smell, it was just…the worst."

Storm shook her head. "It didn't seem like it, did it? With an infection that bad, I wonder how much longer Galen would have survived."

Lincoln shrugged. "Maybe he wasn't infected right at the beginning. Maybe the infection came later. It's not exactly easy to keep things clean here." He waved out his arm. "This whole continent. It's going to go back to having just one person living on it." He smiled at Storm. "And a whole lot of dinosaurs, but maybe fewer than before."

Her stomach clenched. Look what had happened to Blaine when he'd been left here alone. Reban said Blaine had always been strange – but how much did being alone contribute to that?

She looked into the distance at the bay. It looked beautiful again. Peaceful. This place could deceive you so much. It was almost as if Lincoln was reading her thoughts. "You know, in a few years – if the viruses work, and once

Arta is well again – I might actually think about coming back here."

"You would?" She was surprised. She hadn't expected him to say something like that.

He nodded, unaware of the millions of thoughts spiralling around in her head. "That's what they want anyway, isn't it? The Stipulators. That's always been their plan. To start to move people to Piloria." His face lit up. "Just think. Being one of the first groups to come here. The land. The space. Soil that actually grows things! If Arta was sick again, I could just go into the nearest jungle patch to find the evergreens."

"You'd really think about it?" She was amazed.

He touched her arm. "Storm, I live in a cave and work in a lab. It's never been my dream. It's not what any of us ever wanted."

"What did you want?"

His bright green eyes met hers. For a second she thought he might not answer. "My dad and I, we used to talk at night – before we had to house share, before we had to live in the caves. When there were still little patches of green around. When there were still a few trees. Dad used to tell me stories about growing up and running through a forest." Lincoln's smile was sad but genuine. "He was a dreamer, my dad. He had plans." Lincoln broke their gaze and stared back towards the bay. "He just didn't get a chance to see any of them through." He couldn't hide the wistfulness in his tone and Storm moved closer to him, bumping shoulders and sliding her hand into his.

They stood for a few minutes, just looking along the coast towards the bay. In the distance the grey hull of the ship could be seen emerging from further down the coastline.

Time was up. They were finally going home.

FORTY-SEVEN

LINCOLN

Last time he'd been on Piloria, he could have whooped with joy when the *Invincible* had appeared back at the beach.

This time things felt different.

Leif needed some medical attention. They all knew that. And the only place he'd get that was on the ship.

Jesa looked as if she could burst into tears at any second. No wonder. She'd found her father, and lost him all over again.

Reban was pacing again, hands in his pockets. He kept glancing at the ship, and then at Storm.

As the ship grew closer, Storm started to get agitated. She couldn't stand still; wringing her hands over and over, checking the contents of her backpack, and glancing at the others sitting on the beach.

There was a flash of black on the ship. Silas. His blond hair was easy to pick out. Even from far away it was obvious that he was issuing orders to all those around him.

As they watched, a different kind of boat was lowered from the side of the ship. It was bigger than before, more robust, though lowering it to the ocean was obviously more difficult.

A few crew members and one nervous-looking Stipulator rowed quickly across the bay. As soon as the boat landed at the beach they all jumped out.

The Stipulator glanced around the beach. "Where's the other team?" he asked loudly.

They all looked around, as if someone might emerge mysteriously from the forest. But the beach remained silent. An uncomfortable prickle went down Lincoln's spine. It had been like this the last time too. A whole team lost. And this time Froan Jung and Tena Koll hadn't made it back. Very few people made it home from Piloria.

When no one replied, the Stipulator continued. The loss of the other team was obviously not important. "Have the viruses been planted?"

They all nodded nervously.

"Did you see any evidence of them working?"

Lincoln spoke up, choosing his words carefully and glancing towards Reban. "Since we've planted the viruses we've seen a dead raptor, and a dead pterosaur."

"What about the T-rex?"

Lincoln held up his hands. "We planted the virus at the T-rex watering hole. We haven't seen them since."

The Stipulator looked over Lincoln's shoulder towards

the jungle behind them. It appeared he was satisfied with their answers. "Move quickly," he ordered. "Silas wishes to make good time."

The crew scowled at Leif, who was slouched on the sand and grumbled as they picked him up. Lincoln went to pick up all the backpacks.

"Wait a second," said Storm.

She fumbled through hers, taking out leaves and plants, putting them in some of the other packs.

"What are you doing?"

She gulped and looked over at Reban.

"I'm not coming."

FORTY-EIGHT

STORMCHASER

"What?"

Lincoln looked shocked. She didn't blame him.

Reban was by her side in an instant. "What are you talking about? Get on the damn boat."

She shook her head firmly. Now she'd said the words, they actually didn't feel so unreal.

"I'm staying."

"What? Why?" Lincoln grabbed her by the shoulders. "Are you crazy?"

She tilted her chin and met his panicked gaze. "No. I'm not. What is there back on Earthasia for me? A job in parliament where one person wants me to talk about here, and the rest probably want to send me to the mines. How long do you think it will be before they find an excuse to do that?"

"But what about Arta? What about the other kids?"

That was the hard part. It was the only thing that made her feel a duty to go back. "They should be allowed to stay. They should be allowed to keep the rations. Do you remember Kori Tunn? She was a Finalist a few years ago. She brought that weird green fruit back. She got sick and died. But her house isn't far from mine. Her children are still there. They still get extra rations."

Lincoln shook his head. "But you're not sick, Storm. You're not dead. Refusing to go back – surely that will mean a punishment? Can you risk that?"

She gulped. Could she really risk it? What if they did decide to punish Rune's and Kronar's brothers and sisters – or Arta – because of her actions? Silas wasn't always the most rational man on the planet.

"No, she can't," broke in Reban. He pointed to the boat. "Get on board."

Storm straightened her back. "Stop telling me what to do. Both of you."

She looked at Lincoln. "Take the samples. Make some ointment on the way back. Hide it. Keep it for Arta. Jesa has more. Leif has plant samples too." She gave him a hopeful smile. "This is the only thing that might help Arta. You've got to try to grow these. It's not Earthasia's health care she needs. It's proper treatment. It's a cure. This is her chance. You have to go back. You have to try."

Lincoln looked around. The crew seemed to be arguing with the Stipulator about something. They didn't even seem to care what was going on. "This is madness. This place is huge. Even if the viruses work, there might be T-rexes or raptors in distant parts it won't reach."

Storm nodded. "I know." She pointed at the ship. "But you said it yourself, the ship will be back. The Stipulators haven't finished here. They haven't even started. They need to come back and check how well the viruses have worked. The first thing they'll do when they go back is ask for more viruses to be made. They'll want to come back. They'll want to establish a first habitat here." She lifted her chin as she grew more confident. "Who better to tell them what they need to know than two people who already live here?" She lifted her hands towards the ship. "The truth is, no one there really cares if I stay or if I go back."

"I do." Both voices spoke simultaneously.

Storm turned to Reban. "Then start treating me with respect. Start acknowledging who I am. Listen to me. We've wasted sixteen years. Who knows how many we have left?" She put her hand on her chest. "I've spent the last five years with no one – even though I apparently had two relatives I didn't know about. It's payback time." She held out her hands. "I want space. I want green. I want colour. I want a chance to live. I want a chance to be."

"To be what? Dinosaur food?" Lincoln was still shaking his head.

She sucked in a deep breath. "I hope not. But it's a chance I have to take. Blaine lived here for nine years. He survived. He managed. We already have a head start. We have a house – well, a shack. It's something. There's a water supply.

379

We know how to make a basic medicine." She looked around at the weapons lying on the sand. "We have some weapons. And, maybe, we have a few less dinosaurs to hide from."

Lincoln shook his head. "Think about this, Storm. Really think about it. If they're going to come back here in a few years, they'll want volunteers, you could come back then. We could come back then."

Storm could hear the desperation in his voice as he turned to Reban. "Can't you make her come back?"

She smiled. Lincoln couldn't help himself. He wanted to protect her. But that wasn't what she needed. She'd spent too long looking after herself.

Reban held her gaze as he spoke carefully. "I learned a long time ago not to argue with the Knux women. You never win. They always do exactly what they want." He gave a soft smile. "It's one of their most admirable traits."

Storm held her breath. A compliment. He'd said a few nice things before, but she'd always thought them offhand remarks. This time it seemed clear.

Reban kept talking. "She's right." He glanced at the ship. "If she goes back, I don't know how much Octavius can protect her. Silas is on a mission right now. I was part of it, and now Storm is too. Once he goes home with stories of dinosaurs dying, he'll be the hero. Nothing will get in his way." His voice dropped. "I can't control any of that."

She was staying. She was staying on Piloria. With Reban. Her dad.

Storm smiled and stepped forward, lifting her hand to

touch Lincoln's cheek. "Look after Arta," she whispered. "Do whatever it takes. For Rune's brother and sister too."

Lincoln nodded. She could see how conflicted he was. "I could—"

"No." She cut him off. "You need to go back. You need to make the ointment."

He sighed, then leaned forward, pressing his head against hers and closing his eyes. She stood like that for a second. Feeling his soft skin under her palm, sensing the tension in his body. His green eyes flickered open, so close, his eyelashes brushed against her. "This isn't goodbye. I'll be back."

She nodded and stepped back, her voice trembling. "I'm counting on it."

Jesa walked over and smothered her with a hug. "Stay safe," she whispered. Storm nodded, then crossed to Leif, lying in the boat. "Are you crazy?" he said, with a big smile on his face.

"Of course I am," she said, as she bent to kiss his cheek. "Look after the kids. Look after yourself, and" – she glanced at Jesa – "look after Jesa too."

The crew members climbed into the boat. The Stipulator scowled at her as he scanned the bay, before casting a nervous glance in Reban's direction. "Are you coming?" he asked Storm.

She shook her head and stood back. She pressed her lips together as she watched the boat cross the bay to the ship. The bay stayed calm and bright blue, the tylosauruses nowhere in sight. Once the boat was safely winched aboard,

Lincoln stood on the deck staring back at her.

He was safe. He had a job to do. And he was her friend.

Reban nodded at her and gave an ironic kind of smile. "Don't take all day. We have work to do." He turned on his heel, swinging his backpack onto his shoulder, and walked off into the jungle. For the first time, he started to whistle.

Storm breathed in. She wanted to hold this moment. She wanted to keep it right here. The richness in the air, the humidity, the scent of the life growing around her.

In a few years, things would change. Other people would come and start to settle on Piloria. Nothing would be the same again.

She swung her own backpack onto her shoulder as the *Invincible* started to disappear, and followed her dad into the jungle.

Ready to start their new life.

ACKNOWLEDGEMENTS

I'm not much of a planner when it comes to books and I think I might have made my lovely editor Sarah Stewart at Usborne a little nervous when she asked me about the plan for the story and I said, "Oh, I'll find a way to send them back to the dinosaur continent." So thank you for believing in me, for understanding that planning for me kills a story, and for loving the story when you got it!

Huge thanks to Sarah Manning, my lovely agent, for always being supportive, guiding me in the right direction and dealing with all the complicated stuff. It's a real joy and pleasure working with you. Our world takeover is due any day now!

And to the team at Usborne who are so enthusiastic about the *Extinction Trials* books, shout out about them constantly and get them into the hands of bloggers and readers everywhere: Stevie Hopwood and Jacob Dow, thank you so much. Matilda Johnson, thank you for understanding I am completely irrational about copyedits and treating me kindly. Stephanie King and Rebecca Hill, thanks for supporting *The Extinction Trials*.

Also thanks to the lovely Zoe at nosaferplace and the equally lovely Steph at A Little But A Lot, Kelly at Kelly's Rambles, Nicola at Fantastic Book Dragon and Lucas Maxwell at Glenthorne High School all for shouting out about *The Extinction Trials* and encouraging others to read. I never, ever forget that for some children, young people and adults, reading can be their safe place.

STORM AND LINCOLN
WILL RETURN...

LOOK OUT FOR MORE
EXTINCTION TRIALS
COMING IN 2019

#EXTINCTIONTRIALS